CONTEMPORARY AMERICAN FICTION

THE WANDERERS

Richard Price was born in the Bronx in 1949. After graduating from Cornell University and receiving an M.F.A. from Columbia University, he was a Mirillees Fellow in Fiction at Stanford University. *The Wanderers* is his first novel, for which he won both a MacDowell Fellowship and a Mary Roberts Rinehart Foundation Grant. Mr. Price is the author of three other novels: *Bloodbrothers, Ladies' Man*, and *The Breaks* (all available in Penguin Books). He has also done extensive journalism, teaching, and screenwriting. He lives in New York City with his wife and daughter.

THE WANDERERS

A NOVEL BY
RICHARD PRICE

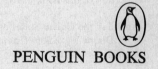

PENGUIN BOOKS

PENGUIN BOOKS
Viking Penguin Inc., 40 West 23rd Street,
New York, New York 10010, U.S.A.
Penguin Books Ltd, Harmondsworth,
Middlesex, England
Penguin Books Australia Ltd, Ringwood,
Victoria, Australia
Penguin Books Canada Limited, 2801 John Street,
Markham, Ontario, Canada L3R 1B4
Penguin Books (N.Z.) Ltd, 182–190 Wairau Road,
Auckland 10, New Zealand

First published in the United States of America by
Houghton Mifflin Company 1974
Published in Penguin Books 1985

LIBRARY OF CONGRESS CATALOGING IN PUBLICATION DATA
Price, Richard, 1949–
    The wanderers.
    I. Title.
PS3566.R544W3   1985   813'.54   85-9969
ISBN 0 14 00.8344 8

A portion of this book has appeared in *Antaeus*.

Printed in the United States of America by
R. R. Donnelley & Sons Company, Harrisonburg, Virginia
Set in Times Roman

Dedications

Roachman, Santos, Stieny, Lance,
and the others

Dion, The Four Seasons

Alice

Margo

Garry

Judi

I would like to thank the Mary Roberts
Rinehart Foundation for the grant
and the validation.

"I shall search my very soul . . . for the Lion"
—Van Morrison

"Good Times
O children think about the good times"
—Lucille Clifton

Contents

THE WANDERERS

The Warlord

THERE HE WAS in Big Playground. Richie Gennaro. Seventeen. High Warlord of the Wanderers. Surrounded by the Warlords of the Rays, Pharaohs, and the Executioners. Touchy allies. Tense convention. Issue at hand —

"We gotta stop them niggers."

"Do you think the Fordham Baldies would fight wit' us?"

"Man, if we get them Baldies it's all over."

"Yeah, but don't forget them Wongs. Them Chinks know judo."

"No Chink judo chop can stop this!"

"Hey, put that back! Jeez, you wanna get us busted!"

"Hey — how about them Lester Avenue guys?"

"Nah, they're fuckin' killers."

"They jus' as soon kill one a us as a nigger."

"I heard the Del-Bombers is comin' in wit' the Pips 'cause Clinton Stitch got a cousin in the Bombers."

"Ever notice how spades got two million cousins all over the country?"

"Del-Bombers . . . shit . . . that's bad."

"Now we *gotta* get the Baldies."

"Antone — you know Joey DiMassi, doncha?"

"Yeah."

"Whyncha go over to Fordham tonight with Gennaro an' see if you can get to talk wit' the Baldies."

"Awright."

Richie felt uneasy with Antone. The Wanderers and the Pharaohs often rumbled, and this emergency peace was only temporary. What if Antone, tonight, while they were waiting for the train pushed Richie on the el tracks? The Pharaohs knew that Richie was the vital spark, the cold logical mind behind the Wanderer war machine. Richie knew that if *he* was a Pharaoh and *he* had the chance he would surely push the Wanderer Warlord into the path of an oncoming train. Maybe they should take a cab.

The meeting was adjourned.

"So you wanna go wit' me to see DiMassi tonight?"

"Awright."

"I'll meet you here about ten, O.K.?"

"Sure, you wanna hop a cab?"

Antone shrugged, he eyed Richie suspiciously. "Ah look . . . I dunno if I got the dough for a cab."

"Awright, we'll see."

"Later."

"Later."

After everyone had gone back to their candy stores, deserted lots, or playgrounds, Richie sat down on a bench and scribbled out a score sheet.

US		THEM	
WANDERERS (GINNY)	27	PIPS (NIGGER)	50
PHARAOHS (GINNY)	28	CAVALIERS (NIGGER)	30
RAYS (IRISH)	42	DEL-BOMBERS (NIGGER)	36
EXECUTIONERS (POLACK)	30	MAU-MAU (NIGGER)	40
FORDHAM BALDIES (MIXED)	40	WONGS (CHINK)	27
LESTER AVE. (VERY GINNY)	50		

Except for the Lester Avenue boys it was pretty even. Richie had to figure out how to get them involved without having them turn on the allies. They hated the niggers but they also hated everybody else. The Lester Avenue gang was older. Maybe twenty-one on the average. Comparing the other North Bronx gangs to the Lester Avenue boys was like comparing the Coast Guard to the marines. The other gangs had a few rumbles; every once in a while some guy would have his jaw busted or need a couple of stitches, but the guys on Lester Avenue were all ex-cons or Mob punks. Last year the heads of their gang, Louie and Jackie Palaya, were up on murder raps but had Mob lawyers fix a deal.

The only other gang worth being scared of was the Fordham Baldies, who were *so* fucking insane that they shaved their heads so their hair wouldn't get in their eyes in a fight. They were older too. About eighteen on the average. The toughest guy in the Baldies was Terror, a huge cross-eyed monster who even beat up on his own gang when they weren't fighting anyone else. But even *he* knew better than to fuck with the puniest guy on Lester Avenue. They'd come down like vigilantes and tear up the whole Fordham area, and they'd go down like that night after night until Terror gave himself up. Then a kangaroo court in some basement and even money Terror would be found in the trunk of a deserted car out in Hunt's Point the next week.

Richie thought about the opposition. Most of the time he couldn't figure niggers out. He once took a prejudice quiz in a comic book, and he had all the right answers except for the question, "Do Negroes smell different?" He checked YES, and the upside-down answer key said the answer was NO. But that was bullshit because he knew they did. As long as he could remember his mother had warned him about coons and razors and knives and going into empty elevators with niggers because niggers would just as soon cut your balls off and pawn them for dope or booze as look at you. One fact that he knew was true was that if you go into a building where most of the tenants are niggers, either the hallway or the elevator is going to smell of piss. One time he went uptown to the Gun Hill Projects to get the homework from a kid in his class and the piss-stink in the elevator made him throw up before he got to the kid's floor.

He could understand them getting all the gangs together because essentially niggers were cowards unless there was a big gang of them. What he couldn't figure out was why the Wongs would team up with them. They were people from two different worlds. They never fought in school, but they never were chummy either. The Wongs were the insanest people of all. Not only were they all Chinese, but they were all related. Twenty-seven guys with the last name Wong. Each guy had a dragon tattoo, and rumor had it they all knew jujitsu and could kill someone with a judo chop.

Except for the Reds, Richie thought most Chinks were pretty harmless, and he liked Chinese food, but these characters were something else. He'd heard that their great-grandfather was a real Warlord — of the Tongs down in Chinatown around World War I — and who'd brought up his family to keep the Tong terror alive. From what Richie understood, the Tong still existed down there, although they were nowhere near as powerful as the Mob — but who really knew what the hell was going on down there, or who was coming off those boats from the Orient every day and slithering into Mott Street. In school, the Wong gang was inseparable. Silent, even among themselves, they walked through the halls like the Imperial Guard, giving off a glow of royalty, a unity that raised them above all other gangs.

"Hey."

"Hey." Richie looked up. C was peering over his shoulder at his notes. C was Richie's girl friend, fifteen, with hair teased into a beehive. She covered her pimples with what appeared to be flesh-colored mud. The C stood for comb — she always carried around a large pink comb and a crumpled Kleenex in her hand.

"What's that?"

"Nothin'."

"If it's nothin' how come you're coverin' it up?"

"Because it ain't none of your business."

"You gonna rumble wit' the Pharaohs?"

"No."

C sat down next to him. Richie folded the score sheet and slipped it into his back pocket. He tensed his chest muscles under his sky blue muscle shirt to catch C's eye. C's jaws worked furiously, popping her Bazooka, which gave her sugar breath. She wore a hot pink rayon blouse, revealing the tiny puckers in her oversized bra. Richie knew she stuffed Kleenex, but always looked the other way when she sneaked the wads out before he felt her up.

Richie's garrison belt had RG & C in a heart followed by TRUE LOVE WILL NEVER DIE. C carved it in with a nail the night she gave him his first hand job in Big Playground. Richie had really wanted a blowjob because he'd heard some guys say that getting a blowjob was better than getting laid, but C had steadfastly refused. Finally after a few weeks of fighting and head pushing, C agreed to give him one the next night. The following day he took two showers, inspected every inch of his prick, and bathed it in some strong cologne. That night when the big moment came, C tentatively gave it a preliminary lick and almost gagged on the cologne. They dropped the subject after that.

C put her leg over Richie's leg and winked. She had on black imitation leather pointy ankle boots. Richie wore roach killers — pointy as a dangerous weapon, curving high over his ankle and low over his heel.

"Whatcha doin' tonight?"

"I gotta go to Fordham."

"How come?"

"I gotta see somebody."

"Can I come?"

"No."

"You seein' a girl?" Her eyes promised violence.

"No, I ain't seein' a girl," he mimicked. "I gotta see this guy."

"About what?"

"About a job."

"Bullshit."

"Bullshit yourself, I ain't kiddin'."

"I need help wit' my homework."

"Whatcha got?"

"Math and social."

"I'll come over about eight."

"Seeya then." She ruffled his hair and walked off.

The sunlight turned to a neutral gray. Six-thirty. Dinnertime. Big Playground was deserted except for the parky in his olive uniform collecting basketballs and spongy red kickballs. Richie Gennaro walked through the housing project to his own building.

His father was already home — which meant Richie was late. He washed quickly and sat down. His mother sliced a cantaloupe in fours and sat down with them.

The dinner table — one bowl mashed potatoes, one bowl broccoli, one plate with four steaks, garlic bread wrapped in silver foil, one bottle Hammer lem'n'lime soda, one bottle Hammer mellow-cream soda, one salad bowl, one jar Seven Seas French Dressing, one unlit candle, one Richie Gennaro — seventeen, one Randy Gennaro — twelve, one Louis Gennaro — forty-one, one Millie Gennaro — forty-one. In the corner, one television, on channel nine — one Dick Van Dyke.

Richie's father produced a paperback — one *Lady Chatterley's Lover*. "Is this yours?"

"Yeah."

"I don't want this filth in my house."

"It's a great book."

"It's filth. Don't talk back."

"Did you read it?"

"I don't read filth."

"Then how do you know it's filth?"

"I worked my way up from nothing. There were times when your mother and I had to go through all the clothes in the closet just to find a quarter to buy milk."

"Hey look, Pop, it's a classic."

"Oh yeah? Read page two-sixty-seven, that's classic filth."

"I thought you didn't read it."

"Goddamn smartass. You break your back to send them onwards and upwards, so they could be and do and have things you never dreamed of, and they reward you like this." He slammed the book down on the table.

"Louis! Get that book off the table! We're eating!"

"You see? Now you've got your mother upset!"

The family ate in silence. No one laughed at Dick Van Dyke. Richie finished and excused himself, heading for the door.

"Sit down and have dessert."

"I don't want dessert."

"Just have some cooked fruit."

"No, seeya."

"Hey, Professor Filth, where you going?"

"Over to C's."

"You coming back this week?"

Richie slammed the door behind him and headed across the projects.

"You lazy sonovabitch I refuse to clean this shithouse anymore if you keep trackin' mud and godknowswhat on my new carpet every time you come in this house. THE NIGGER MAID AIN'T WORKIN' HERE ANYMORE, YOU UNNERSTAN'?"

"Stop your bitchin'. You don't get off your ass all day anyhow, an' don't call me a sonovabitch in front of my children. I GOTTA GET RESPEC' IN MY HOUSE. I AM . . . THE . . . BREADWINNER HERE."

Richie rang the doorbell. Utter silence.

From the living room. "Yeah? . . . whozzat?"

"It's me." He hated yelling through a closed door.

C's old man opened the door. He was fat and bald and mean and short. He was indifferent to Richie. C's parents resumed their argument.

Richie walked through the foyer to C's room. Her little brother Dougie was hiding in the kitchen eavesdropping on the fight. Richie kicked him in the ass, and he stumbled into the dining room. "Hey, you stupid fuck," Dougie hissed. He scampered back to the kitchen before he was noticed. Richie continued down the hall. "The Wanderers are faggots, the Wanderers are faggots."

"Dougie, I'm gonna wash your mouth out wit' soap," warned his father.

"He kicked me . . . he kicked . . . oh, man . . . I'm leavin' home."

"Don't forget your toothbrush."

Richie walked into C's room. She was hunched over a blue loose-leaf notebook: "C & RG" and "True Love Will Never Die" on the cover in her fanciest handwriting.

He peered over her shoulder and saw

Denise Rizzo   Algebra 323
9/12/62   Mr. Lumish

$$2x = 10, \; x=?$$
$$10x = 100, \; x=?$$
$$5x = 65, \; x=?$$

C&RG = Mrs. CG
Denise Gennaro, Denise Rizzo Gennaro
DG,   DRG   DRG & RG = TRUE LOVE
Mrs DRG   If X = RG and Y = C then X + Y = Love

She hadn't heard Richie come in because her record player was blasting the Shirelles off the walls. He poked her in the ribs. She screamed, wheeled around, and crumpled the paper into a ball. They plodded through her homework for an hour. Richie finally wrote out the whole assignment himself. She was probably the only student in the city who didn't know what office Mayor Wagner held in city government.

He left at nine-thirty and waited outside Big Playground for Antone. He showed up at ten.

"Hey."

"Hey."

"You wanna hop a cab?"

"Nah, I ain't got no dough."

"Well, I don't wanna take a train."

They wound up taking two buses over to Fordham.

Even though most of the stores were closed, thousands of shoppers were still walking through the massive shopping area. In the middle of the busiest intersection, on a large traffic island with both navy and army recruiting centers and a row of twenty public phones, lounged the Fordham Baldies, heads shaved and gleaming in the fluorescent overheads, black jackets showered with silver buckles, chains, and studs. They draped themselves over the phones, leaning back lazily, chewing gum or smoking cigarettes in slow motion, their studied poses out of pace with the hustle of the night shoppers.

Both Antone and Richie felt intimidated by the Baldies' sullen presence. Terror spotted them and sauntered over. Richie's stomach grew knuckles. He expected anything, was prepared for nothing. Antone's face was defiant but bloodless. Terror weighed three hundred pounds and stood six-four. His bald head revealed a thick roll of fat at the base of his neck. An asthmatic condition made every breath sound like it came from a steam press. He was a high school dropout, or kickout, because he'd creased a shop teacher's head with a file when he was fifteen. "Whada you want here?"

"We wanna see Joey . . . it's important."

Terror's cross-eyes were black pearls. He never blinked. Tommy Tatti once said that Terror's mother was Mexican. No one would ever dare ask Terror about his mother. No one ever seriously talked about anyone else's mother. Even 'How's your mother?' was no good because the guy would think "What should be wrong wit' my mother?' "Joey ain't here . . . beat it."

"You know where we can find him?"

"He's screwin' your mother."

Richie and Antone walked away. Terror laughed and walked back to the Baldies.

"Stupid fuckhead," Antone muttered.

Richie was silent. He was scared of Terror — he couldn't even bring himself to talk behind his back. They walked down Fordham Road past the blacked-out stores.

"Hey, there's Joey!" Richie spotted Joey's bald head bobbing up the hill toward his gang.

Antone stopped Joey. "Hey, Antone, what's shakin'? I haven't seen you guys aroun'." Joey DiMassi was tall and skinny. A scar slanting across his eyebrow gave his face a permanently dazed expression. He was the leader of the

Baldies. He wasn't the toughest, and he wasn't the smartest in his gang, but he had a good logical head and a great sense of fairness and decency. He had respect.

Antone told Joey about the coming war. Joey smiled, asked some names of the opposition, and told Antone to relax, he'd take care of it. Everyone had implicit faith in Joey DiMassi. When he said he'd take care of it, it was as good as done. Tommy Tatti once said that Joey should run for mayor on the Fordham Baldie ticket.

The next day at lunch, word was out that the niggers had decided not to rumble. No one knew why, but Antone and Richie knew that Joey had a hand in it. The main reaction was a lot of curses and grumbling, palm-pounding and shadow-boxing.

"Ah, I woulda beat their fuckin' skulls in."

"Ah, I had it all planned. They wouldna knowed what hit 'em."

"Ah, them fuckin' coons is cowards."

That night Richie ate two steaks and had two portions of cooked fruit for dessert. After dinner he decided to drop in on the Wanderers' camp — a deserted lot down the block from his house bordered by trees and the backs of commercial garages. The Wanderers had cleared an area about twenty-five feet in circumference where they built campfires and sniffed glue. The surrounding garages were spray-painted with the gang's name and then individual names under that.

A block away Richie sensed something was wrong. He saw too many people standing around the camp. At first he thought they were cops who were always coming around when there was a good fire going, but it was too light yet for a fire. They weren't cops. He raced up to the clearing.

It was the Wongs.

The Wanderers were standing around not knowing what to

do or say. Perry ran up to Richie whispering hysterically.
"It's the fuckin' Wongs!"

"What's goin' on?"

"I don't know! They ain't sayin' anything!"

The Wongs stood there as if posing for a group photograph,
faces expressionless, eyes slits. They didn't move a muscle. If
one of them gave out with a judo shout the Wanderers would
have cleared the place in ten seconds flat. Richie looked
around. His troops were standing in little clusters, staring and
nervously rubbing their arms. Finally Teddy Wong, the leader
of the clan, decided that enough of the Wanderers had shown
up and very softly said, "We came up here to warn you guys
about the niggers."

"We thought the fight was off!" Perry's voice cracked. En-
tranced, Richie stared at the dragon tattoo on Teddy's forearm.

"It is. They're just after one guy. Who's Gennaro?"

Richie swallowed his jaw. He ran up to Teddy. "How
come? Whad I do? Whad I do?"

Teddy stared at him contemptuously. The other Wongs
sneered at such a breakdown in composure. "Come off it,
man. I saw what you wrote on the sidewalk in front of school
and by the bus stop."

"What! What! I didn't write nothin'!"

Teddy turned to leave. The others filed out after him.
Richie wanted to run up and cry on Teddy's tattoo and beg
forgiveness; he was more afraid of the Wongs than of Clinton
Stitch and the niggers. The last Wong to leave turned to face
Gennaro. "That was stupid, man . . . really stupid." They
walked in formation toward the train station.

Panic in the camp. Richie's shirt was soaked with sweat
and his underwear stuck to his prick where a little pee had
seeped out. Everyone crowded around him. He just kept re-
peating, "I didn't do nothin'! I didn't do nothin'." His voice

broke and the steak and cooked fruit started coming up. Suddenly he jerked around. The others danced away as he puked. Buddy Borsalino ran to get his father's car. The other guys helped Richie into the back seat, careful not to get too close — he smelled pretty bad. They drove to the school and saw in at least seven different sidewalk squares in white paint:

NIGERS STINK
RICHIE GENNARO

He had no idea who wrote it. He had no enemies to speak of. He hadn't had a fight in months. At the bus station the same story — this time on the walls. They went back to the camp.

"Hey, lissen, man, if you gotta fight then we're fightin' too."

"Yeah, we gotta stick together."

"I didn't *do* it, I didn't *do* it." His voice had settled into a tired whine. He wanted to go to sleep.

"Don't worry, man, we won't letcha down."

That night, Richie had a nightmare:

He was naked, getting the shit pounded out of him by gigantic muscular blacks wearing sunglasses, his head slowly sinking into Big Playground concrete. Voodoo drums. He began choking in the pungence of elevator piss. He was being cooked in it — in a big black kettle, with a blazing fire underneath. Clinton Stitch, head of the Pips, stirred the pee around him with a huge ladle that had a skull on the end. Then he was stretched out on a rack getting judo-chopped by the Wongs. Teddy Wong was standing there dressed in an embroidered ceremonial gown and a black silk skull cap. He had a two-foot stringy black mustache and wore eyeliner. His hands were hidden, folded in the sleeves of his garment. Suddenly they appeared with two-inch fingernails painted black. He clapped twice and two bald fat Chinks appeared dragging C, nude, hands tied behind her back. She was yanked by the hair and forced to kneel in front of Teddy who parted his gown. His huge prick stood straight out with tremendous fire-breathing dragons tattooed on both sides. C was commanded to suck it, which she did greedily, stopping momentarily to gasp for breath and moan, "I love it, I love it!"

Richie awoke with the biggest hard-on of his life, which he promptly pounded into mother-of-pearl-colored drops that flew around the room like scatter pellets.

The Wanderers arrived at school grim-faced. Richie cursed himself for not at least painting over his name last night. As Richie slaved over "who" and "whom" in the dread *Warriner's English Grammar and Composition,* a fat sophomore came into the English class with a call slip from Mr. Mulligan's office for Richie. He had forgotten about disciplinary action.

Mr. Mulligan, or "Biff," was a huge hurricane of a man. He was dean of discipline, football coach, and top ballbreaker of the school. Richie walked on rubber legs to the basement office.

"You Gennaro?" Richie noticed the two cops. Big and solemn with guns as huge as horsecocks. "Answer me!"

"Yes, sir."

"So you're the sick sonovabitch who did that!"

"I didn't do that, sir! I didn't!"

"You're lying."

"No I ain't, sir."

The cops looked bored, their thumbs tucked into their gun belts. Richie's disciplinary record lay in its beige folder on Biff's desk.

"You . . . are . . . one . . . arrogant sonovabitch. Wipe that smirk off your face before I wipe it off with the back of my hand!" Richie wondered where Biff saw a smirk since he was almost in tears. "You're in big trouble, boy."

"I didn't do it!" His lower jaw started to tremble, a sign that he was going to cry. Biff saw this and eased up a bit.

"Can you prove you didn't do it?"

Richie thought. "For one thing . . . I know nigger has two g's."

One of the cops cracked up but quickly regained composure. Even Biff started to smile.

"Another thing I know is that I'm gonna get killed this afternoon."

"Awright, get outta here, go back to your class. This isn't over yet, Gennaro."

As he closed the office door he heard one of the cops laughing and Biff saying, "Ah, the kid didn't do it. I'll get the custodian to tar it over."

In the cafeteria the Wanderers, feeling puny and defenseless, sat hunched over a corner table. Everyone knew about the vandalism now, and it seemed like the whole school was staring and snickering. Every few minutes a black kid would walk past the table with an evil grin. Richie threw his tuna sandwich in the garbage and buried his head in his arms.

At three o'clock the Wanderers met in front of the principal's office and left the building together. It seemed like every black kid in the school was waiting for them. They formed a large ring open at one end, the end the Wanderers walked into. Except for Richie the rest of the gang was hustled away and told not to come back or their ass was grass. Richie's gang was left across the street helplessly craning their necks to see what was happening over the woolly heads of the crowd.

Richie was alone. Clinton Stitch emerged from the crowd and faced him. "Hi, Clinton." He smiled nervously. There was laughter from the crowd. A chorus of "Hi, Clinton's" in falsetto. He felt like a faggot and angry at himself, some strength returning to his body and soul. Clinton was so muscular that his arms and chest looked like round stones were sewn under his skin. "I didn't do it!" More laughter. "I didn't do it." More laughter. He became furious. "Hey, fuck you guys, man. Hah? I didn't do it!"

Clinton spoke. "Don't worry, man, you ain't gonna have to fight everybody. Just me."

"I ain't fightin' *you*, man."

"Then I'm just gonna kill you standin' there . . . man."

The kids in the crowd were gleefully giving each other taps and fighting for a front-row spot. Clinton started for Richie but was distracted by the sound of screeching brakes as five beat-up Buicks came to screaming halts in front of the school, and ten guys scrambled from each car shouting and yelling, swinging tire chains, aerials, and baseball bats, scattering the crowd. Clinton punched Richie in the gut. "I'll get *you later*, motherfucker!" and vanished. Richie was sitting, dazed, his hands folded over his stomach. Tutti Frutti, one of the Lester Avenue boys, grabbed Richie by the front of his shirt. "Lissen 'ere . . . if any a those black cocksuckers ever lay a hand on you again you call us, awright? Awright?"

"Yes, sir." He felt like a little kid. The only faces Richie saw now were white. The Lester Avenue boys stood around laughing. Three or four of the slower black kids were getting the shit pounded out of them on the broad lawn. In the distance he saw a black kid chased toward the parkway by a crazy guinea who was whooping and hollering, swirling a baseball bat over his head.

"Where the hell were you? I was gonna call your father to go look for you."

"I had a meetin'." Richie pushed past his mother and went into the kitchen.

"Don't gimme none a that. I was gonna call the cops in ten minutes."

"Lay off, Ma."

"I thought maybe God forbid some a those niggers . . ."

"Will you lemme alone? Jesus Christ!" He opened the refrigerator, grabbed a bottle of orange soda, and took a long swig.

"Animal! We all gotta drink from your lips now, hah?"
She slapped him on the back of the head.

He stared at her balefully, belched, and walked out the door
with the soda.

"*Now* where you goin'?" She followed him into the hallway.

"Over to C's."

"You ain't back by six you ain't got no dinner . . . I don't
care." She shrugged.

"Good."

"Oh, Richie!" C pulled him in from the foyer.

"Hey, what's happenin'?"

"I passed my math."

He offered her a shot of orange soda.

"*I'll* take some." Dougie came running in and snatched the
bottle from his hand. Richie watched almost four inches of
the stuff disappear in one gulp. Dougie's white shirt hung out
of his pants, and his Holy Rosary School clip-on tie was hanging from one collar. His narrow, freckled imp face was covered with chocolate, and when he finished drinking, his thin
lips glistened red. "Whadya starin' at?" Dougie said.

"When you gonna get braces?" Richie asked. Dougie had
front teeth like Bugs Bunny.

"Fuck you!" Dougie screamed. "If I had a dog with a face
like yours I'd shave its ass and teach it to walk backwards!"
Dougie was so pissed he had spit on his chin. Richie was serene. "If you had braces you wouldn't spray spit on people."

"Richie!" C admonished.

Dougie rushed at Richie, trying to kick him in the balls, but
Richie caught his foot and waltzed him around the room in a
mad hopping dance. Dougie could only scream in impotent
anger. Richie let go, and Dougie fell on his back. "I hope the
niggers kicked your ass!" Dougie hissed.

"What!" Richie grabbed his sticklike arm. "What'd you say?"

Dougie got scared and clammed up.

"Richie, let go! You're hurting him." C tried to pull him away, but Richie ignored her.

"How'd you know about the niggers? I'll break your fuckin' arm, Dougie!"

Dougie struggled to get loose. Richie saw the white paint on Dougie's fingers. He smiled and twisted Dougie's arm behind his back, whispering in his ear, "Whadya do it for, Dougie?"

"Leggoleggoleggo, oooh, Denise!"

"Come across and I'll let you go."

"Duh-*neese!*"

"Richie, stop!"

"Who else did it, Dougie?"

"Duh-neese!"

Richie jerked Dougie's twisted arm another two inches.

"IdiditwithScottie, leggoleggoleggo, puh-leeze!"

Richie let go. "Scottie Hite?" Dougie got up, rubbing his arm. "Scottie Hite!" Richie repeated. Dougie made a motion for Richie, thought better of it, punched his sister in the tit, and ran into the bathroom locking the door.

After dinner, the Wanderers met in Big Playground.

"How you feelin', man?"

"O.K." Richie rubbed his stomach. "Lissen, I found out who did it."

"Antone?"

"Nah."

"Terror?"

"Nah, you'll never guess . . . Dougie Rizzo."

"Dougie?"

"Yeah, an' his friend that kid Scottie."

"Scottie Hite?"

"Yeah."

"Jeez, they're like . . . ten!"

"You wanna kick their asses?"

"Nah . . . I got a better idea."

That night Richie and Perry walked through Bronx Park to the cave near French Charlie's field. Six bicycles were strewn in front in a daisy pattern. Painted on the outside of the cave were a skull and crossbones with the legend:

WARNING! WHOEVER ENTERS THIS CAVE WILL DIE A DEATH AT THE HANDS OF THE ZORROS

RANDY	GLEN
CARY	GENIE
STEVE	PHIL

Richie stuck his head into the dakrness. "Hey, Randy!" his voice echoed off the walls. Randy Gennaro emerged. He had his brother's sleepy bug-eyes and pouting lips, but instead of Richie's curly waterfall hairdo he sported a six-inch-high pompadour.

"Hey, Richie!"

"Hey, babe, what's goin' on?"

"We're havin' a meetin'."

"Lissen, we gotta job for the Zorros."

"Hey!" Randy shouted back into the cave. "C'mere, guys." The other five Zorros came out. They all sat powwow style in the damp evening grass. The Zorros were a bunch of sixth graders from Holy Rosary School. They rode their bikes like a motorcycle gang around Bronx Park and Big Playground.

"Lissen up . . . we gotta job for the Zorros," said Perry.

"What kinda job?"

"Revenge," said Richie, sending a white pearl of spit arching between his front teeth.

"We want you guys to rub out an enemy," said Perry, cleaning the dirt from his thumbnail with a pocketknife.

"A big guy?" asked Phil, a fat blond kid.

"Nah . . . a little guy."

"Two little guys."

"What grade?"

"Fifth."

The Zorros laughed easy.

"We'll give you a slice of pizza and a pack of butts."

"Each?"

"A slice each and a pack for the whole gang," said Richie.

"Two packs," offered Perry.

Richie gave him a dirty look. "O.K. Two packs."

"Done."

The next day, six Zorros wearing Lone Ranger masks and riding English Racers swooped down on Dougie and Scottie in Big Playground and whisked them off to Bronx Park. Outside the cave the two kids were blindfolded, their hands tied behind their backs.

"C'mon, Randy, I know it's you," said Dougie. Scottie, a skinny little kid like Dougie, with a blond almost white crew cut, was weeping.

"Silence!" Cary slapped Dougie on the back of his head.

"C'mon, lemme go, man!" Dougie whined.

At a signal from Randy, they were shoved inside the cave and made to sit with their backs against a wall. The six Zorros sat facing them. The blindfolds and the ropes were removed.

"I know all you guys," said Dougie. "I'm tellin'."

The Zorros were silent. Randy produced a big fat earth-worm. He held it on a stick in front of Dougie's face. "If you open your mouth one more time this goes in it."

Dougie clammed up.

"Now!" Randy took a piece of loose-leaf paper from his pocket. "Dougie Rizzo and Scottie Hite, you are formally charged with high treason. How do you plead?"

Before Dougie could open his mouth, Randy picked up the earthworm stick and waved it in his face again.

"Nothing to say? Ah . . . contempt of court. Very good." He waved the stick in front of Scottie. "How 'bout you?"

Scottie puked in his own lap.

"Hmm, spitting at the judge."

Randy turned to the Zorros. "How do you find the defendants?"

"Guilty!"

"Kill 'em!"

"String 'em up!"

"Plan C!"

"No, Plan A!"

"Plan B!"

"Kill 'em!"

Rubbing his hands, Randy faced the defendants. "You have been found guilty on all accounts . . . do you have any last words?" He made a motion for the stick but didn't have to pick it up. "Hey, someone clean that guy up." One of the Zorros took off Scottie's shirt and wiped his face and chin. "Now, as judge I decree that you can pick your punishment from three options. A." He counted on his fingers. "We tie you up naked on the cave floor, and in the morning we pick up what the worms and spiders didn't eat." He put the earthworm on Dougie's shoulder. Dougie screamed. "No . . . I guess you wouldn't want that. Well, anyway, Plan B." He flicked open a pocketknife and rested it on Scottie's cheekbone. "We scoop your eyeballs out." Scottie screwed up his face like he was going to bawl again. "I guess that leaves us with Plan C."

"Plan C!" everyone shouted.

They were marched out of the cave and taken to a bridge that crossed over a dried-up stream. When they reached the center of the bridge Randy ordered their pants and underwear removed. One of the Zorros produced two lengths of twine. He tied one length around Dougie's little prick. Then he tossed the other piece to another Zorro who did the same thing to Scottie. The ends of the twine lay in curled piles at their feet.

"Whadya gonna do?" blubbered Dougie.

"We're gonna make you inta girls." A Zorro marched up to the bridge with two large rocks — one resting on each shoulder. He dropped them with a loud thud. Randy tied the loose ends of the twine around the rocks. Dougie and Scottie were pushed to the edge of the bridge, the dry riverbed twenty feet below. Randy and Cary each picked up a rock, checked the tightness of the knots on both ends, and held the rocks over the edge.

"Do you have any last words to say to your pricks?" Scottie peed all over his legs. Randy tugged slightly on the twine and watched Dougie's prick jump like a marionette. "Look a' that! It'll probably rip right off before the rock hits the ground!" He laughed.

"Hey! I wanna hear you guys say goodbye to your pricks. Say . . . goodbye, prick . . . nice a you to hang around so long. Say it."

Dougie said, "Goodbye . . . nice a you . . . c'mon, Randy, I'm sorry."

"Scottie . . . now you."

"Goodbye . . . so long . . . I — I — "

"One . . . two . . ."

Dougie and Scottie screamed at the top of their lungs.

"Three!" The rocks flew over the side, landing with a dry thud on the cracked mud. Dougie and Scottie stood paralyzed but intact. If the drop was twenty feet the ropes must have been thirty feet long.

Randy peered over the side. "Hmm, I guess the ropes were too long. There's only one thing to do." He took out his pocketknife, walking slowly toward Dougie. Dougie trembled, making high-pitched squeals. With one swipe Randy cut the rope off Dougie's prick. Then he cut Scottie's rope. "Well . . . I guess we'll have to find shorter ropes." He tucked the two pairs of pants under his arm, and the Zorros marched off, leaving Dougie and Scottie bare-assed and shivering on the bridge.

2

The Party

EUGENE CAPUTO was having a party. The Wanderers met on Burke Avenue.

"Awright, Perry, you goin' in again?"

"How come I always gotta go in?"

" 'Cause you look like a fuckin' forty-year-old degenerate."

"So does your mother."

"You ain't got one."

"Your's got a mattress on 'er back for curbside service. Hey! Get it while it's hot."

"Hey, c'mon, Perry, you gotta go in, you look the oldest."

"Awright, awright, what's it now? Two Tangos, a bottle of Seven . . ."

"An' some vodka."

"Ugh!"

"Well fuck it, I ain't drinkin' any a that orange piss."

"Awright, awright, get a pint a vodka."

"Lessee, that's two, three, four, four-fifty."

"O.K., there's five of us so that's . . . ah . . . ah, hey somebody gimme a pencil."

"Ninety cents each, asshole."

"Awright, get it up."

"Shit . . . all I got's a fifty-dollar bill."

"Yeah right, you can't even count that high."

"Oh yeah? It's more money than your old man sees in a week."

"Oh yeah? Your mother gets that for spreadin' her legs."

"Oh yeah? Your mother gets that for closin' 'em."

"C'mon, c'mon, we ain't got all night."

Once the booze was bought they split to pick up their girl friends. Richie walked back to the projects to get C.

"Yeah? Whozzat?"

"Richie."

C's father opened the door, stared at Richie through leather eyelids, grunted. Richie walked past him through the foyer of the narrow apartment into C's room. C was standing in front of her mirror picking at her hair with a teasing comb. He stood in the doorway watching her.

The party was in Eugene's wood-paneled basement. C and Richie came early. Only Eugene's date Terry, his cousin Ralph from Queens, and Ralph's girl friend Anne were there.

"Hey."

"Hey, Richie, this is Ralph."

"Howarya."

"Howarya."

"An' this is C."

They all nodded. Eugene pulled Richie over to the record player. "Check this out." He handed Richie a stack of 45s. He looked them over: "Soldier Boy," "Ten Commandments of Love," "Sealed With a Kiss," "Patches," "Tell Laura I Love Her," "Tears on My Pillow," and ten more of the slowest songs imaginable. Eugene nudged him. "This is gonna be a *grindin'* night!"

"Hey, you know what C said to me? She said she was so horny she might go all the way!"

Eugene slapped his forehead. "You shittin' me?"

"Would I shit you? You're my favorite turd."

"Hey, up yours."

"Be nice to me and I'll let you smell my finger."

"Hey, watch this." Eugene flicked off the master switch and all the lights went out except a small red bulb in a corner. "Atmosphere."

"Hey, cut it out!" Anne yelled.

Eugene turned the lights on. "We'll save it for later, when they're all horny."

"Hey, ah, lissen . . . if, ah, things get goin' between me an' C, you know, can I use yer room?"

Eugene frowned. "You really think you might go all the way?"

"Maybe even farther."

"Well, O.K., but don't use it unless you really have to."

"Don' worry." Richie slapped Eugene on the shoulder.

The front-door chimes rang. Eugene took the rickety basement stairs four at a time. The stairs rattled again a minute later as five guys and four girls came down yelling and shouting. Each guy had a bottle conspicuously hidden under his coat. Everyone gave their booze to Turkey. He went to work making quart shakers of Seven, screwdriver, and rum and Coke.

"Hey, Turkey, put in that Spanish fly I gave you, heh-heh." Joey laughed and squeezed his date's shoulder.

While waiting for the drinks, everyone grabbed at potato chips, M&Ms, pretzels, and Fritos.

"Hey, man, me an' Margo saw *West Side Story* at the Valentine last night, you see that yet?" Buddy asked.

"Yeah, that was boss."

"Yeah, I dug the Jets."

"Yeah, but the coolest dude was Bernardo."

"Yeah, he's cute."

"Ah, my ass is cute."

"You see those shirts and jackets them P.R.s was wearin'?"

"I just got me a jacket in Alexanders like Chico's."

"I liked Tony. He was cool."

"Yeah, he was boss."

"Yeah, but howdja like them bazooms on that P.R. chick?"

"Perry, you're such a pig."

"Who you mean, Natalie Wood?"

"No, man, the other one."

"Natalie Wood, a carpenter's dream."

"Flat as a board an' easy to screw."

"I thought Richard Beymer was cute," said Margo.

"Hah! You shoulda seen Margo bawl at the end," said Buddy.

"I didn't know Margo balled," Joey said.

"Drinks are ready," said Turkey from the other side of the room. The guys charged up to the portable bar.

"Hey, you know, they shoulda asked the Wanderers to be the white gang for that movie."

"Yeah, Perry woulda been A-Rab, Joey coulda been Action, Richie coulda been Riff, Turkey coulda been Baby John."

"No! Turkey could be Anybody's." Everyone laughed except Turkey.

"I coulda been Tony," said Buddy.

"Yeah sure, my ass would be a better Tony," said Richie.

"I'd a like to be Bernardo," said Joey.

"What for? He was a P.R."

"He ain't a real P.R. That George Chakiris, he's Italian."

"No he ain't, he's Jewish," said Perry.

"Bullshit, he's too good-lookin' for a Hebe."

"Maybe he got a nose job," countered Perry.

"Maybe he got a handjob," said Joey.

"Maybe he got a blowjob," said Richie.

"There's no job like a blowjob, there's no job that I know," the three sang.

"An' now ladies an' gennelmun, will you please rise for the national anthem," Eugene announced, standing at attention by the record player. A static riddled piano brought on Dion's gutty voice.

> Oh, I'm the type of guy who will never settle down,
> Where a pretty girls are, a well you know that I'm aroun'
> I a kiss 'em an I love 'em Cause to me they're all the same
> I a squeeze 'em and I hug 'em, they don't even know my name
> They call me the Wanderer, yeah the Wanderer
> I roam aroun' aroun' aroun'

After their theme song, Eugene put on a stack of 45s, mixing the slows to fasts in a two to one ratio. The party was on. The first record was the Marcels' "Blue Moon." None of the guys wanted to dance yet, so C and Pat, Perry's date, started doing the Slop. Then Margo, Buddy Borsalino's date, and Barbara, Joey Capra's date, started dancing. The guys were getting high, especially Perry, chugging Sevens as fast as he could. The next record was slow.

C and Richie were alone on the floor. Perry started throwing M&Ms at Richie's head.

"Cut it out, asshole."

Perry laughed and went back to drinking. Half an hour later almost everyone was dancing. Most of the guys were high except Turkey, who never drank. Eugene sat in a corner of the couch with Terry on his lap, making out. Turkey flicked off the master switch, and the room glowed a soft red. Some of the girls yelled in mock protest, but no one told Turkey to put the lights on. Joey and Barbara took the other corner of the couch. Buddy and Margo sat down on a big chair. Ralph and Anne settled for the stairs. C and Richie were the only ones left dancing. Someone turned off the red light and the room was as dark as a closet.

C and Richie started to tongue. He pushed his knee between her legs, and she responded with a nice rotating grind.

"You wanna go up to Eugene's room?" he whispered in her ear.

"What's up there?" she asked.

"You ever see his rock collection?"

"Yeah." He tried to usher her to the stairs. She resisted. "Hey, we can make out down here."

"There's no room." He stuck his tongue in her ear. "C'mon." He took her hand. She held back.

"You sure he won't mind?"

"Nah, he said it was O.K."

They groped their way through the darkness. Climbing the stairs unsteadily they fell over Ralph and Anne. They sorted who belonged to whom, and Richie and C continued upstairs.

In the kitchen, Turkey made himself a sandwich. Perry was throwing up in the bathroom. Richie and C found Eugene's room and locked the door. The lights were out. They sat on the bed and started necking. Richie eased C down and climbed on top. They began to grind in a slow, mechanical motion. Richie stuck his tongue in her ear again and put his hand on her small breast. Groaning, she grabbed him around the neck. He unbuttoned her blouse and ran his fingers along the contours of her bra. He tried slipping a finger inside her bra, but it was as tight as a steel trap. She sat up and unhooked it. Richie went to work flicking and sucking just like the guys in the French films. He threw in some more heavy grinding before putting his hand up her skirt, feeling the wetness of her underwear. She reached between his legs and rubbed his cock. He frantically unzipped his fly and whipped it out. She stroked his balls. He pushed her skirt above her waist and slipped his hand inside her panties. Running his fingers lightly through her tight curls he suddenly plunged his middle finger into the fleshy wetness. She moaned and squirmed like a fish on a hook. He moved his finger around trying to find the clit. Tommy Tatti said it felt like a marble covered with oil, but Richie would be goddamned if he could find anything like a marble down there. He could tell when he was close because she would gasp and squeeze his balls. This hurt, but was a good indicator. He tried to take off her panties but couldn't get them past her knees. He took her hand off his cock and tried to put himself in. She froze. He felt her tenseness and tried to put his fingers back in to see if she was still wet.

"Don't." She twisted her legs.

"Oh Christ! C'mon, I won't come in you."

"Not yet."

"Whadya mean not yet? You mean inna half-hour? Or do you mean in five years? I don't know whatcha mean by not yet."

"Just not yet."

He sat up, looked at his hard-on, and plopped down again. "Jesus Christ, I'm gonna die!" He tried to lick her ear. She turned her head away.

"I'll do it with my hand."

"Great! *I* can do it with my hand. I don't even *need* you for that."

She started to cry. He lost his hard-on in degrees like a descending car jack.

Suddenly they heard shouts and screams. Richie zipped his fly and ran out of the room leaving C sitting on the bed, her clothes on in all the wrong places. In the basement the lights were on. The girls were crying hysterically, Perry was sprawled on the couch, one side of his face covered with blood. The Wanderers were shouting out the window; other guys outside shouted back. Rocks thudded against the side of the house.

"The Pharaohs," Joey Capra said, looking up at Richie.

"So let's get 'em!" Richie started for the door. Turkey stopped him. "They got chains. Perry went out awready."

Eugene came downstairs with two baseball bats and a souvenir bullwhip.

"What're you crazy! There's eight of 'em out there!" said Joey.

Eugene threw his arsenal on the floor. "Great! So what the fuck are we gonna do, let 'em tear down the house?"

"C-call the cops," Anne said between sobs.

"No!" Richie was livid. "We ain't callin' no cops for the fuckin' Pharaohs!" He flung the door open. "Antone! I'm gonna kick your fuckin' ass!"

"C'mon out, Gennaro! C'mon out!" A rock smashed into the door over his head. Eugene dragged him back in.

Perry started moaning, "I'm gonna kill 'em, I'm gonna kill 'em."

A rock sailed through the window sending a shower of glass into the room. Richie grabbed a quart bottle of booze and threw it at the window. In his fury he missed, smashing the bottle against the wall.

"That's a great help," said Ralph.

"Hey, wait!" Turkey picked up a bottle half-filled with rum and Coke. "Yeah." He looked around at the other guys. "Grab a bottle and come upstairs."

"What?"

"Just do it." They each grabbed a bottle and ran upstairs after him. He emerged from the bathroom with a roll of toilet paper. "Grab off some and stuff it into the mouth of the bottle like this." He unrolled a foot and a half, shoving it into the bottle, leaving some hanging over the top. They copied him.

"C'mon." He ran to Eugene's bedroom. "Fuck! The door's locked!"

C opened the door. She was dressed now, and her eyes were red. They barged past her. Richie stopped. They looked at each other for a moment, then she ran downstairs. The window overlooked the front of the house; they were directly above the Pharaohs. Turkey eased up the window about halfway and motioned everyone to stand back. He took a lighter from his pocket and lit the toilet paper in his bottle. Standing flush against the wall, he lobbed the bottle grenade-style out the window. It crashed against the pavement, exploding into a sheet of flame. The Pharaohs screamed. Antone's pants caught fire, and he ran in circles in front of his horror-stricken gang until he had the presence of mind to take his pants off. Turkey, still against the wall, held his lighter out. Richie raised his bottle to the flame and whipped it out the window, sailing it over their heads. This time the Pharaohs took off. Lights went on all over the block.

The Wanderers filed downstairs. Eugene and Richie stood outside, waiting for the police. Buddy Borsalino took Perry to the hospital. When the cops arrived, Eugene said they were having a party when some drunk guys came around and tried to crash. He showed them the broken window. He had no explanations for the fire. He didn't know who those guys were. Richie added that they had Puerto Rican accents, maybe Simpson Street dudes.

When the cops left, Eugene and Richie went back inside. C was gone. Anne said Turkey took her home. Richie said, "Fuck'er."

Turkey was a real turkey. He was in all the honor classes at school, but the other smart kids would have nothing to do with him because he was such a creep. He had a face like the French Angel and a thick, hunko body. His skin was yellow like bad teeth and he dressed in dirty-gray clothes. The Wanderers thought he was a creep too, but they weren't used to his intelligence. He knew about things like astronomy and war stories. He collected Nazi paraphernalia (even though he was Jewish) and could speak German. He could draw. Once he did a pencil portrait of C on loose-leaf paper that they swore looked good enough to hang in a museum. He could sing. He sang "Some Enchanted Evening" like Robert Goulet and wasn't ashamed to sing in front of people. So occasionally he hung with the Wanderers. Everyone knew his mother and father were flippy. That his sister was a royal skank who fucked for a dime. That his house was covered with tissues and dirty magazines.

That night, he walked slowly and silently under the streetlights painfully aware of C at his side. When she left the party, he impulsively ran after her. She was crying. He offered to walk her home. "The Pharaohs might still be around," he said. She said nothing. After a few blocks she stopped crying. Once in a while she would sniff. She didn't look up at him, didn't raise her head. Turkey wracked his brain for something to say. They reached Big Playground.

"Did you have a good time tonight?" he asked.

She started up again, her sobs ripping into him. She plopped down on a bench. He sat next to her — not too close. "I'm sorry, C. I was only tryin' to make conversation."

She looked up at him with watery eyes, wiping her nose, smiling bravely. "You're sweet, Turkey. Thank you for walking me home." He placed his arm on the top of the bench behind her shoulders. "I'm gonna go up now."

"I'll walk you upstairs." He stood up.

"No, it's O.K., I can go myself. Thanks for walking me home. I mean it, you're really sweet." She smiled at him and walked toward her building.

He sat on the bench watching her shaded bedroom window until the light went out.

*

"I'm sorry."

"For what?"

"For Saturday."

C examined her nails. "Sataday?"

"You know."

"Know what?"

"Goddamnit, don't be a cunt!" Richie said it louder than he planned, and a few little kids stopped their basketball game to watch the show on the bench. Richie knew C would be bitchy when he apologized, so he'd rehearsed that line for half an hour, and now he'd said it too loud, and too uncool, and he blew it.

"Why not, Richie, what else would a prick go out with?"

Richie was impressed. That was even a better line than his. "That hurts, C, that really hurts." He looked hurt. The kids went back to their basketball game.

"Aww," she pouted, "Richie's hurt."

Richie stood up and surveyed Big Playground. C remained on the bench, crossed her legs, and continued to study her nails. "I can't talk to you," he said to no one in particular as he scanned the basketball court. "I never could."

"You're talkin' now," she said in a singsong voice.

He sat back down. "Look, I said I was sorry an' I ain't gonna say it again. You don't like it you can gimme back my fuckin' ankle bracelet."

"That's the way you apologize, Richie? You call me a cunt an' say if I don't like it I can give you back your fuckin' ankle bracelet?" She finally looked up and he saw she had tears on her cheeks. Something in Richie folded like a flower.

*

Friday night.

"C'mon, C."

"No!" She rolled onto her stomach. Richie had to be satisfied with stroking her back and grabbing her ass.

"Look," he compromised, "I'll only stick it in . . . this much." He narrowed the space between his fingers. She lay motionless like a corpse.

"O.K., forget it." He started getting dressed, but she didn't move. He put on his socks and shoes. Then he put on his T-shirt. But she wasn't budging until she heard the metallic zip of his fly being closed.

She turned over and Richie in his socks, shoes, and T-shirt dove between her legs like a sea gull swooping down for a clam in the ocean. His pants were on the floor, the zipper zipped. As he worked between her thighs with a maniac determination, there was a tremendous explosion and the room filled with smoke. C screamed. Richie jumped to his feet, his heart going crazy, his erection shrinking like a speeded-up film of a blooming flower shot in reverse. An acrid thickness filled the air. C clutched the blanket to her in wild-eyed horse terror. Richie saw the shreds of a firecracker by the door. On the other side of the door Dougie and Scottie made sounds of idiot glee. Richie's anger kicked the film forward, and he had a blooming-rage hard-on. C grabbed him by the T-shirt before he could fling open the door and drown them in the bathtub like two kittens.

*

Lenny Arkadian had a sign-painting shop on Olinville Avenue. The Wanderers sometimes hung out at the shop after school because Lenny was a young guy who cursed like a sailor and knew the best dirty jokes. He was a big flabby shipwreck of a person who'd won a William Bendix look-alike contest in high school. He was usually covered from head to toe with red paint — the only color he ever used for his signs. His store had been condemned by the Board of Health six times since he'd opened up. This was no small accomplishment as the only things around were a splattered workbench, a few reams of blank poster board, and a pyramid of red paint cans. He'd framed the six citations and hung them around his expulsion notice from Rhode Island School of Design. He considered himself an artist, a cocksman, and a real card — in that order. He'd had a barber pole tattooed on his cock when he was in Tangiers with the navy, he could give out with a fifteen-second fart, and he didn't give a shit about business. He'd do anything for an audience. One time when the Wanderers were hanging around, an old lady came into the store for a sign. Lenny got down on all fours, barking and howling, snapping at her heels, chasing her into the street. Then he went after the guys, growling and snarling, scuttling across the floor like a crab until Joey emptied a gallon of red paint on his head. In five minutes, the walls, the floors, the reams of white paper, and everybody present were soaked with paint. Lenny ruined two days' work and fifty dollars worth of finished signs, but a good time was had by all. Since that day, Lenny had been known as the Wolfman.

"Wolfman!"

"Gennaro! How's she hangin'?" Lenny hadn't looked up when the sleigh bells over his door jangled, and Richie barged in, throwing his schoolbooks on the workbench. Lenny, up to his armpit in the stuff, was mixing a barrel of red paint with a wooden salad fork. He wore a paint-stiffened sweatshirt and gray chinos.

"You seen Eugene?" Richie asked.

"He was just here about ten minutes ago. I heard that was some wild party you guys had Saturday. How come you didn't invite me?"

"It was a full moon."

"Ah, you guys crack me up." He grimaced as the paint crept up to his shoulder. "Oh, Gennaro, I heard you got laid. I don't believe it but that's what I heard."

"I didn't get laid. Who told you that, Eugene?"

"Yeah, he says you got balled in his room."

"Right, my fist got balled in his room." After wiping his sweatshirt and hand reasonably dry, Lenny laid out a blank poster on the workbench. "It was this close, Lenny." Richie held his thumb and index finger almost touching. "Ah dunno, I'm gonna join the monks." He shook his head sadly.

"Gennaro, not to make you feel any more inadequate than you are, but I gotta tell you what happened to me last night." He worked as he talked, carefully printing the details for a linen sale at Lipschitz's department store down the block. Richie laughed. He knew a good story was coming. "I went out with this chick last night, a nurse from Jacobi. You know them nurses. You know half them operations where the patients die is because the doctors are too tired to hold a scalpel straight because they just been in the, I dunno, the sterilization room sterilizin' with the nurses? That's a fact. Yeah, I read it in *Argosy*. Anyways, I think Rochelle — that's the nurse I went out with last night as I started to say — Rochelle I think was responsible for half them losin' operations at Jacobi."

"Hey, fuck you! My mother was a nurse."

"Yeah, well, I got a story about her too. Anyways this Rochelle, like I picked her up in Manny's last night. You know, just put the old moves on an' I swear to God, in fifteen minutes I was back in my place, an' in twenty, I'd say twenty-seven minutes, I was gobblin' her clam like it was the last supper." Richie doubted the timing since Lenny lived in Westchester and the drive alone was thirty minutes. "An' I'm tellin' you I musta hit the bullseye because I never got hit with as much clam juice in my life. I mean my chin was drippin' just like this brush."

He dipped his brush in the barrel. The paint dripped obscenely over the floor and his blue canvas shoes. "Anyways, I get this idea. I get up and I got a butter knife and a piece of Wonder Bread, you know, builds your body twelve different ways and all that bullshit. Anyways, I get this knife an' some bread an' I stuck the knife up her ol' patoot, got a nice gob of clam squirt, an' I spread it on the bread." To demonstrate he slapped the wet paintbrush slowly back and forth across his palm. "Like this, see?" Richie shook his head in dumb amazement. "An' I did it until I got me a nice pussy on white sandwich. Then I folded the bread over an' I ate it. An' you know what that fuckin' cunt says to me after I finish? She says, 'Lenny, you shouldna done that . . . I got gonorrhea.'"

"Bleagh!"

"I got gonorrhea," Lenny repeated grimacing, finishing the new poster.

"Wolfman, you are not to be believed."

"Yeah, that's what your mother said when I was done with her." Before Richie could protest Lenny continued. "Anyways, Gennaro, about your problem. You have come to the right party for help. I guarantee you if you follow the good doctor's orders your seemingly incurable virginity will be cleared up in a week."

"You shittin' me?" Richie squinted skeptically.

"I shit you not. We may not clear it up in the first treatment, but then again . . ." Lenny shrugged, looking at Richie.

"Keep talkin'."

"Now, are you talkin' about Miss Denise Rizzo alias C?"

"Yeah, yeah." Lenny finished the sign and held it in front of him examining his work. "C'mon, c'mon."

"Patience, mah man. You been waitin' sixteen years for this you can wait five more minutes. Besides, I gotta make a livin'."

Richie sighed and looked to heaven.

"This is a nice poster, ain't it?" He held it facing Richie.

"Lenny," Richie begged.

"You know how much that fat fuck Lipschitz takes in a year? A week? A day?" Richie scratched his head. Hard. Pulled at his hair. "I don't know either, but I betcha it's a titload," Lenny said. Richie got up to leave. "Vaseline a carrot," Lenny said quickly.

"You talkin' to me?"

"Vaseline a carrot, shove it up her snatch. It'll give her a taste of what the real thing's like."

"You talkin' to me?" Richie pointed a finger at his own chest.

"Make sure you stick the right end in. A banana's too soft. It might break off in the middle, then where'll you be?"

"You ain't a Wolfman, you're a . . ."

"I knew this girl once whose cunt muscles were so strong she could pick up a carrot off a table with her snatch and make it disappear. Of course an unpeeled banana will do the trick too but sometimes the ends are too rough. You see, the trick with getting laid is you gotta be gentle."

The next day Richie went food shopping. All he wanted was a carrot, but just so the cashier wouldn't get suspicious, he bought two pounds of squeeze oranges, a pound of turnips, and four heads of iceberg lettuce.

*

Every Friday night, C's parents went to their cousin's club meeting, and every Friday night Richie would slip into C's bedroom for his weekly wrestling match. So far C was undefeated, but this time Richie brought brass knuckles into the ring. The warm-ups went as usual. With lights out and television on he took off her blouse and bra to the theme from "Seventy-Seven Sunset Strip." He took off her dress and drawers to the theme from "Twilight Zone" and by the time Zacherle's "Shock Theater" came on they were in the middle of a one-fall-no-holds-barred-Texas-Death-Match-winner-take-all, although all C had to do to win was hold Richie to a draw.

"Hey, C?"

"Huh?"

"I'll be right back." Richie got up. He felt for the carrot, which he'd slipped into one of his socks while undressing. He dropped the carrot into the front of his pants and made it to the bathroom. The light made him squint as he searched through the Rizzo medicine cabinet for Vaseline. They had a large family-size jar. He smeared a fistful over the carrot until it had a dull, slimy glaze. He put the carrot in his pants, turned off the light, and went back to the bedroom. His strategy was to slip it in while fingering her, taking advantage of the darkness to pull the old switcheroo. He undressed again, keeping the organic dildo within easy reach. As he worked his fingers inside C, like the master finger-fucker that he was, and as a big-titted blonde was being eaten by Roachmen from Mars on "Shock Theater," he grabbed the slippery vegetable with his other hand and was about to make the switch from index finger to food when C turned on the light, catching him with the goods.

"I just wanna . . . what the hell is that!" Her eyes widened in disbelief.

"What?" Richie said dumbly, his hand paralyzed, the carrot six inches from C's nose.

"That!"

"This?"

"That."

"Oh, that. Oh, it's a carrot. It's a, uh, it's really good!" Richie took a large bite, chewed enthusiastically, wiped a dab of Vaseline from his chin, and offered it to C, a grin on his face like a mule eating shit. "Want some?"

"Lenny! You fucker!" It was three in the morning, but Lenny answered the phone on the first ring.

"Whosis? Sounds like Gennaro." Lenny was wide-awake. "Gennaro, say hello to Dolores." The phone exchanged hands and a husky female voice said, "Hi."

"Lemme speak to Lenny," Richie said, for once unimpressed and unamused.

"Gennaro, what's up?"

"Me, you, Dolores, an' my dinner, you bastard."

"What're you talkin' about?"

"Glazed carrots."

"You dope, you ain't supposed to eat 'em. Come in Monday, we'll talk." Lenny hung up the phone before Richie could say anything.

*

"Gennaro, how many times I gotta tell you? I'm in your corner." Lenny put his arm around Richie's shoulders.

"You really are a Wolfman, you know that?"

"O.K., that's it, no more bullshitting around with amateurs, we go pro."

"Whadya mean?" Richie felt a frightening tightness in his gut.

"I'll be right back." Lenny left the store. Richie sat on the workbench feeling like he was on a doctor's examining table. Five minutes later Lenny returned. "It's time to harvest the cherries."

"Whadya mean?" Richie's lunch was doing a mambo up his throat.

"Whado I mean, whado I mean, whadya think I mean?" Lenny put the "will be back at" sign on the door, setting the movable clock hands for four thirty.

"Whadya gonna do, close the store? C'mon, Lenny, don't go to no expense like that."

Lenny slung his jacket over his T-shirt. "You comin'?" he snickered.

Richie shrugged, took a deep breath that turned into a nervous shudder, and followed him out of the store. He walked behind Lenny, staring at the back of his gray chinos, the big ass, the wide shoulders, the bird's nest of blond hair. Sensing Richie's stare, Lenny turned his head and smiled, motioning

Richie to walk beside him. He put his arm around Richie's shoulders.

"Hey, Lenny? I don't need no bag or nothin' do I?"

"Nah, just relax. You'll be O.K."

They stopped in front of a grocery store. Lenny went inside. "A fuckin' grocery!" Richie muttered to himself. Every woman coming out looked like a hooker. All the delivery boys were pimps. A police car pulled up and a cop went inside. Richie sprinted across the street into a pizza shop and waited for the paddy wagons: The cop came out munching a banana. "Payoff," Richie thought, going back across the street. Lenny came out carrying a small green bag. "Let's go." He started down the street. Richie declined a tangerine.

They walked six blocks to a quiet residential street of old two-story wooden homes. Lenny ushered Richie onto the porch of a brown and yellow house and opened the door. They climbed a narrow, wooden stairway. Richie felt like he'd just sniffed glue. He held onto the banister for support. When they reached the landing they were faced with six doors.

"Rhonda?" Lenny yelled, peeking into a few rooms.

"Here, Lenny," said a voice from the room at the far end.

He put his hand on Richie's shoulder.

"O.K. I'm leavin' — the kid's here," he shouted.

"O.K., send 'im in."

"See you later, champ," Lenny winked.

"Hey! Take my books?" He looked at Lenny with pleading eyes.

"Sure." He took the books, winked again, and left. Richie knocked on the door.

"C'mon in." Rhonda lay on an unmade bed in her underwear reading a copy of *Cosmopolitan*. She looked up. "Hello," she smiled, "I'm Rhonda."

Richie felt like apologizing.

She wheeled her legs off the bed and sat up, patting the sheet next to her. "Have a seat."

Richie sat.

She unzipped his ski jacket and began to undress him, all the time talking in a smooth, calm voice. "What's your name?"

"Gregory."

"Do you have a girl?"

"Yes."

"What's her name?"

"Mary."

"Is she pretty?"

"No."

"Do you like school?"

"Yes."

"What do you wanna be?"

"A frogman."

She put her hand in his underwear and played with his prick. He looked at her for the first time. She was about thirty, blond, with nice tits. She reminded him of a nurse. "Help me take my bra off?" She turned her back, looking over her shoulder at him. He unhooked her brassiere and felt the warmth of her back through his fingers. He hoped she wouldn't ask him to take off her panties. She stood up, slipped them off, and faced him. He stood up. She pulled down his shorts.

"Do you want me on top? Or do you want to be on top?" she asked.

"Huh? What? I dunno. Whatever you think is best."

"We'll do you on top."

She lay back, spread her legs, and brought her knees up to her chest. "Allaboard!"

Lenny walked back wondering if he'd done the right thing. Shit, the kid's old enough. I got it when I was twelve. It didn't hurt me none. Rhonda's a good kid, she'll take care of 'im. He reached his store at four o'clock. The sign read "will be back at 4:30." He shrugged and walked two blocks to Manny's. The bar was deserted.

"How you doin', Lenny?"

"Awright. Gimme a Jack Daniels, John." The bartender poured a jigger over ice. "Hey, John, how old was you when you got laid?"

"Thirty-six."

"No, c'mon, I'm serious."

"You lookin' for some action?" John's voice went down a few octaves as he placed the drink in front of Lenny.

"Nah, nah. You know those kids always hangin' aroun' my place? I just brought one a 'em over to some hooker I know on Colden Avenue."

"First time?"

"Yeah. The kid's sixteen. That's old enough, ain't it? I mean shit, I was twelve when I got my first piece."

"I was twenty-one," said John. "In Japan, I was in the occupation troops, I'll never forget. Cigarettes use' to be six-fifty a pack in Tokyo. We use to get 'em for a dime in the PX. You'd go over to Madame Soo's or the Blue Moon, and you could get a girl for five bucks." He laughed. "We use' to give the madame a pack of butts and we'd get a girl and a dollar fifty change."

"You was twenty-one?"

"Yeah. A beautiful girl named Sooky."

"When I was twenty-one I had the clap twice awready." He finished his shot and motioned for another. "You think sixteen's too young?"

"Who's the kid?"

"Richie Gennaro."

"I know his old man. He comes in here every once inna while."

"What's his old man like?"

John shrugged. "Nice guy. Drinks his drink and watches the fights."

"Hey, don't tell 'im, awright?"

"I'm gonna tell 'im?"

Lenny threw a dollar-fifty on the counter. "Take care."

John gave a quick wave as the cash register kachangged.

Lenny went back to his store, knocked off two "sale" signs, and started to lock up. As he turned off the lights, the sleigh bells on his door jangled. Richie stood in the doorway.

"How'd it go?" Lenny asked softly.

"Awright . . . awright." In the semidarkness Richie walked to the workbench. "Lenny?"

Lenny's heart was pounding in his ears. "Can I have my books back?"

"Sure, kid." Richie took the books and headed for the door. "Hey, Richie?"

Richie didn't turn around, but he stopped, one hand on the doorknob. "Didja like it?"

"It was fine."

"You ain't a virgin no more. I don' hafta hear none a your bullshit no more." Lenny laughed weakly.

"Yeah." Richie walked out the door.

3

The Game

JOEY CAPRA was a zip. Short, wiry, always moving, blinking, smoking, chewing. A hook nose and bad posture made him look like a comma. He never idled — he was always in gear, springing up and down on the balls of his feet even when standing in one spot. Any second like a road runner he was off, had a need to GO and FLY. Pure raw nervous energy; a precision honing job done by his father, Emilio Capra, Mister New York City — 1940, who over the years would suddenly lash out with a punch, a kick, a slap, a word that would make Joey vibrate for a week. And Joey learned to duck, bob, weave, twirl, and dance to avoid pain. Now he was like a deer — trip wire reflexes to the slightest sound, sensitive to the smallest change in atmosphere, ready to zoom off, jump up, or leap out. In short he was a nervous wreck and one hell of a broken-field runner. The best hustler in the league, the league being a six-team North Bronx competition between the Stingers, Paragons, Velvet Sharks, Imperials, Red Devils, and Del-Bombers, no sponsor or officials. The teams were made up of different gangs and their nongang associates. The Wanderers were the Stingers with Buddy, Eugene, Richie, Perry, Joey, and some part-time guys, George and Vincent Tasso, Lenny Mitchell, Jo-Jo Kelsey, Ralph Arkadian, Lenny's younger brother, Ed Weiss, Ray Rodriguez, Peter Rabbit, and others. Every Saturday three games were played in various parks in the Bronx — Bronx Park, Van Cortland, Macoombs — each team bringing a caravan of nonplaying friends, fathers, girl friends, and assorted neighbors.

And Joey Capra was everybody's choice for all-league halfback. A scrambling, hustling zip who could squirt through defensive lines like Jell-O between clapped hands.

Except for his thick brush mustache, Emilio Capra looked just like Kirk Douglas. Arrow features, obsidian flecks for eyes, a white line for a mouth. Rich black hair dashed back in waves from his forehead. Neck, arms, legs, torso bulging like a weightlifter gone berserk. Joey was skinny — muscles looking like something trapped between skin and bone. The same face of a hawk but without the glinting power behind the corners of the mouth and the eyes. Father and son played a perpetual game of tag. When Emilio was home, Joey never sat, he crouched; he never walked, he trotted. Always locked his door, slept with one eye and both windows open. Emilio played frog to Joey's fly. Emilio would be immobile, following Joey only with his eyes then suddenly lash out with a quick left, a quick right. Pretend to read a newspaper, and when Joey tried to sneak past, Emilio would snake out a foot — Joey would start to fall but regain his balance and dance triumphant into his bedroom. Emilio would wait for next time.

*

Perry was fullback — slow but unstoppable. A Mack truck rolling downhill. He was best friends with Joey like Little John and Robin Hood. It was envy at first sight — Perry wanting Joey's lithe speed, Joey wanting Perry's bulk and power.

"You wanna have a catch?" Perry and Joey were walking home from the el station on a nice enough November Friday afternoon.

"Awright, yeah." They deposited their schoolbooks and made sandwiches at Perry's house.

"I ain't diggin' the idea of playin' the Del-Bombers tomorrow." Perry tore off half a ham and ketchup sandwich.

"Maybe they ain't diggin' playin' us," Joey said. The Del-Bombers were an all-colored team from the North Bronx near Mount Vernon.

"How'd you like Terry Pitt on top a you in a pileup?" asked Perry.

"Pitt's a pile of shit. He couldn't catch me with a dragnet." Joey was a cocky bastard.

"Don't be too sure."

"Hey! What is this? We're gonna kick their asses." Joey patted Perry on the knee reassuringly. "C'mon, man, don' be such a faggot."

"You wish."

"I know."

"You blow."

"You wish."

They got the football from Perry's room and headed toward the elevator. Perry wore ankle-high, dagger-toed, peau de soie shoes with Cuban heels and heavy taps that made him clop down the hall like a Clydesdale.

"Whyncha put on sneakers?"

Perry started back to change, but the elevator came. "Ah, fuck it."

As they walked to Big Playground they flipped the ball between them. Perry scooting ahead of Joey, Joey scooting ahead of Perry. They played in the basketball courts, which were wide, long, and empty.

"Long bomb!" said Perry, scrambling like a quarterback. Joey streaked across the concrete, catching Perry's pass Willie Mays-style.

"Tittle to Shofner. T.D.!" shouted Perry, snagging Joey's

pass. For thirty minutes they ran at oblique angles to each other catching good and bad passes, announcing the names of the great and near-great quarterbacks, ends, halfbacks, and linebackers.

"Hold on!" yelled Joey, trotting to the bench. "Rest time. Don't wanna get knocked out."

"C'mon," said Perry. "One more long bomb!"

"Forget it."

"C'mon . . ." He flipped the ball to Joey. "Do me. Long bomb." Perry ran as fast as he could looking over his shoulder for Joey's pass. Joey threw a high spiral. Perry stretched his arms — mouth and eyes open for a great catch — Bart Starr to Marv Fleming, Unitas to Berry. His slick shoes slid across the cold ground, the taps on concrete sounding like roller skates, and his legs slipped from under him. Skidding, he crashed heavily into the mesh playground fence, the football hitting the same spot on the fence a second later. Perry rolled on the ground screaming. Joey ran over. "Oh God, it's broke, oh God, oh Jesus, oh God." Tears splashed his face, running into his ears. His teeth chattered in shock as he held up his right arm, his hand hanging too loosely. "Oh Jesus, oh Jesus, owww."

"Sssh." Joey stared at Perry's broken wrist in horror. "Walk on it."

"Oh, it hurts, Joey, it hurts, it hurts."

"Sssh." Joey helped Perry to his feet. They walked through a six-foot-high triangular hole somebody had clipped in the mesh fence and hailed a cab for Jacobi Hospital.

"EEEEEEEEEEE!!!!!" Perry's mother tore out a healthy fistful of her hair when her son and Joey walked into the kitchen two hours later — Perry's hand encased fingertips to elbow in plaster of paris. After two Nembutals Perry was serene and barely heard his mother shrieking. Joey was feeling no pain either because he'd also taken Nembutal from the packet the doctor at Jacobi gave Perry. Perry's mother started working up her panic an hour earlier when Perry hadn't shown up for dinner. She'd called his friends' houses, then the police, and she was just about to call the morgues when they waltzed in on a cloud of tranquilizers. They watched benignly as she ran in small circles around her son, staring in horror at the cast.

"Relax, Ma, it's only a busted wrist, I don't got cancer."

She continued to circle around him, eyes now toward the ceiling, clapping her hands slowly, calling on divine help. "Help me, Saint Ant'ny. Saint Ant'ny, help me, I'm gonna die, I'M GONNA DIE, EEE!!!"

Joey giggled.

"Ma."

"It's only a broken wrist," she informed the refrigerator.

"Ma."

"Don' worry, it's only a broken wrist," she reassured the cold, greasy hamburgers — Perry's dinner.

"Ma."

"It's only a . . ."

"MA!" Perry shouted.

She jerked erect as if she'd been slapped.

"Ma, it's only a broken wrist. I went to Jacobi wit' Joey an' the doctor said it would be O.K. in a couple of weeks." He dug his good hand into his tight black dungarees and pulled out a Nembutal. "Here. The doctor said you should take this pill or my wrist'll get worse."

*

Joey sat down to dinner. His mother brought wine to the table for Emilio, sat down herself, and waited for her husband to start eating. Emilio was in a decent mood tonight because he'd just gotten paid and his two-week vacation started on

Monday. Joey and his mother waited until Emilio cut a piece of steak, chewed and swallowed, and started on a second piece before they began to eat.

"Was a fire today on Bathgate." He downed half a glass of wine. "Carried out two kids." He tore off a piece of bread from a long loaf. "They was cooked more well done than this." He tapped the steak with his fork. Then he finished the wine in his glass. Joey and his mother were silent. They often had to listen to Emilio's horror stories at dinner. He was a fireman, and he would always compare somebody's burned body to something on his plate. "Hey." He stared at Joey. "You playin' football tomorrah?"

"Yeah. Joey didn't look up.

"What?" He put his silverware down and stared at his son.

"Yes." Joey made the "s" hiss. Emilio grabbed his son's chin and jerked it up, his fingers digging deep into Joey's cheeks and jaw. "Yes. I am playing football tomorrow." Joey was scared because he wasn't sure what his father wanted.

Emilio dug his fingers deeper and pointed at Joey's nose. "You look at me when you talk."

Joey tried to meet his father's burning stare, but the pain was distracting.

Emilio turned his attention to his dinner. Joey's mother had learned never to interfere. "Whadya play, water boy?" Emilio laughed at his own wit.

Joey had no trouble staring at his father this time. "I'm halfback."

"Who you play . . . cripples?" He laughed loudly, slapping the table. "Cripples," he chuckled, returning to his meal. Joey controlled himself, although he'd lost his appetite.

"Joey, eatcha dinner," his mother almost whispered.

"Yeah, eatcha dinner so you can get big an' strong an' beat the cripples."

"Whynchoo come down tomorrah an' watch me play?" Joey said with a mixture of anger and pride. Emilio looked amused. "Twelve-thirty at French Charlie's field."

Emilio was stumped for a comeback, so he just chuckled, mumbled something about cripples, and ate in silence.

Friday nights before the Saturday games were the best part of the football season. Each team in its own neighborhood would have a torchlight parade with banners, chants, and crowds. If the neighborhoods overlapped one procession would often collide with another, and nuclear war would break out. This happened in the past season between the Velvet Sharks of Olinville Avenue and the Red Devils of Gun Hill Road. The next day the game was canceled since the entire Red Devil backfield and half the Velvet Shark defensive team were in the hospital.

At ten, the Stingers assembled in Big Playground. Joey and Eugene had the rolled-up banner, a twenty-foot-long, six-foot-high piece of canvas, each end sewn around a mop handle. Two guys carried it through the streets, stretching the canvas so the road was blocked. Twenty team players were there, fifty or sixty younger kids, some older guys living in the project, a few curious adults, girl friends, and a few neutrals from nonfootball playing gangs. Every Stinger was there except Perry, who was K.O.'ed on Nembutals and couldn't have played the next day. Mops, brooms, and baseball bats were distributed. Joey sprayed lighter fluid on the mops and brooms, and everybody lit their makeshift torches. Dozens of small, fiery whoosh sounds were drowned out by a tremendous roar from the crowd as the banner was unfurled. It was a beauty. Lenny Arkadian fixed it up. The banner had STINGERS in dripping red letters. By each of the "S's" Lenny had painted giant black and yellow bees wearing white gloves on tight fists, scowling faces, and a week's growth of beard stubble. The bees had giant cigars clamped between dagger teeth, and stingers coming out of their asses like golden scimitars. Lenny got the idea for the faces from the Woody Woodpecker racing decals.

Joey and Perry were supposed to carry the banner, but Joey wouldn't carry it without Perry, so the Tasso brothers were recruited. George and Vincent Tasso were twins, non-Wanderers, and according to consensus, good guys. They were the split ends — tall and fast, hands like baseball gloves. Joey stood in front of the unfurled banner, the roaring torches, the roaring crowd. He raised his hands. Silence except for the crackle of flames.

"GIMME AN S!"

"S!"

"GIMME A T!"

"T!"

They roared back the letters in lusty bellows.

"WHAT'S THAT SPELL?"

"STINGUHS!"

"WHAT'S THAT SPELL?"

"STINGUHS!"

"LOUDER, YOU MOTHERFUCKAHS!"

"STING-GUHHS!"

"LOUDER, YOU CRIPPLE BASTADS!"

"STING-GUHHHS!!!"

"LAUDAHHHH!!!!"

"STING-GUHS! STING-GUHS! STING-GUHS! STING-GUHS!"

Joey was crying and screaming, and the crowd marched down the street chanting, torches blazing, the banner held high. Joey bellowed and roared, his neck veins swollen with blood and hate, and they caught his passion, trading him howl for howl. Even the little kids were foaming at the mouth.

"STING-GUHS! STING-GUHS! STING-GUHS!"

Every twenty feet they would pick up a few more people —
people who didn't even know who or what the Stingers were
but were swept into the radioactive net of emotion. They
marched down Burke Avenue across White Plains Road. Joey
stopped them in front of his building.

"STING-GUHS! STING-GUHS! STING-GUHS!"

Joey looked up at the windows of his apartment through
red eyes. "LAU-DAHHH!" He screamed until he couldn't
hear himself anymore, but no one came to the three windows
on the third floor — although almost every other window had
a face in it. They marched twice around the projects, and
people started getting tired. Joey still screamed but they
weren't screaming back as loud anymore, and people dropped
off at every block. Finally, the Tassos rolled up the banner
and torches were snuffed.

"STING-GUHS! STING-GUHS!" Joey was the only one
chanting now. "C'mon, Joey, it's bedtime."

"C'MON, YOU GUYS!"

"HEY, JO-WEE!" Eugene shouted in his ear. Joey acted
drunk. "C'mon, Joey, it's eleven-thirty."

Everybody went home. Joey stared down the street. He
tried to shout one last time but his throat felt like a razor
strop. He staggered to his apartment. Just let musclehead say
one word. His father was probably shitting pickles. He didn't
come to the window because he was scared, scared bad. Cripples, yeah, they sounded like cripples all right. There's gonna
be some changes around here. Joey found his mother's note
on the kitchen table.

> Joey
> We went to the movies. Be back late.
> > Love you
> > Mom

"That movie was sick," Emilio declared. Sitting in the dinette, he lit a cigarette and studied his wife's ass while she

made coffee in the kitchen. Twelve-thirty. "It was filth." His wife didn't answer. She never knew how to answer her husband. Eighteen years of walking on eggshells. "It was pornography." He picked a crumb from his mustache. She brought in the coffee and a box of Danish. "Cream."

She got the cream and sat down, taking a cigarette from his pack. He trapped her hand. "Where's yours?"

"I forgot to buy some."

"You forgot to buy some? You just had a full pack this morning."

"They're gone."

"Gone? Whadya mean gone? They vanished? They marched out of the pack into the elevator and took a train somewhere?"

A headache the size of a dime settled behind her eyes. "I smoked them."

"Ah. Ah. You smoked them," he said with mock enlightenment.

"Could I please have a cigarette?" Her hand was still caught under his — the pack under everything.

"You smoke like a chimney." She said nothing, the headache branching out. "You're like a junkie, you know? Like a drug attic'. You're a tobacco attic'." Her free hand fluttered up to her forehead. "See? You need a fix!" He took his hand away. "G'head, junkie, have your fix." As she lit the cigarette he poured coffee. She was surprised that he poured her a cup too.

Joey's mother was a beautiful woman. She had the tight, smooth skin of a twenty-year-old girl and clear, large brown eyes. The constant fear and tension of her domestic life kept her slim. Her manner was gracious and graceful. She never raised her voice. The only time she had defied her husband, the only time she stood up to him, he had beaten her so badly she couldn't get out of bed for a week. She knew he wasn't a cowardly woman beater. He'd fight anybody, man, woman, or child, with equal fury and violence. She had forgotten what led up to the beating, but Emilio liked to remind her of "what happened when you got out a line that time."

Emilio saw his wife was having one of her headaches that hurt so badly she sometimes cried. He felt guilty and decided to be a little nicer. "Hey, junkie . . . you want another fix?" He offered her the pack. She smiled no. She was still smoking the first one. He left the pack on the table and went to the bathroom.

Emilio undressed and stepped into the shower. He liked to feel the water on his body. He loved his body. He still worked out with weights every other day at the firehouse. He stepped from the bathtub, admiring himself in the full-length mirror on the back of the bathroom door. His muscles and his cock always looked bigger in the mirror, although, God knows, he didn't need any mirror to look big. He had kept the physique that won him the title of Mr. New York City twenty-two years ago as well as a forty-eight-year-old man could. His waist was only thirty-two, his chest measured forty-seven-and-a-half, biceps holding steady at eighteen inches, cock at nine, although it fluctuated between eight and ten. He knew muscle-bound guys with dicks the length of his little toe. There were plenty of those guys around too. Not him though. He was hung like a grandfather clock. He massaged his dick until it got hard. He tensed all his muscles, flexed his biceps, watched them dance, watched his thighs undulate at his mental command. He made his pectorals rotate under his skin. His erection stiffened — at least ten inches.

His wife waited patiently for him to finish in the bathroom. She hoped he wasn't going into one of his body-beautiful routines. They sometimes lasted half an hour. She had a weak bladder, and coffee made her pee. Once when Emilio was in the bathroom she had to go so bad that she dropped her drawers and sat in the kitchen sink. Then he came out as if he'd been waiting to catch her. It took two years for him to stop digging into her about that. Once at a party he'd told all their friends. She felt so ashamed she didn't do laundry or go shopping for a week. She'd given up Wednesday mahjong for good. Now, ten years later, she still flinched when she thought about it. She waited, listening for the noises that meant Emilio was finishing up.

Emilio lightly patted his body with a towel. He put a hand under his balls and contemplated their weight. Meatballs. That's what they were — meatballs. Two meaty balls. Must weigh a pound each. Maybe a pound and a quarter. He slapped his buttocks. They didn't wiggle. They were taut and hard. And small. When he was in the navy some chippy told him he had an athletic ass. And he'd made sure his ass stayed nice and athletic ever since. He thought of Joey. He had to admit that Joey had an athletic ass too, but that hardly counted because the rest of him was so goddamned puny. The only time he'd seen his son with a hard-on he almost puked. It couldn't have been more than five inches — maybe five and a half.

When Joey woke up the next morning he was sure he had cancer of the throat. He sat up in bed with his hands on his neck like a man who'd just taken a shot of homemade redeye. He stumbled into the bathroom, flipped up the toilet cover but not the toilet seat, and pissed. Swallowing was agony. He took the Vaseline from the medicine chest, scooped out a fingerful, and put it in his mouth. Bracing himself, a hand on each side of the sink, he gagged and swallowed simultaneously. He couldn't remember if his grandmother used Vaseline,

Vicks VapoRub, or Ben-Gay for sore throats, but he imagined they all tasted the same.

Emilio sat in a bathrobe listening to the radio, smoking a cigarette, and staring out the dinette window. Nine-thirty. Saturday morning sunlight splashed onto the bright red-and-white oilcloth leaving a swath of brightness across Emilio's chin, neck, and seminaked chest. Joey brought in a cup of coffee for himself and sat down in his underwear at the far end of the table. Emilio glanced briefly at his son and returned his gaze to the street and the el tracks, which were eye level with the window. Joey sipped his coffee and watched his father. He was dying for a cigarette but afraid to ask for one.

"Jo-wee! Jo-wee!"

"Fi' minutes!" He dashed into his bedroom, crammed his equipment into a duffel bag, and slipped on a sleeveless sweat-shirt and black dungarees. Yanking the bag over his shoulder he tramped into the dinette and gulped down the rest of his coffee standing up. "Twelve-thirty at French Charlie's," he said to his father. Emilio didn't turn around. Joey stood there for a few seconds staring at his father's back, then left the house.

Emilio watched his son emerge from the building. Buddy, Eugene, the Tassos, and Richie waited for him on the bench, duffel bags strewn at their feet. Eugene threw the football at Joey, who one-handed it and flipped it behind his back. A perfect spiral. Emilio felt a strange rage building up inside him, a restless blackness at watching the six boys. He lit an-other cigarette and turned off the radio. He felt a little better when they tramped up the hill toward Bronx Park. His anger turned to a mazelike boredom. Hearing his wife in the bath-room, he slipped into the bedroom, dressed quickly, and left the house.

It was a beautiful day, and he decided to take a walk toward Allerton Avenue. The el train roared overhead but he'd stopped hearing it years ago, after he'd moved into the projects. Sometimes his whole life seemed to be made up of loud noises — el trains, sirens, alarms, screams from burning windows, but he didn't mind noise that much, at least he preferred it to the silences in his life. He bought a *Daily News* on the corner of White Plains Road and Allerton Avenue under the el station stairs and walked down Allerton toward the park. A block from the entrance he stopped. He didn't mean to go to the park to see the game. He was going to read the goddamn paper and have a smoke. He felt as if he had to convince an invisible audience in his head of this fact. The game had slipped his mind, and he was just going for a goddamn walk. He became angry again. He cursed Joey. Little bastard. Can't even go into the park for a little relaxation on a Saturday morning. Emilio folded the paper, jammed it under his arm, and wheeled back toward White Plains Road. He went home, made it to the elevator, turned around, stormed out to the street again, his face as red as a blood boil, and walked back to the park. He sat on a bench for ten minutes staring at the sports page without one score or photo registering in his enraged head. He flung the paper onto the narrow asphalt bicycle path, scattering it like tumbleweed. He kicked furiously at a pirouetting page that the wind blew across his legs. He marched back to the newspaper stand. He had nowhere to go. The anger drained away, substituted again by the baffling boredom. He didn't want to go home, but there was nothing to do. He thought of going down to the fire station. He thought of taking a nice ride through Westchester. He thought of going out to Brooklyn to visit his parents. Everything seemed incredibly boring and meaningless and stupid and fuck Joey anyway, the little bony rat, rat shit.

Ten-thirty. Emilio stood at the bar beside Lenny Arkadian in Manny's. Lenny and John the bartender disliked Emilio.

He made them nervous the way most bullies make people nervous. They didn't like him, but they made sure they were nice to him.

"How's your kid?" Lenny twirled the ice in his drink.

Emilio looked away, annoyed. Lenny shrugged. John absently wiped the counter in the subdued almost brown light of his bar. "What time's the game, Lenny?"

"One o'clock, John."

"Twelve-thirty," said Emilio, still not looking at them.

"You goin'?"

"No" — a clipped sound cutting off all debate. Lenny was relieved. He didn't want to watch the game with Ivan the Terrible. "You know why I'm not goin'?" Emilio challenged Lenny and John. "I'll tell you why . . . I'll tell you why . . ."

Lenny ran his finger along a scratch in the bar top. He wished Emilio would go away, drop dead or something.

"Because . . ." Emilio looked at them now, pointing a finger like a gun. "Because that kid, that little bastard . . ." The finger wavered, folded into a fist, and Emilio returned to his beer. Lenny and John looked at each other and shrugged.

"Ralphie playin'?" John asked.

"Yeah, the kid runs like a stallion. They're puttin' 'im in as halfback," Lenny said with pride.

"No kiddin'?"

"No kiddin'. You haven't seen 'im in years."

"Christ, lemme think, the las' time . . . the las' time he was like . . . thirteen, maybe fourteen."

"Jesus, you're in for a shock."

"Got big?"

"Big and fast. They're puttin' 'im in as halfback."

"Fast too, hah?"

"Runs the hundred in ten-two."

"Jeez, that's fast."

"Yeah."

"Ten-two . . . wow."

"Goddamn stallion."

"No, he's not," said Emilio, again looking away.

"Not what?" asked Lenny.

"Joey's halfback." Emilio sat erect, his back to his audience.

"But . . ." Lenny started.

"Joey's the fucking halfback." Emilio's voice came out loud and flat.

Lenny was going to say that there were two halfbacks — Emilio's son and his own kid brother — but decided it wasn't worth it. Anything he said would be a goddamn major production. Fuck it. Fuck Emilio. Goddamn asshole. He threw a dollar on the bar and waved to John. As he passed Emilio he involuntarily flinched as if half expecting a punch in the back of his head.

*

Bronx Park was a plain of high weeds, weeping willows, and sporadic swamps stretching for miles in every direction. The only area cleared enough to play ball was French Charlie's field — a rectangular patch of land almost bald from generations of football cleats. It looked like an old oriental rug. No one knew who French Charlie was. Some said he was a farmer in the area before it became Bronx Park, but unless he raised mosquitoes and rats that didn't seem likely. Some said he was a murderer who lived in the woods and killed people strolling through the park during the 1890s. The cops had him holed up one night, and when they couldn't flush him out of the woods they set fire to the area. He was presumed dead although the body was never found. Over the years the burned-out land became known as French Charlie's field. The reason he was called French Charlie instead of just Charlie was because all his victims were women. But this legend was probably bullshit too.

French Charlie's was surrounded by a small forest of willows and other more shapeless trees. When football teams arrived for a game, they dumped their gear on the borderline between the forest and the field and changed behind the trees.

When the Stingers showed up the Del-Bombers were already in uniform, doing push-ups and wind sprints on the far side of the field. The Stingers watched the enemy in anxious silence: the most intimidating thing about the Del-Bombers was their full uniforms. The Stinger outfit was a silky green jersey, shoulder pads, a protective cup, a helmet, and tight black dungarees. Half the team had cleats, the other half wore converse sneakers. The Del-Bombers weren't richer than the Stingers. They had uniforms because Winston Knight and Raymond Firestone held up a sporting goods store last year and took everything from ace bandages to teeth guards for twenty-five guys. As a matter of fact the Del-Bombers were on the average poorer, if for no other reason than they were spades.

Joey tossed his duffel bag against a tree and yawned. The Del-Bombers looked big. He wished Perry could play. But Perry was in that fingertip-elbow cast. Richie and the Tassos started throwing around a football. In the distance Joey saw Jo-Jo and Ralph with duffel bags. Ten minutes later Peter Rabbit, Ed Weiss, and Lenny Mitchell showed up. They had an hour until game time. Everybody was silent. The Del-Bombers finished their warm-ups and left the field.

"Anybody wanna run?" Joey asked. Joey, Buddy, and Ralphie started jogging around the field. Joey felt tight. He felt fast. On the third lap he fell into some fancy broken-field running. So did Ralphie. Buddy trotted back to the Stingers.

"How you feelin', Joey?" asked Ralphie.

"Good. We're gonna run their asses off."

"Yeah."

They ran two more laps. Joey saw Perry standing with the guys and shouted in delight. Perry wore his Stinger jersey. "Hey-y, mah man, you playin'?"

"Nah, I just came in case you guys got in a fight."

"How's your arm?"

Perry shrugged. "Busted."

Four more Stingers showed up. Each time somebody else came the Stingers felt a little looser, a little more relaxed. Soon rooters showed up from the projects, and when the girls, C, Margo, Laine, Anne, and a few others, came, it was time for the Stingers to get the show on the road.

The first thing they had to do was get into their gear. This was an important ritual because changing into their uniforms was all they could offer in the way of a pregame show. Each player had a different specialty. Richie liked to stomp around naked to the waist in subfreezing temperature while he looked for his shoulder pads. He would isometrically tense his gut, puff out his chest, and parade in front of the girls in a flurry of preoccupation, making sure the wind caught his hair just right so he could frown heroically like a raw-muscled Viking on the prow of a raiding ship somewhere in the North Sea. His whole show was pretty effective; seeing a guy seminude in the winter was the equivalent of seeing a girl in a bikini in the middle of Manhattan. Joey was a cup insertion and ball adjustment man. His thing was to open his fly, peel his briefs to the curly perimeter of his pubic hair, and make a major production of inserting the large white diamond-shaped protective cup. One hand up to the forearm in his pants, he would jiggle his balls, align his cock, and do little dances of adjustment to secure and anchor his goods against the coming violence of the afternoon. If Richie liked to frown heroically, Joey's expression was a grimace of Herculean labor like he was moving two cannonballs inside his briefs. Some guys did shoulder-pad slamming duets. Like mountain goats butting heads, they would square off, ramming shoulders together to make the pads set better. Then they would walk around shrugging, making small circles with their shoulders to signify they were ready. Perry's forte was the most impressive. Perry never really enjoyed being a big guy except for football, and before a game he liked to come on twice as big and mean as he was. After he put on his shoulder pads he would wrap his arms around a big tree and slam his shoulders against the trunk to settle the pads. The whole tree would shake and nuts, squirrels, leaves, bird's nests, and whatever else was up there would rain down on the fans. Last year Perry got so carried away he separated his shoulder and missed four games.

At midfield Richie and Ray Rodriguez, the co-captains of the Stingers, met Leslie Frances and Toby Barrett, the co-captains of the Del-Bombers, and shook hands.

"G'luck, man."

"G'luck."

Walking back to the sidelines, Richie made some comment to Ray about niggers. Ray, the only Puerto Rican playing for either team, didn't know whether to be pissed at him or agree.

Fifty yards from the fans, Emilio Capra stood alone. He saw that Joey was playing halfback, and Ralphie Arkadian wasn't even playing offense. He saw Lenny Arkadian with the rest of the assholes cheering their heads off, and he resisted an urge to ask him how his half-assed halfback kid brother was doing.

Today was Joey's day. He saw daylight every time he got the ball and near the end of the first half, he had racked up over 120 yards. Ed Weiss, the quarterback, was throwing like Y. A. Tittle, and the Tassos had golden hands. Defense was

holding steady and so far nobody had gotten hurt. The Stingers led, 14 to 6. Full uniforms or no, the Del-Bombers would
have to hold up a few more sporting goods stores to look good
that day.

Lenny Arkadian noticed Emilio about twenty-five yards
down the line of trees that served as a boundary. He nudged
Perry. "You know that guy?"

"Emilio?"

"He's a real douchebag."

Perry shrugged, not in the habit of cutting down any of the
guys' parents.

Coming off the field at half time, Joey noticed his father
standing about ten yards from everybody else. In spite of himself, Joey felt excited but resisted an impulse to run up to Emilio and ask how he had looked on the field. Fuck it. He knew
how he looked. Like always. The best. Joey walked over to
the rest of the guys, tossed his helmet by the duffel bags,
grubbed a cigarette from C, and out of the corner of his eye
watched his father watch him out of the corner of his eye.

Perry's bottle of Tango was passed around. Joey took a
slug and walked past Emilio to the Del-Bomber camp. He
handed the bottle to two guys and bullshitted with some other
guys from Tully. Watching his father across the field, Joey
suddenly wished that Emilio was talking to the other people.
For a strange moment Joey felt depressed and sorry for him.
He took back the Tango and walked toward his father.

Ray Rodriguez was sitting alone drinking a soda and still
debating whether he should be pissed at Richie when he saw a
midget run from the woods and snatch the football. Ray
jumped up in pursuit and tackled the midget. The football
went flying; the midget ate dirt. Ray got to his feet, pulling up
the thief by his jacket collar. "Whadya think you're doin',
hah?" (slap). "Hah?" (slap). "Hah?" (slap). The midget

was trying to fend off the slaps. He pulled out an old-fashioned razor and went for Ray's face. Ray was startled and fell backward on his ass. The midget jumped on his chest and was about to rearrange Ray's eyes when a football whipped the blade from his hand. He leaped to his feet, stomped on Ray's crotch, and disappeared into the woods. Joey and Ed Weiss ran to Ray and helped him up.

Joey had been walking toward Emilio when he saw Ray Rodriguez beating up a dwarf. Then he saw a flash of silver, and Ray fall down. He thought the dwarf had killed Ray. Panicked, he dropped the Tango and ran blindly toward the bizarre scene. Ed Weiss was throwing footballs at a tree trunk. He'd pitched three no-hit games for the Evander Tigers, and he threw the pigskin with the speed of a baseball. He was reaching into the duffel bag full of footballs at his feet, ready to drill one into the tree again, when he saw Ray Rodriguez laying on the field about twenty yards away. A little kid was sitting on Ray's chest. At first he thought Ray was fucking around with one of the younger kids watching the game, but then he saw the knife. Ed grabbed a football and fired it at the glinting reflection.

Ray was trembling as Ed and Joey helped him to his feet. Some Del-Bombers and Stingers came over.

"Shit! What the hell was that all about?" asked Perry.

"I dunno. I saw this . . . I think he was a midget . . . grab the ball an' . . ." Ray's hands were shaking.

"Midget my ass." Toby Barrett walked over to the small crowd, the razor in his outstretched palm.

"Oh, shit . . . Ducky Boys." Joey felt his stomach tighten. The Ducky Boys were stone killers that always attacked in droves to compensate for the fact that few of them were over five feet.

"You sure?"

"Yeah, man . . . lookit the fuckin' blade."

"Oh, my God." Ray closed his eyes and held his forehead.

"You think they'll be back?"

"Yeah."

"Maybe not."

"Well, I ain't hangin' around to find out."

"What's happenin'?" C poked her head into the group.

"Nothin'."

"Get lost."

"Whada we gonna do?"

"What happened?" Richie and Jo-Jo came over.

"Ducky Boys."

"What?"

"Ray just slapped aroun' a Ducky Boy."

"Richie, I'm goin' home," C declared. Richie ignored her.

"Where'd he go?"

"Into the woods."

"You think they'll come back?"

"They always do."

"So what? We got fifty guys here," said Perry. They looked at him like he'd broken his head instead of his hand. Perry laughed, swishing his cast through the air. "I'm ready."

"Somebody take 'im home before he gets hurt," said Jo-Jo.

"We playin' or not?"

"I ain't takin' no chances," said Raymond Firestone.

"You guys just don't like losin'," said Perry.

"Motherfucker, we gonna whip yo' asses so bad you gonna have to shit out the other end."

"I thought you was goin' home," Perry continued. Raymond shrugged.

"C'mon, what's wit' you faggots?" Perry asked. No one said anything. Guys kept coming over to find out what was up. When almost everybody was standing in the center of the field, Perry shouted, "O.K.! Half time's over! Let's get the fuckin' show on the road!" and walked to the sideline. The guys looked at each other, shrugged, and went for their helmets.

Joey saw his father standing with the rest of the spectators. He felt better. He wondered what happened to the bottle of Tango. He wondered what his father would do if the Ducky Boys came. When he picked up his helmet his eyes locked with Emilio's. He waved a short wave, but Emilio quickly looked away. Joey got hard and tight. He grabbed his helmet and marched onto the field.

Emilio had watched the crowd gather in the middle of the field. He moved closer. When people started drifting back he picked up something about a fight and some ducks. All he knew was if those niggers started a fight or anything he would kick their asses. Fuck the ducks.

Ray Rodriguez was tall and fast. He played safety good enough for any high school team in the city. But like Ed Weiss, he'd wound up at a school without a football team, so he played with the Stingers. His close call during half time gave him nervous superspeed during the second half. And he played like a pro. He kept seeing that razor in front of his face and that Ducky Boy sitting on his chest with a cloudiness in his eyes that signified a conscience and an intelligence the size of peanuts. The Del-Bombers threw a long bomb, and Ray outran Leslie Frances, intercepting the pass in the end zone for a touchback. As he caught the ball, he slipped to one knee on a wet patch of grass. Facing away from the field, he looked up into the face of the Ducky Boy who tried to kill him. He was standing ten yards away against a tree, staring expressionlessly at Ray. Ray froze. The Ducky Boy motioned Ray forward. Ray stood up and backed into a goal post. The Ducky Boy drew his thumb across his own neck and clenched his teeth. Ray turned and ran.

"What's with you?"

"They're here!"

Richie's eyes widened. "Where?" Ray pointed to the end zone. Nobody there. "Where?"

"I ain't fuckin' around, Gennaro. He was there."

"What now?"

"What happened?"

"Ray saw the guy."

"I ain't shittin', I'm goin' home."

"Hey, c'mon, man. The game's almost over."

"I don't care, like . . . hey! There he is!" Not only was the Ducky Boy back but six or seven of his friends were standing by the goal posts. "Goodbye. You guys can hang around."

"There's only six there. We can take 'em."

People started leaving. The football players congregated in the center of the field with Perry in the middle. "Lissen, I ain't runnin' from midgets."

"They ain't midgets. Whynchoo knock down a tree, Perry."

"I'll knock your fuckin' head off, man. I ain't leavin'." Perry startled himself with his own bravado. He didn't know why he was coming on tough.

"Oh, my God, look," said Eugene.

The six Ducky Boys had multiplied into hundreds, lining the woods and the football field. The remaining fans packed up and hightailed it for the park entrance except Lenny Arkadian and Emilio Capra.

"Jesus Fucking H. Christ!" Richie strapped his helmet on.

"I think my mother's callin' me," said a Del-Bomber.

"I'm thirsty, anybody wanna get a Coke?" asked Ed Weiss.

Leaving their street clothes behind, about twenty football players ran after the fans.

"What the fuck," Eugene said, "let's get the hell outta here." Eugene wanted to run, but his fear of violence was less than his fear of losing face.

Joey saw his father and Lenny walking toward them.

"Let's hang around," he said, feeling a terrible sense of excitement.

Perry put his cast around Joey's shoulders. "All faggots can go home." Every time Perry started feeling scared he came on louder and braver.

"What's goin' on?" Lenny looked pretty big and tough. He saw the Ducky Boy nation down the field. "Friends a yours?" Lenny was disappointed and relieved that his younger brother had disappeared.

About thirty guys were left including Perry, Joey, Richie, Raymond Firestone, Eugene, Buddy, about half the Del-Bombers and half the Stingers.

"Where's my brother?" Vincent Tasso asked.

"He split."

"Goddamn!" Vincent looked hurt.

Emilio strolled over and took off his coat, displaying a physique that silenced everybody. Joey felt like crying. "Who a' those guys?" Emilio asked with casual disinterest. Nobody answered.

He shrugged, walked over to a tree, and tore off a fat branch, swinging it lazily. He returned to the group, resting the club on his shoulder. Impressed, Perry winked at Joey. Joey strapped on his helmet and adjusted his shoulder pads. Some guys, imitating Emilio, tore off tree branches. The Ducky Boys were motionless, waiting to see who stayed and who ran. Now they were on the move — almost walking in formation down the field like a marching band. Some of them carried baseball bats, some car aerials, some tire chains. Joey inched closer to his father. Emilio exhaled heavily through his nose and tightened his grip on the club. The football players didn't know whether to fan out or to bunch together, and they started bumping into each other, shouting strategies. Perry took practice cuts in the air with his cast. Joey ran for the trees. He tried to pull off a branch but couldn't snap it loose.

He ran back empty-handed, standing between Perry and his father. Ray Rodriguez stayed because Richie had made a comment about fuckin' nigger cowards when half the Del-Bombers ran for the hills. It didn't seem to make a difference that half the Stingers had suddenly developed a strong thirst about the same time.

"What the fuck am I doin' here?" asked Lenny.

"Get 'em, Wolfman!" Perry laughed.

When the Ducky Boys got to midfield, they broke rank and charged, swinging everything they had. The football players were outnumbered five to one, but Ducky Boys came small. Emilio ran to meet them and swung his branch in someone's face. A fountain of blood arched from the kid's nostrils, spraying Emilio's arms. Emilio plowed through five or six Ducky Boys before someone got him from behind with a base-ball bat, and he went down thrashing under a sea of foaming rats.

Twelve Ducky Boys tried to jump Perry and Lenny because they were the biggest. Perry swung his cast like the jawbone of an ass, piling up bodies at his feet. Lenny grabbed a Ducky Boy by the legs and used him as a club, swinging him face-first into the attackers.

Joey, inspired by Emilio and fear, was doing O.K. for a lit-tle guy until he saw his father go down. Then he got hit in the face with the tip of a car aerial — a curtain of skin and blood blinding him. Perry saw Joey go down, and bellowing in anger, he waded through Ducky Boys, smashing bones and heads until his cast was red. He peeled Ducky Boys off Joey, yanking him to his feet and shoving him toward the safety of the woods. But Joey couldn't see and walked right into a wait-ing Ducky Boy and went down again under a flurry of kicks and punches. Perry grabbed the Ducky Boy and rammed his head into a tree. His cast shattered, and the pain from his throbbing wrist made him cry.

Raymond Firestone, a Golden Gloves boxer, was having an easy time until a tire chain smashed his fingers, and he sank to his knees staring in disbelief at the mangled remains of his life's dream.

Richie, Eugene, and Buddy stood back to back in a defensive triangle, but for some reason no one was interested, much to their relief.

Under the mountain of Ducky Boys, Emilio pumped his fists and eventually cleared an opening so he could sit up. He grabbed a Ducky Boy and using him as a support leaped to his feet. He lost his club but he wasn't hurt, except for the throbbing lump at the base of his skull. He grabbed another Ducky Boy with a tire chain and broke the kid's arm in one quick twist. Emilio wrapped the tire chain around his hand and, using it like a bolo, broke ribs and legs. After a while he stood untouched and unchallenged.

Ray Rodriguez punched Richie in the nose.

Lenny found Emilio's club, and when he got tired of swinging the Ducky Boy he tossed him away and used the stick, but he lost his balance, and they were all over him and suddenly things weren't so funny anymore.

Joey lay on his stomach, whimpering. He thought he was blind, and his father was dead. But Emilio was still swinging, and Joey only had a superficial cut across his forehead. For the first time in the afternoon he felt hopeless, overpowering terror. He was too scared to lift his head and tried to belly-crawl away — his body moving slowly across the cool grass. He bumped into the broad roots of a tree and held onto the base of the trunk with all his strength.

Blood was seeping from the inside of Perry's cracked cast. Shreds of gauze hung in festoons from his arm. The pain overcame his bravado, and he stumbled into the woods howling in anguish. Hidden from view, he sat on the ground, held his arm, and rocked back and forth.

Raymond Firestone lay curled into a ball, crying softly, holding his smashed hand against his chest. He'd lost a shoe, and his helmet was half off his head.

After Ray Rodriguez punched Richie in the nose he felt much better and ran home.

After Richie got punched in the nose he ran home.

When Buddy and Eugene saw Richie run home, they ran home.

Lenny was out cold and dreamed he was painting miles of canvas with a brush the size of a toothpick.

Between those decked and those running, Emilio was the only one still fighting. When the Ducky Boys saw that the only one left to fight was the maniac with the steel whip, they decided their job was done and began to vanish as abruptly as they had appeared. Emilio ran after them like a lunatic gladiator, the burning ball at the base of his skull driving him on to mow down and plow through anything that moved.

After the Ducky Boys had gone, Stingers and Del-Bombers crept timidly out of the woods. Joey sat up. The blood had dried and except for the stinging band over his eyes and the shakiness of fear, he was more or less O.K. He saw his father, his back to everyone, standing alone in the field. Elated, Joey struggled to his feet and ran to him. At the second before contact, Emilio wheeled around, slamming him square in the gut. Joey made a noise approaching a snarl and sank to his knees. He stared at Emilio with unblinking eyes and vomited slender ropes of hateful black.

4

The Roof

THE HITE BROTHERS were idiots. Scottie, ten years old, was best friends with Dougie Rizzo, C's brother. Scottie's brother, Rockhead or Frank, was as old as the Wanderers but was considered a maniac jerk-off, and a leper.

The Hite boys were so blond they seemed white-haired. They always went around moving their lips wordlessly and squinting like they were figuring out a calculus problem. Only a fellow maniac, though far more evil, like Dougie Rizzo could have befriended Scottie Hite — but only so he could use Scottie as Igor for his fiendish plots. As for Frank, he was friendless although he had many enemies. Mr. Hite worked in a factory that made roller skates. His job was checking that the right number of rollers were on each skate. He was on probation because he once let a three-wheeled skate get by and a fifty-year-old lady in her second childhood broke her leg zooming down a hill. The lady sued, and the company traced the error to him — so if he let one more faulty skate go past him again he'd be canned. They were purposely sending three-wheeled roller skates down the assembly line, but he caught every one. He was a conscientious worker.

Mrs. Hite was in charge of the projects' laundry room in the basement of her building. She'd been living in this country for twenty years and still spoke almost unintelligible English. She was from Ireland.

*

The day Dougie and Scottie were left nude in the park, Dougie convinced Scottie to run to the highway and try to stop a car for help. While Scottie was standing bare-ass-naked on the edge of the road, almost getting run over by shocked motorists, Dougie found and beat up a smaller kid, took his clothes, and went home.

*

"Hey, Hite!" Dougie came up behind Scottie in Big Playground and clapped a hand on his shoulder.

"Hiya, Dougie."

"You wanna havva contest, Scottie?"

"Yeah?"

"I got a good contest. Let's see who can hit each other the softest."

"Hah?" Dougie ushered Scottie behind the Parks Department building, a small brick supply house in the middle of the playground.

"We'll see who can hit each other the softest, you get it?"

"Nah." Scottie squinted, working out pi to the tenth decimal place.

"Look, asshole . . . like this." Dougie grabbed Scottie's arm, and as Scottie cringed, he drew back his fist and, faking a furious punch, tapped Scottie lightly on the biceps. "Like that . . . see?" Scottie nodded. "O.K. You go first." Dougie stuck out his arm. Scottie made an angry face, snarled, drew back his fist — and for a second Dougie got scared that Scottie didn't understand — and tapped his friend lightly on the arm. "O.K., now it's my turn." Dougie grabbed Scottie's arm again, drew back his fist, and punched Scottie as hard as he could. "You win." He laughed as Scottie held his bruised arm and howled like a wolf, his head thrown back, his eyes clenched in pain. "Hey, I gotta 'nother one."

"No!" said Scottie.

"C'mon." Dougie rubbed his friend's arm. "Hey, Scottie!" Scottie stared at him.

"Eeeeuwww! You got a booger on your shirt!" Dougie pointed to a spot on Scottie's chest, and when Scottie looked down Dougie flicked up his finger, smacking him in the nose.

"Rotten shit!" Scottie chased Dougie around the playground, but Dougie was faster, eluding his flunky with laughable ease. Finally Scottie got tired and called it quits.

It was one of those gray, cold Sunday afternoons when bored kids are at their most dangerous, Scottie and Dougie no exceptions. As they rambled through the angular housing project they broke a window, started fires in three garbage cans, and jammed the elevator in Scottie's building.

"I wish I was a marine," said Dougie. Scottie squinted as if thinking about reorganizing marine troop distribution in the Pacific. "I wish I was a marine so I could torture Nazis . . . do you like torture?" Dougie asked.

"I dunno, what is it?"

"C'mere, I'll show you." He took Scottie into the hallway of a building. "O.K. I'll be the marine and you be the Nazi." He faced Scottie. "Where are your tanks?" he barked. Scottie looked confused and shrugged. "You lie!" Dougie slapped Scottie hard across the face.

"Auuu! You fuck!" Scottie grabbed Dougie's ears and slammed his head into a cinder-block wall. Hearing a satisfying BONK, Scottie's anger left him. Dougie sat dazed on the concrete floor, his head vibrating.

"You shouldna did that, Dougie," he said, groping for an apologetic tone of voice. Dougie looked up at Scottie, who panted and picked his nose. Dougie was filled with a cool hate that calmed his impulse to strangle and replaced it with a sweet sense of time and revenge. Scottie had never hit him before, although Scottie was Dougie's punching bag; this was a clear case of mutiny. "Help me up, Hite." Dougie extended a hand. Scottie backed away. "You gonna hit me?"

"Nah."

"Swear to God."

"I swear."

"Cross."

Dougie crossed.

"Swear on your mother."

"I swear." Dougie smiled amiably.

"Swear on Brother Timothy and Sister Theresa at Holy Rosary."

"I swear," Dougie said patiently. Nervously, Scottie extended a hand. Dougie resisted pulling Scottie headfirst into the wall and struggled to his feet. "So you don' like torture, hah?"

"What?"

"C'mon, I'll buy you a Coke." He ushered Scottie through the projects into the Pioneer Candy Store. As Scottie sipped his Coke, Dougie spun himself around on the rotating counter stool until he was dizzy. "Hite, ain't I your best friend in the whole world?"

"What?"

"Ain't I your greatest buddy?" He put an arm around Scottie's shoulders.

Maxie, the bald immigrant soda jerk whose glasses reflected every bit of light they could catch, came over to them. "Twenty cent."

"I'll pay for the whole thing." Dougie made a big deal of extracting a quarter from his jeans. "He's my best friend, and I'll pay for him any time." Maxie failed to be stirred and gave Dougie a nickel.

Outside, they walked across the street to Big Playground. Dougie nudged Scottie with an elbow.

"What?"

Dougie pulled a dirty magazine from the front of his pants and gave it to Scottie. "I took it when he wasn't lookin'."

"Wow!"

"You din't see me take it either, you . . ." He stopped himself from calling Scottie a jerk. "It's yours."

"Wow."

"You like that, hah? You like them big titties there?" Dougie snickered.

Scottie giggled idiotically as he stared at a seminaked girl with big jugs.

"You wanna go up onna roof and look at the pictures?" Dougie suggested in a nasty whisper.

"Yeah, O.K."

"C'mon."

They trotted through the projects to a building they'd never been in before near the park, Scottie chortling and giggling, Dougie silent. They took the elevator to the top floor, then took the stairs to the roof. Dougie pushed the big iron door with his shoulder.

The roof was square, bordered by a jail-like four-foot-high iron grill. The ground was covered with a carpet of gravel, and the gravel was usually covered with a fine layer of black cinders that floated up from the mouth of an incinerator chimney. The only two structures on this flat terrain were the chimney and the huge iron door that led to the stairs.

The boys felt a delicious sense of terror because sneaking onto a roof was the most forbidden thing they could do in the projects. Any second a big black porter could kick open the iron door or dash from behind the chimney in his dark blue work uniform and drag them down seven flights of stairs and over to the housing police. Scottie whooped and hollered as he ran to the iron grill and looked down to the impossibly small street.

"We're on toppa the world!" he squealed.

"How 'bout that?" Dougie stared serenely across the sea of dirty buildings. Scottie ran around the roof making noises of nervous delight.

"Hey, Hite! C'mere wit' that magazine." Dougie squatted on the gravel. Scottie sat down next to him, and they thumbed through the pages, Dougie making cracks, Scottie drooling and laughing. "Hey, Hite, look a' that ass!"

"Yeah!"

"Hey, Hite, watch!" Dougie lifted the magazine to his mouth and kissed the winking girl's behind.

"Wooo!" Scottie waved a limp wrist meaning shame-shame.

"You do it."

"Nah." Scottie giggled in embarrassment.

"C'mon, g'head." Dougie shoved the magazine into Scottie's face. Scottie tried to twist away, then gave the magazine a quick peck. He redoubled his noises, approaching hysteria. Dougie smiled contemptuously. He held the magazine in front of his own face, the nudie photos facing Scottie, and spoke in a high-pitched voice, "Oh, Scottie Hite, you naughty boy! You kissed my tushie!"

Scottie waved weakly in helpless, salivating, embarrassed laughter. Dougie got up and started chasing him around the roof with the pictures and squeaking, "Oh, Scottie! Kiss my tushie!"

Scottie, howling and wiping his chin, stumbled away from Dougie. Suddenly Dougie stopped and tossed the book over the iron grill.

"Ah, this sucks . . . let's go downstairs," and as Scottie stood bent over with laughter, Dougie trotted over to the iron door and turned the knob. Nothing happened. He yanked and pulled but the door was immobile. White-faced, he ran to Scottie. "The door's locked! Whada we gonna do?" He started whining in terror. Scottie started whining also, his eyes big and wet. "Whada we gonna do! Whada we gonna do! Whada we gonna do!" He grabbed Scottie by the arms and shook him.

"Whada we gonna do!" Scottie echoed weakly.

"ANNNNNNH-NNN-NNNH," Dougie sniffled, starting to cry.

"MAAAA! MAAAA!" Scottie ran over to the iron grill and bleated in dull oxen terror to the empty street far below.

"Scottie! Scottie!" Dougie ran to him eyes glistening. "I got it! I got it!" Scottie's face was coated with tears, his breathing labored, his lips shivering. "Scottie! Lissen! We . . . can . . . jump!" Dougie's lips were shivering too.

"What!" Scottie gasped in horror.

"We can jump! Look!" He pointed to Scottie's sneakers. "We got P.F. Flyers! We'll bounce up like kangaroos! Like on 'Terrytoon Circus'!"

Scottie, sensing salvation, nodded excitedly. "Yeah!"

"We'll be safe!" Dougie shouted.

"Safe!" screamed Scottie.

Dougie climbed the iron grill and crouched on the top rail. "C'mon, Scottie!"

Scottie hoisted himself up to Dougie. Both boys grasped the top bar. Crouched, they looked like swimmers waiting for the starting gun. Scottie's eyes were shut tight. Dougie looked at him.

"O.K., now when I say three we jump, O.K.?" Scottie started sniffling again but wouldn't open his eyes. "Ready? One . . . two . . . three!" Dougie jumped backward onto the gravel but Scottie pitched himself clumsily off the roof. About four stories down he started to scream. Hearing a WHAP like a splattering coconut, Dougie ran to the rail. Looking down he saw Scottie sprawled on the pavement like a bloody Howdy Doody with cut strings. Dougie pressed his face between the cool bars of the grill and stared off to the park. After a while he trotted back to the iron door, opened it, and disappeared down the stairs.

5

The Love Song of Buddy Borsalino

THE GUYS were hanging around Big Playground with nothing to do. It was Thanksgiving, and almost everyone went away to see relatives. It was getting too dark to play basketball and it was too cold anyway. Richie sat beside Buddy on the bench. Perry and Joey were idly throwing rocks through the mesh fence.

"You wanna go to White Castle?"

"Got no dough."

"I'll lend you a quarter."

"You *owe* me a dollar."

"No, I don't."

"Who bought the Tango last night?"

"O.K. I'll lend you a quarter and I'll buy you a pack of cigarettes."

"See that shit?"

"Hey, you wanna go elbow titting?"

"Too cold."

"Bronx House is havin' a dance."

"Got no dough."

"We can hang aroun' outside."

"An' freeze your titties off."

"You wanna go to Eugene's house?"

"He ain't home."

"Let's go elbow titting."

"What the hell."

They started walking down to Allerton Avenue in search of girls. The street was deserted, and all the stores were closed. A block away they spotted two women walking toward them.

"Who goes first?"

"Perry."

"I went first last time."

"Joey."

"Nah, I don't wanna."

"G'head. Just pretend it's your mother."

"At least my mother *got* tits."

"Yeah . . . three."

"Two more than your's got."

"Least they ain't hairy."

The girls walked past them while they were arguing.

"See that shit?"

"Fuck it, you guys are pussies. I'll go," Buddy said. Richie helped him off with his jacket. "C'mon, c'mon." Buddy jumped up and down to keep warm. They were now standing out of sight in a storefront. A fat woman was walking down the street toward them.

"Get 'er, Buddy."

Buddy put his hands in his pockets, his elbows stuck out from his body. He winked at the guys and walked slowly toward the fat lady. When he was five feet from her, he cut in front of her path, bumping into her. As they stood facing each other, figuring out how to pass, Buddy moved left and rubbed his right elbow across her left tit. He mumbled "sorry" and moved right rubbing his left elbow across her right tit. He was trying the right elbow again when she caught on and belted him with a beefy forearm. He fell down. She cursed him in a foreign language and marched away. The Wanderers were on their asses laughing. Passing them she shouted, "You bois a' peegs! Feelty peegs!" Perry started grunting. Then they all got down on their hands and knees and grunted their way to Buddy's prostrate form, crouching around him like hyenas.

"Hey . . . I tink dis feelty peeg he got knocked down." They crawled around him, grunting and sniffing.

"Hey, peeg, I tink maybe you should get up now." Buddy raised his hands, curling them into clutching claws, squeezing invisible flesh.

"Oh, my lovely titties . . . oh, my *lovely* titties!"

"I think dis peeg he want seconds."

They stood up and helped Buddy to his feet.

"You wanna go again, man?"

"Believe it! Except maybe this time I go for a smaller size."

They retired to the storefront. Buddy put his jacket on. A few minutes later, a girl walked toward them, and Buddy was on the move again. The closer he got, the more he liked what he saw. She was about sixteen and had jet black hair piled high on her head. She had a nice figure, as much as he could see, and her face was Cunty Italian — small dark features, dark eyes, high cheekbones, and a lot of eye makeup. He was so involved in checking her out he almost forgot to cross her path. When he did, it was so abrupt that she bumped her nose on his chest. He stood there looking at her, intoxicated by her Juicy Fruit breath. She looked up at him quizzically. He realized that he wasn't moving his elbows, and he started twisting them back and forth ineffectually like the pumper in a washing machine.

"What's wrong with you?"

"Huh?" He stood in front of her doing the twist with his hands in his pocket.

"You gotta go to the bat'room?" She walked around him. He started after her, his tongue thick in his mouth, and caught up to her.

"Uh . . . what's wrong wit' me?" His mind worked feverishly. She stared at him.

"Uh . . . what's wrong wit' me? Uh, nothin'."

"You O.K.?"

"Uh . . . yeah." He had a brainstorm. "Except I just got jumped by two guys."

"What!"

"Yeah. Uh . . . they jumped outta a Cadillac down by the park and jumped me . . . I fought 'em off but they sapped me with a blackjack." He held his forehead and shook his head dazedly. "I'm sorry I bumped into you . . . I'm a little dizzy." He leaned against a parked car and suffered. "Lissen, do you wanna have a slice of pizza wit' me? I gotta talk to somebody," he said.

"I think you oughta see a doctor."

"Nah . . . I'll be O.K."

"I still think you should go."

"Nah . . . this ain't the first time it happened . . . I'm O.K. What's your name?"

She laughed out loud. "What kinda line is this?"

"It ain't no line! I swear to God!"

She looked at him amused and started down Allerton. He walked by her side past an astonished group of Wanderers. Suddenly he remembered he had no money. He grabbed her arm. "Wait here, I'll be right back." He ran back to the Wanderers, obscured from her sight. He grabbed Richie. "Lissen! Gimme that dollar now!" He shot a quick glance to see if she was still waiting for him. She was.

"Buddy! What's happenin', got your elbow stuck?"

"Lissen." He grabbed Richie by the front of his jacket. "Gimme the dollar or I'll tear your fuckin' heart out!"

"All I got is half a buck." Richie was shook by Buddy's panic.

"Give it here." He leaned backward to check on the girl and at the same time stuck his hand out, wiggling his fingers impatiently. Richie laid it on him and Buddy was off like a shot. "Thanks for waitin'."

"You lose your wallet?"

"Yeah."

The Wanderers watched them walk down the street, looked at each other, and walked up three blocks past bars and gas stations to White Castle.

Buddy and the girl walked into a pizza shop by the park and sat at a littered table munching on dripping slices.

"What's your name?"

"Despie."

"Despie . . . like in Despinoza?"

"Yeah. What's yours?"

"Buddy."

"What's that short for?"

"Mario . . . Where you live?" he asked, scooping up some cheese.

"Up by White Castle."

"Hey . . . do you know Fat Sally?"

"No."

"Do you know Eugene Caputo?"

"No."

"Do you know . . . Toby Becker?"

"I think so."

"He's my best friend."

"Oh yeah?"

"Yeah, we was in ninth grade together."

"You go to Olinville?"

"Yeah. I graduated."

"Where you go now, Evander?"

"Nah, Tully."

"Do you know Phillip D'Allessio?"

"What grade?"

"Tenth."

"I'm in twelfth."

"Do you know . . . Donna Palombo?"

"No."

"Do you know . . . Marie Gueli?"

"Yeah, she's in my English class. A real skank."

"She's my sister."

"Oh . . ." He turned red.

She laughed. "I'm only kiddin'. Where you live?"

"The projects."

"Do you know Barry Jacobi?"

"No."

"He's my boyfriend."

Buddy's heart dropped into his gut. "Oh yeah?" he said weakly.

"Well . . . we broke up."

Resurrection.

"Yeah, he was seein' another girl on the side."

"I would never do that," he said righteously.

"He begged me to go back with him but I got my pride, you know what I mean?"

Buddy nodded solemnly. "I had a girl friend who was two-timin' me. I dropped her like a hot potato. I got pride too."

"Pride's important."

"Yeah . . . you gotta hold your head up high."

"Yeah."

"I saw this movie once where this guy is bein' tortured by the Japs, but he won't give 'em any information. Everytime they tortured him he just started singin' 'The Star-Spangled Banner.' "

"Wow! What happened?"

"They killed him."

"That's pride."

"I would never give out information to the Commies if they was torturin' me," said Buddy.

"My father was a marine," said Despie.

"Mine was in the navy," said Buddy.

"Do you like the Four Seasons?"

"Yeah . . . my brother knows Frankie Valli."

"A friend of mine met Dion."

"I got Smokey Robinson's autograph."

"I once went up in an elevator with Murry the K."

"Jackie the K's a real piece. No offense."

They walked outside and up Allerton toward Despie's house. Buddy put Despie to a test. She carried a pocketbook in her left hand, so he walked on her left. If she moved the pocketbook to her right hand she was leaving her left free for handholding. At first she didn't, so he casually brushed his knuckles against the back of her hand. The third time he did this, she hoisted the pocketbook strap over her right shoulder. A block later they were holding hands. When they passed White Castle they bumped into the Wanderers.

"Hey!"

"Hey!" He greeted them like long-lost friends.

"Mah man Buddy!" They devoured Despie with their eyes, taking special note of the fact that Buddy was holding her hand.

"Hey, this is Despie . . . this is the guys."

She stared at Richie. "Are you Denise Rizzo's boyfriend?"

"Yeah."

"I know you . . . me an' Denise are in the same homeroom at Evander. I saw you one day after school."

"No kiddin'. Hey, maybe we could double sometime," suggested Richie.

Buddy flinched. He hadn't asked her for a date yet, and Richie could blow the whole thing.

"Sure!" she said.

"Yeah, we could go bowlin' or somethin'."

"Hey, ah . . . lissen. I'll see you guys later, O.K.?"

"Later."

"Later."

After Buddy and Despie walked a quarter of a block, Buddy looked back at the Wanderers, made crazy-eyes, and let his tongue hang out. They thought that was cool and cracked up.

"I live on the next block."

"Nice street."

"It's O.K."

They stopped at her door.

"Ah, lissen . . . whyncha gimme your phone number, maybe we could double with Richie and C."

She took a soiled piece of loose-leaf paper and a funny-looking oversized pen out of her pocketbook. "Here."

"Hmm." He studied the number, stalling for time. "Despie Carabella. TU-six, four-two-three-one."

"That's right."

He studied the note a little longer, then stuffed it into his pocket. "Well . . ." He shuffled his feet.

"G'night."

He put an arm across her shoulder and brought his mouth to hers. She resisted for a second, then closed her eyes and put her arm around the back of his neck. She tongued like a pro and stood right up against his body. They mingled tongues for a full five minutes, until both their chins were dripping with spit.

"I like you, Despie."

"I like you too."

"Maybe we could go out Saturday."

"Sure."

She turned to go inside. Buddy walked away, wiping his chin on his jacket sleeve. After he crossed the street he shouted to her loud enough to turn on some lights.

"I'll call you tomorrow!"

She waved, and he took off like a jack rabbit for White Castle.

In homeroom the next day Despie slipped a note to Denise three aisles over:

DO YOU KNOW A FRIEND OF YOUR BOYFRIEND'S NAMED BUDDY? I MET HIM LAST NIGHT AND WE ARE GOING OUT SATURDAY. DO YOU WANT TO EAT LUNCH TOGETHER AND TALK? — DESPIE

Denise wrote back:

YES, I KNOW BUDDY. I LIKE HIM AND I THINK HE IS CUTE. I WILL MEET YOU IN THE BACK OF THE LUNCHROOM NEAR THE WINDOWS — DENISE

"So how'd you meet Buddy?" C asked, taking a bite out of a thin bologna sandwich.

"Well, last night I had nothin' to do so I was walkin' down Allerton when I saw Buddy walkin' up the other side of the street. I thought he looked cute. He didn't see me or nothin'. Anyways, he bumps into this fat lady an' starts elbow tittin'. This lady knocks him down. It was really funny. She started yellin' at him an' then I see he's wit' these other guys."

"Was Richie wit' them?"

"That's your boyfriend?"

"Yeah . . . I'll kick his ass if he was elbow tittin'."

"He was there but he was just hangin' aroun'. Anyways, I figure I'll play along, so I walked around the block and come down on the other side of the street, and Buddy starts walkin' toward me."

"What happened?"

"He bumped into me but he didn't do nothin' else."

"So then what happened?"

"He asked me if I wanted pizza. But first he gave me this bullshit story about gettin' jumped by two guys in a Cadillac."

"That sounds like Buddy."

"Then he walked me home an' asked me out for tomorrow night."

"That's too much."

"Yeah. What's he like?"

"Well, he's cute, he's in the Wanderers, he lives in the projects."

"Did he have a girl friend that he broke up with because she was seein' someone else?"

"Well, he was goin' wit' this girl Margo that was seein' someone else, but she broke up with Buddy. Buddy didn't break up wit' her."

"He told me he broke up wit' her."

"Sure."

"Is he on any teams?"

"Nah, but he's a good bowler, they all are," said C.

"Do you wanna double tomorrow?"

"Yeah, we're goin' to the Globe. You wanna come?"

"Yeah. He's gonna call me tonight."

"Howdja do on the Social?" C asked.

"I passed. I copied offa that creep Barry Jacobi."

Buddy was late coming down to the lunchroom. The Wanderers were already eating at their table.

"Hey! The man of the hour!"

Buddy sat down and took out a ham sandwich.

"You goin' out wit' Despie tonight?" Richie asked.

"Nah, I gotta call her."

"Lissen, me an' C are goin' to the movies tomorrow night. You wanna come?"

"O.K. As long as we can split up later, if you know what I mean."

"Yeah, well, my parents won't be home tomorrow night. They got a Cousins' Club meetin'."

"Dynamite!"

"Yeah, you can have my room. Me an' C will take my parents' bedroom."

"You got any bags?"

"My old man does. Hey, wait. Whadya mean do I got any bags. You ain't gonna need 'em."

"Don't be too sure."

"Five dollars."

"You ain't got five dollars."

"That's O.K. You ain't gonna get laid."

Buddy couldn't get his father's car, so they walked to the Allerton Globe to see two good horror pictures, which was fine with Buddy because Despie shrieked a lot and buried her head in his armpit. With his arm around Despie's shoulder, Buddy leaned his head over the back of the seat and caught Richie's eye. Richie did the same, wiggling his tongue obscenely. C excused herself, and she and Despie split for the john.

"Hey, man!" Buddy jumped over two seats. They slapped palms loudly. "I got such a fuckin' hard-on I'm bustin' my drawers!" Buddy squeezed his crotch in mock pain. Two elderly people turned around to give him dirty looks.

"Ja get tit?" Richie whispered.

"I din't try yet."

"She got nice ones."

"Hey," Buddy said, "I got your bedroom, right?"

"You get gizzem on my bed I'm gonna make you eat it with a spoon."

"We'll do it on the floor."

"You got class."

"Yeah, I'm elegant," said Buddy.

Buddy put records on Richie's record player and turned out the light. Despie almost pulled him down on top of her. Buddy excitedly started grinding, and she groaned appreciatively.

"Buddy?" She tapped him on the back and whispered huskily, "Get me a glass of water."

"Huh?"

"I'm thirsty."

"Yeah . . . wh . . . yeah." He stood up, his shirt half out of his pants, his hair messed up. He padded to the bathroom, took a piss, and brought Despie a glass of water. Despie put the glass on the floor.

"I thought you wanted water."

She took his hand and placed it between her legs.

"Jesus God!" Despie was naked. Buddy had never been with a naked girl before. She unbuttoned his shirt as he sat paralyzed, his hand frozen where she placed it. "Are you a virgin?" he whispered. She didn't answer but started on his pants. " 'Cause if you are, don't be scared." She pulled down his shorts and caressed his hard-on. "I don't got no bags but I'll pull out before I come." She put an arm around his neck, slid under him, and with her other hand guided his prick. The moment he was in, he came a bucket.

Early the next morning, Buddy lay in his own bed thinking about Despie. He looked at his alarm clock. Five-thirty. He got up, went into the kitchen, and dialed her number. He prayed her parents wouldn't answer. The phone rang four times; he was about to hang up when she answered.

"Hello?"

"Despie?" he whispered.

"Who's this?"

"Buddy."

"Whassamatter?" Her voice was thick with sleep.

"Nothin'. I just wanna talk."

"Wha' time is it?"

"I dunno, about two."

"Whadya wanna talk about?"

"I dunno. I miss you."

"That's nice."

"Do you miss me?"

". . . yeah."

There was dead silence for a minute.

"Despie?"

"Yeah?"

"Can I come over?"

"Tomorrow?"

"Now."

"Now? Everybody's sleeping."

"I gotta talk to you."

Another silence.

"O.K."

"See you soon." He hung up, got dressed, took his father's car keys, and drove over to her house. She was waiting for him on the porch. "Hi."

"Hi." She wore a quilt bathrobe and a kerchief over rollers.

"Let's go inside," she whispered, taking his hand and guiding him up the steps to her room. "Don't talk out loud. You'll wake them up." She closed the door, and they lay on the bed.

"I missed you, Despie."

"Me too."

"It was a good date."

"I had a good time."

Sitting up, he took off his coat and shoes. She lifted the cover, and he slipped in, right up next to her.

"Despie?"

"Yeah?"

"That was numero uno for me."

Another silence.

"Me too."

"Did it hurt?"

"A little."

"I tried not to hurt you . . . did you have an orgasm?"

"I don't know."

"Whadya mean?"

"I dunno . . . I couldn't tell."

"Did it feel good?"

"Yeah."

"I came pretty quick."

"That's O.K."

"I won't come so quick next time."

"It's O.K."

"That was your first time?"

"I told you yeah."

"Did you bleed?"

"I didn't look."

A light went on in the hallway. Slippers shuffled toward Despie's door. Buddy jumped out of bed and hid in the closet. A soft knock. Despie pretended she was asleep. Her mother opened the door, poking her head into the room. "Despie?"

She peered into the darkness for a moment, then softly closed the door. Twenty minutes later Buddy came out of the closet. Despie was fast asleep.

The next day in Big Playground Buddy was moody and quiet. He couldn't play basketball or join in with the every minute bullshitting. Thinking of Despie made him miserable. He thought of her with intense longing, yet there was something about her that made him wish they'd never met.

"Hey, man." Richie sat on the bench next to him. "Why ain'tcha playin'?"

"I dunno." He shrugged. "Don't feel like it."

"Despie give you a bad time las' night?" Buddy smiled. If Richie only knew Buddy lost his cherry he would flip. Buddy himself was amazed that he wasn't shouting it from the rooftops. Sex wasn't anything like he thought it would be. It was a bitch. "Despie give you trouble?"

"Nah."

"How far you go?"

"Far enough."

"Don't wanna talk?"

"I guess not, man."

Richie shrugged and got up. "O.K., man, it's on you."

Sunday was always a drag. It was cold and windy. The few trees in Big Playground were leafless. Buddy still hadn't finished the report due Monday for social studies. He couldn't concentrate on anything but Despie. He walked across the basketball courts and through the hole in the fence to the street. Fishing in his pockets for a dime, he went into Pioneer's Candy Store and sat in a phone booth. He hated the panicky feeling in his gut. He had nothing to say, yet he had to talk to her.

The number was busy.

No one answered.

Wrong number.

No one answered.

No one answered.

Buddy left the candy store, his clothing soaked with nervous sweat. Everyone had left the playground. He went upstairs and tried to call Despie. Still no answer. He took out his loose-leaf, opened it to a clean page, and wrote

Mario Borsalino	Social Studies 402
11/27/62	Mr. Finnerty

The XYZ Affair

He took out the WYC-XAU volume of the *Home and Hearth Encyclopedia*, opened it to the XYZ Affair, and began copying verbatim. After every ten sentences he would get up and call Despie's number. She hated him. He bored her. She wasn't a virgin. She fucked Nazis and niggers before breakfast. His dick was too small. He loved her. She gave head to all the guys on Lester Avenue. Terror liked to shit in her mouth. When he was in the closet she laughed herself to sleep. She told her parents, and they all had a good laugh. Lenny Arkadian knew the inside of her cunt like the back of his hand. She was out fucking *right now*. He loved her. He did. He really did.

"Hello?"

"You're home."

"Who's this?"

"Buddy."

"Hi."

"Where were you?"

"I was at my uncle's house."

"What were you doing there?"

"Whadya mean what was I doing there? He's my uncle. We went to visit my uncle."

"Sorry."

"Buddy, is something wrong?"

"Nah."

"Look, I gotta go, my friends are waiting for me. Bye."

Before he could say goodbye, the phone clicked. His stomach frosted over. Friends. What friends? Boyfriends? Probably. But he'd be cool. The fastest way to lose a girl is to be possessive. What uncle? She didn't say anything to him before about an "uncle." Uncle my ass. Uncle Sam maybe. Fucking for the troops. Uncle Sam wants you.

That night Despie sat at her desk doing her homework and listening to the Scott Muni Show on the radio. She couldn't figure Buddy out. She liked him and maybe would like to go steady with him in time, but he acted so goddamn weird. Maybe they shouldn't have done it so soon. She wasn't sure he could handle it. Maybe after he calmed down a little they'd have a talk. On the radio a slow piano led into a song. "O.K., gang, this is a dedication from Buddy to Despie. Listen to the words. Smokey Robinson and the Miracles doin' it to ya."

I don't lak you, but ah luh-uv you,
Seems that I'm all-way-yays thinking uv you
Though-wo-wo you treat me badly,
I love you madly,
You really got a hold on me
You really got a hold on me

Despie sat in stunned silence. The words went in one ear and out the other. The phone started ringing, and in two hours Despie got calls from six girl friends. Despie didn't think about the words of the song. It could have been "Duke of Earl" or Beethoven — it didn't matter. The only things that mattered were that Scott Muni mentioned her name over the radio and Buddy dedicated a song to her.

Buddy sat at his desk in a pool of sweat. He hoped Despie had heard the song, but he was afraid she would be mad at him for declaring the agony of his love in public. He hoped she wouldn't take offense at the "I don't like you," and he hoped she wouldn't be scared by the "but I love you." The phone rang, and he almost took a chunk out of his thigh scrambling from the desk to answer it.

"Hello?"

"Lissen, man, are you buckin' for a section eight?"

"Hey, Eugene, you heard the song?"

"Though-wo-wo you treat me cruelly, I luv you true-el-ly," he mimicked with a nasal nastiness.

"You don't like the song?"

"Man, it's a very pretty song, a delightful song, really. Lissen, you sap, if I was a chick lissenen' to that song, I would think . . . man, that guy's one fuckin' rag. Look, I don't know this Despie chick, all I heard is she's nice-lookin' but man, I'm tellin' you, a chick likes to be pushed around, man, she likes a guy wit' balls not no . . ." He sang another nasal verse from the song. "Do you know what I'm talkin' about?"

"I dunno." Buddy got depressed listening to Eugene.

"Look, Buddy, do you wanna remain a virgin all your life?"

"Hello?"

"Buddy?"

"Despie!"

"Hi, I heard the dedication. That was really sweet."

"You liked it?"

"Yeah, that was really nice of you."

Buddy sighed from the innermost part of his soul. "So you liked it, hah?"

"Yeah. Did you talk to Scott Muni on the phone?"

"Yeah."

"Ooh! What's he like?"

"He's O.K. Do you wanna meet tomorrow after school?"

"Did he say anything about what a funny name Despie was?"

"Uh . . . nah. Do you wanna meet tomorrow after school?"

"What time?"

"Four. I'll come over to your place."

"O.K. Did he say anything else to you?"

"Nah. Despie?"

"Yeah?"

"I really . . . really like you."

"Me too."

"See you tomorrow."

"See you."

Buddy lay on his bed, smiling at the ceiling. What the hell did Eugene know?

6

Super Stud

EUGENE CAPUTO ran his dry lips over Barbara Berkowitz's un-extraordinary nipples, lowered his mouth to her ribs, then her navel, and hesitated before moving on to the warning track. He waited for her hand to yank his head up, but she lay para-lyzed with anticipation, so he continued down until his nostrils were stuffed with pubic hair — then lower still until his tongue tasted and his nose smelled the acrid pungence.

"Oh, Eee-yew-gene! Eee-yew-gene!"

Eugene gagged on her stench and the sound of her ecstasy. He sat up and picked a few pubies like flecks of tobacco from the tip of his tongue. "Jesus Christ, Barbara, you oughta use Right Guard down there!"

She sat up, head slightly cocked in a questioning, shocked, open-mouthed stare as if he'd said, "Your parents are dead." "What?" squeaked from her constricted throat, her eyes glis-tening in mortification.

"Oh shit, don't cry," he sighed.

As if to spite him she cried so hard it actually sounded like "boo-hoo."

He debated whether to console her by patting and caressing her, or to just light up a cigarette.

"Hey look, Barbara, it's perfectly normal for girls to stink down there," he said, taking a long drag and blowing a smoke ring. She arched her back and hitched up her skirt. "Besides, you ain't *that* bad. I once ate out a girl who smelled like she stuffed small dead animals up there." He laughed at the memory.

"Eugene," she said coldly, her features like four deadly straight lines, "shut your filthy mouth and take me home."

He shrugged, started the car, and pulled out into the deserted street. He drove in silence. When they reached her house she got out, slamming the door as if to make the car crumble from shock waves. Eugene winced, leaned over the shot-gun seat, and shouted out the window to her back, "Nice meeting you, Barbara. Good night."

When Eugene came home his father was still up watching television. Eugene plopped down on the couch and started undoing his tie.

"How'd it go, Ace?"

"Thirty-four," Eugene answered without taking his eyes from the set. His father smiled and lit a Marlboro. He offered one to his son from a flat silver case with A.C. initialed in swoops and swirls like Louis XIV silverware. Eugene declined, sticking one of his own Kools between his lips.

"Thirty-four, hah?" Eugene stared at the television. "When I was your age, I was up to forty-six. You're catching up." Eugene shrugged, unnecessarily cupping his hands around his father's lighter. "You want coffee?"

"Nah, I'm gonna turn in. School tomorrow."

"Later, Ace." His father tipped an invisible cap to Eugene and changed channels.

Eugene studied his face in the bathroom mirror. His complexion was soft olive — a mixture of his father's Mediterranean swarthiness and his mother's Lebanese duskiness. His hair was jet black with a blue sheen. The hairline was low and even, the hair straight, looking more manicured than cut. He examined the pores of his skin with his fingertips. No blemishes — not even a blackhead. His eyes were hooded, yet they didn't bug out like Gennaro's. They were sleepy Robert Mitchum eyes with a husky liquid color like good dark rum. His nose was narrow and straight. His lips were thin and perfectly defined by a nearly invisible slightly less olive line. He stepped back to take in the whole face — a real Michelangelo job his grandmother used to say. He massaged his face and neck with the blue soap his grandparents had sent from Spain for his birthday. Before turning in, he sat at his desk and opened his little black book to the page headed "E.B." — "Everything But." A long list of girls' names was followed by initials ranging from "D.H.T.I.C.," which stood for "Dry Humped Till I Came," to "H.J." — "Handjob," "A.O." — "Ate Out," "B.J." — "Blowjob," and "F.J." — "Foot Job." He wrote Barbara Berkowitz under "A.O." and turned to the next page, headed DIAL, which read backwards, LAID. The rest of the page was clear, as unblemished by ink as his own skin was by blackheads.

*

The Wanderers met on the el platform next morning, each wearing a black jacket with yellow piping and "Tully" written on the back in yellow letters.

"Where the fuck's Caputo?" asked Buddy.

"Prob'ly sleepin'," answered Richie.

"Yeah, gettin' his energy back," said Perry with a tinge of envy.

"That guy's gonna screw 'imself to death."

"He mus' get laid more'n Elvis Presley."

"More'n Al Capone."

"Yeah, but he shouldn't miss so much school," said Perry.

"Ah, so what. Whad you rather do — sit on your ass in homeroom or sit on Barbara Berkowitz's face?" asked Buddy.

"I'd like to sit on your face, you stoopit dip."

Buddy made sucking noises at Perry, and Perry chased him around the platform until the train came.

"You-gene, You-gene." His little sister shook his shoulder. He turned over in bed and stared at her through quarter-mast eyes. "Al forgot to wake us again. It's ten o'clock," she nagged.

Eugene sat up and rubbed his face, then reached across his desk for a cigarette. "Ah, shit."

His sister was dressed. She left the room and went into the kitchen to make herself some breakfast.

"Dinky? Did he leave the car keys?" Eugene yelled.

"I dunno," she yelled back.

"Well, whyncha look then? I'll drive you to school." He lay back in bed, scratching his balls.

"Yeah, they're onna table."

"Awright." He got out of bed, and like every morning he had a hard-on, and like every hard-on, it pointed straight down between his legs. He stared at it — no longer shocked and dismayed, but with a hopeless resignation, a passive sense of doom. He staggered into the bathroom and out of habit tried to pull it up to a more natural position. As soon as he let go, it snapped back, pointing rigidly at the ground like a divining rod that just discovered an underground ocean. He pissed, washed, brushed his teeth, and got dressed. He wore a yellow button-down shirt with gold cuff links, cocoa brown skin-tight slacks, gold Banlon socks, and brown suede ankle boots.

Dinky sat in the dining room eating chocolate-flavored dry cereal. Eugene came in with two cups of coffee. A cigarette hung from the corner of his mouth. He put one cup in front of his sister and sat down. "Did Al leave you money today?" Eugene extracted a five from his wallet.

She held up a tiny hand to signify she had enough. "Al

gave me a five yesterday," she said, sipping coffee. "Can I have some more sugar?"

"No, your teeth'll rot. Did you do your homework?"

"Yeah."

"Lemme see."

She pushed away from the table and primly walked across the living room to her books stacked on the coffee table. Eugene chuckled. He really dug his eight-year-old sister — she tried so hard to be sweet sixteen. When she bent down he saw a flash of white.

"Dinky. Your drawers are showin'. Pull down your dress."

She stood up with her hands on her hips, tapping her toe impatiently and staring at him crossly. "You-gene," she said in a stern, lecturing voice.

Eugene laughed. She returned to the table with a black-and-white composition book, opening it for him. As he perused her arithmetic, she stood with one arm around his neck and one hand on her hip, studying his face for any sign of a mistake in her homework.

"How'm I doin'?" she asked.

"Good . . . good . . . ah . . . ah . . . how much is eight and six?"

She squinted at the ceiling, her lips moving. "Fourteen."

"Whad you put?" He pointed to a problem. She leaned over, her arm still around his neck. "Ah, shit," she said.

He bolted upright in his seat and stared at her. "Hey!"

"What?" she asked, wide-eyed.

"You know what," he said menacingly.

She shrugged, staring at her shoes. "You say it, and Al says it all the time . . . last night he said shit to Mommy, and he said shit twice over the phone and this morning when you got up you said ah, shit."

She imitated him rubbing his face. He stifled a laugh.

"Well I'm older'n you, I can say anything I want."

She was impressed. "Can you say fuck?"

He grabbed her roughly by the elbows. "Dinky, if I ever hear you say another bad word, I'm gonna whack your behind an' wash your mouth out wit' soap."

She frowned at the table. He was afraid she would cry so he let go of her arms. "When'll I be old enough?" she asked.

"For what?" he said with a vague fear.

"To say anything I want."

"Never," he said, the nagging unnamed fear setting up house somewhere inside him.

He drove her to the public school though it was only four blocks down the street. "Gimme a kiss."

She planted a sloppy one on his cheek. "Seeya."

"Seeya."

He sat parked at the curb and watched her walk up the steps to the main entrance.

Eugene drove through the park across the parkway and pulled up in front of Tully. The gigantic, gray, block-long factory that passed for a high school filled him with dread. Eleven o'clock. If he went in now he had to see the late monitor, then he had to see Mulligan. Eugene had already been sent to his office four times for lateness, and Mulligan would break his ass. School really bit the hairy banana these days. Eugene ran his hands along the steering wheel, then lit another cigarette. Fuck it. He drove up to Jerome Avenue and bought a knish at a deli. At this point it would be better to stay out all day than to waltz in at noon. He could get Al to write a note saying he was sick. He wasn't feeling that well anyhow. He sat at the back table and watched three flies have a party with a dry spot of mustard. Eugene shut his eyes, screwing up his face. After a few seconds he had a headache and composed a mental note for his father to sign.

Dear Mr. Bitch Mulligan:
 Please excuse my son, Ace, from missing school yesterday. He had one fucker of a headache.
AL "THE MAN" CAPUTO

Eugene took out his wallet and thumbed through his I.D. cards and photos. He always did this when he felt fucked up, just to make sure he knew who he was. He came across Barbara Berkowitz's number. She was on early session at Evander, which meant she would be home by now. He could use a nice blowjob. If he called her first she'd probably scrub her clam so damn clean it would win a *Good Housekeeping* award. Then maybe he'd do a decent job eating her out. But what if she wanted to fuck? The old familiar demon straddled his heart and squeezed. He couldn't finish the knish. Now he had a real headache. Ever since the guys had a circle jerk at Gennaro's house three years ago, and he saw that everybody else's hard-on went up and his went down he was convinced he could never get laid. He was built wrong. The girl would have to stand on her head, and he would have to lower himself into her snatch. He had plenty of chances to get laid in the last two years, but he always got scared of not being able to get it inside like a normal person. When it looked like piss or get off the pot, he would insult the girl incredibly, and she would get mad and split. This saved his reputation as a stud but was hell on his nerves.

"Hey . . . Barbara?"

"Yeah?"

"Ah, look, this is Eugene."

Silence. A good sign. If she really didn't want to see him she would've hung up. "Look . . . ah . . . I'm sorry about last night. I got outta line."

An angry inhale of breath, more of a hiss than a sigh.

"Ah, my grandfather was dying yesterday an' I was upset."

"Oh?" Coolly, "And how is he today?"

"He's dead."

A gasp. Hook, line, and sinker.

As Barbara noisily gobbled his rod, Eugene lay back and studied the pictures on her wall, all cut out of *16* magazine. Fabian, Frankie Avalon, Neil Sedaka, Bobby Rydell, and Johnny Tillotson. Jesus Christ. He stifled a belch. His own taste ran to Dion, the Four Seasons, the Dovells, and some of the new Motown stars like Smokey Robinson and the Miracles, Marvin Gaye, and Mary Wells. That new blind kid, Little Stevie Wonder, wasn't so bad either. Eugene debated the diplomacy of lighting a cigarette.

*

Eugene's mother, although a looker, did not have the confidence and security that some beautiful women have. She always suspected her husband of cheating. He usually was. They had running epic battles all the time. They argued in the bedroom, at the dinner table, in the street, in the car, in front of neighbors, in front of strangers, and in front of their children.

Eugene remembered when he was ten going down to the basement to shut himself away from a big fight his parents were having upstairs. He sat in the oversized upholstered rocker like an old man, rocking back and forth at a furious pace. His father had descended the wooden basement stairs, angrily pointed a finger at his son, and said, "My advice to you, Eugene, is never marry for pussy." Two years later Eugene found out what pussy meant, but only now was he slowly beginning to understand the whole sentence.

*

That night after dinner the Caputo family, except Dinky, simultaneously took out their cigarettes. The ritual was always the same — Al offering Eugene a Marlboro from the fancy silver case, Eugene declining and lighting up a Kool, and his mother, Eleanore, puffing away on a Parliament in an ivory cigarette holder. Except for the dirty dishes, the atmosphere was more like a high-stakes poker game than a family meal.

"How was school today?" Al asked.

"Awright," said Dinky.

"Ace?" Al nodded his head at Eugene.

"I din't go." Eugene dug his fingers deep into his mouth and extracted a shred of steak from a back molar.

"Eugene, that's a disgusting habit," his mother said evenly. "Whyncha go?"

"Headache," he said flatly, studying the food on his fingertip.

"For God's sake, use a toothpick at least."

"Headache, hah? What's 'er name?"

Eugene ate the steak. "Nah, really, had a headache," he said as if he didn't give a shit whether or not Al believed him.

"Thirty-five?" Al winked.

Eugene shrugged.

Eleanore snapped to, staring narrowly at Al. "Thirty-five? Thirty-five what?"

Al stubbed out his cigarette. "Forget it."

"No, no, no, Mister, I want to know. I'm his mother. Thirty-five chippies maybe?" Al shot her a look that could stop a heart, but she was just warming up. "Well," she smiled, shrugging, "I guess it's to be expected." She fitted another Parliament in the holder. "Like father like son?" She blew a small funnel of smoke in Al's face. His eyes burned through the fog around his head.

"Who the hell you think you are, Bette Davis?"

"Who the hell you think *you* are, Humphrey Bogart?"

"Bitch!"

"Chippy chaser!"

"Ball-breaker!"

She raised herself slightly from her seat, her voice trembling with passion, "Whoremonger!"

"Ha! I never had to pay for it in my life!" He lit another cigarette with a flourish.

"Oh, ho! Oh, ho!" she laughed dramatically to an invisible third party in the chair Dinky vacated somewhere between "Bitch" and "Whoremonger." "*He* never *had* to pay for it!"

Eugene lit another cigarette. This was even better than the last time.

*

"Your bosoms are golden mounds of margarine
  your nipples are like a cherry if the A-bomb
  fell on us right this instant this is wherein
  my head I would bury."

Frowning, Buddy perused his poetry. He crossed out "bosoms" and wrote "breasts." He crossed out "mounds" and wrote "lumps." He crossed out "A-bomb" and wrote "H-bomb."

The doorbell rang.

"Ma!" he bleated. "Ma-a-a, get the door. Shit!" He got up from his desk and trotted down the narrow linoleum foyer. He looked through the peephole but couldn't see anyone.

"Yeah?" he shouted, keeping the door locked.

"Do you believe in God?" asked a high-pitched nasal voice.

"Fuckin' Jehovah's Witnesses," he muttered. "Go 'way. I'm Jewish." He was starting back to his room when whoever was out there pounded on the door with thunderous force. "Jesus Christ." Buddy grabbed an umbrella and threw the door open, holding the umbrella over his head like a spear. No one was there. He took a tentative step into the hallway.

"BLEAH!" Eugene shouted in Buddy's ear as he jumped

from his hiding place. Buddy leaped back, almost stabbing himself in the head with the umbrella.

"Jesus Fucking H. Christ, Eugene!" Buddy dropped the umbrella and clutched his heart.

"Howya doin', man?" Eugene smiled. "You got a leaky ceilin'?" He picked up the umbrella and walked into the apartment.

Buddy followed him. "You're a fuckin' lunatic, you know that?"

"Tell it to the marines." Eugene walked into the bedroom. "Whadya doin'?"

Buddy bolted into his room and grabbed the poem from his desk.

"Hey, what was that?"

"Ah, nothin'."

"Borsalino, you bullshit so much your back teeth are brown." Eugene looked around the room.

"Meanwhile, asshole, you almost scared me to death." Buddy tried to change the subject as he slipped the poem into his back pocket.

"Don't change the subject. Wha' was that, a love poem?"

"Fuckin' guy. You come into my house, wanna put me inna hospital wit' a coronary."

"Whyncha read me your poem?" Eugene made himself comfortable at the desk. "C'mon, I'm a pretty good poet myself, I'll help you out."

Buddy stared at Eugene for a long minute, shrugged, and sat cross-legged on the bed. "O.K., pretend you're Despie, awright?"

"C'mon, c'mon, read the fuckin' poem awready." Eugene put his hands behind his head and wiggled seductively.

Buddy brought out the crumpled paper, flattened it on his bed, and cleared his throat seven times. "You ready?" he asked.

"C'mon!"

"Ahm . . . your breastsaregoldenlumps ofmargarine . . . ah . . . yournipplesarelikeacherry . . . ah . . . no, wait . . . uh, yeah, if the H-bomb . . . ah . . . fellonusrightthis-instant . . . thatiswhere . . . inmyheadI . . . wouldbury — whadya think?"

Eugene couldn't answer because he was convulsed with laughter. He shook silently, his face red. He held in his stomach and in an attempt to catch his breath sucked wetly through his nose. After a few seconds he exhaled wearily, cradled his forehead in the bridge of his hand, and exploded into loud laughter. Buddy frowned, examining the paper. Flipping it over he examined the back, like maybe there was a joke written there that he couldn't see.

"You din't like it?"

"No, n-no." Eugene tried to calm down. "I-it w-was very m-moving." He started laughing again, rocking back and forth in the chair until it tipped backward and he went crashing to the floor, his feet raised in the air like a victory signal.

"Good for you, ya bastard!" Buddy helped him to his feet.

"Oh God!" Eugene took deep breaths to stop laughing and rubbed the back of his head. "That was some fuckin' poem there, Buddy! Knocked me outta my seat!" He wiped a tear from his eye. "Enough a this bullshit, let's get outta here," he said.

"Where you goin'?"

"I got the car. Let's go up to Yonkers."

"Where? It's Tuesday."

"I dunno. You wanna hit Papo's?"

"I got no proof."

"Here." Eugene showed him a fake I.D.

"It's Tuesday though," Buddy protested.

"It's the best time. Only the horniest ones go Tuesdays."

"I dunno."

"C'mon, you ain't married yet. I won't tell Despie."

"It ain't that."

"Yes, it is. I'll wait for you downstairs." Before Buddy could protest Eugene left the apartment.

"Hullo?"

"Hi."

"Hiya, babe, whatcha doin'?"

"Ah, nothin'." Buddy cradled the phone between his head and shoulder. "I wro'cha a poem."

"Really?"

"Yeah, you wanna hear it?"

"Whyncha come over an' read it to me?"

Buddy got terribly depressed thinking of Eugene in the car. "Uh, I can't now, I gotta lotta homework."

"Well, come over tomorrow."

"O.K. . . . Despie?"

"Yeah?"

"I love you."

"Me too."

"Bye."

"Bye."

"Oh, Despie?"

"Yeah."

"Uh . . . the phone's outta whack, so don't call me later because it don't ring on this end."

There was a long silence. "O.K."

"O.K."

"Bye."

"Bye."

Eugene sat behind the wheel, checking his breath with a cupped palm. Buddy's poem didn't make him laugh — it made him jealous. As far as he knew Buddy wasn't fucking Despie, but he envied Buddy for having a girl he thought enough of to write her poetry. Even if Buddy wasn't getting laid, neither was Eugene — so what the hell difference did it make?

Buddy opened the car door, and Eugene jumped involuntarily. "Let's go," said Buddy.

Eugene pulled out onto White Plains Road under the el tracks heading for the Bronx River Parkway.

"You know, Buddy? I been thinkin' about your poem."

"Spare me."

"No really."

"Fuck off."

"I liked it."

"Sure."

"It had heart."

"You shittin' me?"

"Would I shit you? You're my favorite turd."

"Fuck off."

"Hey, no, I din't mean to say that. I was only kiddin'. I really dug it!"

"Get lost."

"Hey, lissen, you stoopit jerk! I'm givin' you a fuckin' compliment!"

Papo's was a shoe box on Central Avenue in Yonkers surrounded by a miniature golf course, a Robert Hall drive-in clothing store, a Knapp shoe store, an Aunt Jemima pancake house, eleven gas stations, and Rickey's Clam House. Papo's squatted on the shore of a four-lane main drag that looked like an endless Christmas tree laying on its side adorned with traffic lights, fluorescent overheads, and bubbling neon.

"C'mon, let's go, there's no one here," Buddy whispered to Eugene as a refugee from professional wrestling studied the fake I.D. at the door. His lips moved silently as he tried to calculate Buddy's age, subtracting his phony birth date from the current year.

"Oh fuck it, you eighteen?"

"Sure! Can'tcha read?"

He gave Buddy the I.D. and nodded hello to Eugene. Eugene nodded back, then hustled Buddy to the bar.

"Hey, no one's here, Eugene."

"Shaddup, it's early. Whadya drinkin'?"

Before Buddy would answer, Eugene ordered two Seven and Sevens. The bartender looked like Moose from Archie comics.

The place consisted of a long bar, six or seven card tables covered with tablecloths, and a twenty-by-twenty-foot dancing area bordered by a juke box on one end and a small raised bandstand on the other. Caricatures of the regulars done in pencil and pastel covered the walls. Large faces with exaggerated hairdos and names like Tony, Gino, Ralph, Diane, Pat — about twelve Pats — Rosemary, Dominick, and Vinny. At the darkened table area beyond the bar, newly formed couples felt each other up on crowded weekend nights.

"Call it," Eugene flipped a coin.

"Heads."

"Cunt!" Eugene slid the quarter to Buddy, who walked over to the juke box and studied selections. He put on his three favorites, Ben E. King's "Spanish Harlem," Lee Dorsey's "Ya-Ya," and his all-time favorite, Dion's "Little Diane." Buddy shuddered involuntarily as the first, trembling prolonged guitar note filled the room. He sat down, closing his eyes. Dion, not singing but wailing in anguish against the trembling guitar:

"D-I-I-I-A-N-N-E, DEEP DOWN INSI-I-I-DE I
   CRY-Y-Y-Y-"
"D-I-I-I-A-N-N-E, WI-THOUT YAW LUV AH'D DIE-E-"
"D-I-I-I-A-N-N-E, YOU DRIVE ME-E- W-I-I-I-L-D,
   D-I-I-A-N-E"

Buddy downed half his drink in one gulp.

Awww . . . Lissen to mah heart (D-I-I-A-N-N-E)
Awww . . . yah tearin' it apart (D-I-I-A-N-N-E)
Awww . . . it's mah heart, Di-Ane (D-I-I-A-N-N-E)

Eugene had to grab Buddy to keep him from falling off the barstool in a swoon of musical passion. When they first started going together, and Despie was giving him a hard time — those endless days of agonizing hunger and self-doubt, Buddy had played "Little Diane" over and over on his record player, and now the words were so supercharged with meaning the song was almost unbearable in its symbolism.

"Let's get outta here." Buddy dragged Eugene to the door. He wanted to fly into Despie's arms and kiss and hug and fuck till dawn.

"Hey! Hey! Hey! Whereya runnin'?" Eugene put on his brakes. 'Relax, willya?" He stared at Buddy. "Christ! Finish your drink at least."

"I ain't thirsty."

"Awright. I tell you what . . . we wait . . . fifteen minutes . . . an' if no tail shows we go home, O.K.?"

Buddy checked his watch. "Fifteen minutes."

"Shee! You're a real prize, you know that?"

Fifteen minutes went by and no tail showed. On their way out Football Eddie stamped blue turkeys on their hands so they could come back in without paying. In the parking lot, a VW pulled in beside Eugene's car and two girls popped out.

"Hey! Hey! You see that?" Eugene grabbed Buddy's arm.

"I ain't blind. C'mon, let's go home." He reached for the car door but Eugene grabbed his other arm.

"Let's go back inside."

"I got homework."

"C'mon, don't be like that."

Dragging Buddy by the forearms, Eugene hustled him back inside. They showed their blue turkeys to Football Eddie, and Eugene headed for the girls' table, Buddy bringing up the rear.

"Hi!" They sat down. It was too dark to get a good look at the girls.

"What're you drinkin'?"

"WHAT?"

"What're you drinkin'?"

"WHAT?" The girls adjusted what looked like transistor radio earphones in their hair. Buddy and Eugene exchanged glances.

"What . . . are . . . you . . . drink . . . king?"

"SCOTCH," they shouted.

Eugene ordered four Scotches from a new bartender named Crazy Salad Face, whose skin had a gangrenous tint.

"What's your names?" Buddy asked halfheartedly.

"WHAT?" they both asked in unison.

"Let's get the fuck outta here," Buddy said to Eugene.

One of the girls made another adjustment on the plug in her head. "I'M SORRY," she yelled as if trying to be heard in a hurricane, "WE GOT NEW HEARING AIDS TODAY AND THEY'RE NOT WORKING RIGHT."

"WHAT?" Buddy asked. Eugene elbowed him. The other girl pulled out her hearing aid and and whacked it a couple of times. When she put it back it made a high-pitched whine, and all four of them jumped.

"C'mon, Eugene, I ain't drinkin' wit' robots." Buddy got up.

"IT'S O.K. NOW," the girl said.

Buddy was standing; Eugene yanked him down to his seat. One of the girls winked at Buddy, and he thought he saw the tip of her tongue dart out and back in like the head of a snake.

"I'M NANCY," said the girl with the sonic-boom hearing aid, "AN' THIS IS MARIE." Marie was the winker.

Suddenly Buddy became very interested. Crazy Salad Face fed the juke box a quarter, playing "Patches." "WANNA DANCE?" Buddy invited Marie. Eugene was taken aback but recovered nicely as he grabbed Nancy's hand, nodding in the direction of the dance floor. These girls didn't fuck around. They slammed crotches, bit ears, and licked necks. Buddy tried to lick Marie's ear but got a mouthful of plastic transistor for his troubles. In the light on the dance floor the girls didn't come off too hot. Marie had skin like a pizza pie, and Nancy was cross-eyed. It pained Eugene to dance with somebody so uncunty as a cross-eyed girl, but when he crossed his eyes she looked normal. Buddy was too far gone to care either way. He was nibbling on Marie's transistor wires, giving her tiny shocks with each nip.

After the dance Buddy grabbed Eugene. "WE'LL BE RIGHT BACK, GIRLS." He shoved Eugene into the john.

"Whadya doin', you asshole?" said Eugene.

"Lissen." Buddy's lips were parched. "Let's take 'em home!" He was so excited that when he leaned against the wall, he put his hand in the high urinal.

"Nah, they're dogs."

"C'mon, Eugene, my parents ain't home. I *know* we could score!" Buddy wiped his hand on a revolving towel holder.

"Oh, man, ain't you got no pride?"

"Bu-u-u-ulshit, man, my pride's right here." He grabbed his crotch.

"I dunno." Eugene crossed his eyes in the mirror.

"C'mon, c'mon, whadya say?" Before Eugene could answer, Buddy had led the girls halfway to the car.

*

One of the reasons Eugene had so many girls was because of his attitude. He never allowed himself to feel anything for any female because if he got involved he eventually would have to

fuck and then the show would be over. Also, he was afraid of really liking a girl and having to insult her to save himself, so he always came on with an I-don't-give-a-shit attitude, and he never slobbered over women like some lovesick people he knew. He had perfect control over his sex drive — he couldn't afford not to. Girls liked him — his aloofness challenged them. Of course, many thought he was conceited and his former "conquests" hated him, but the truth of the matter was that Eugene was just plain scared shitless.

*

Eugene lay naked on top of a naked girl, stone deaf without the hearing aid, which dangled over Buddy's parents' night table like a used intravenous tube, and he couldn't talk his way out of this because she couldn't hear a word he was saying. She was holding him on top of her with arms of steel and his fucking hard-on pointed down at his feet as usual. And he knew this girl wouldn't take no for an answer. All of a sudden, she reached between his legs, grabbed his cock, and yanked it toward her cunt. In it went, and Eugene was no longer a virgin.

The first thought Eugene had after the shock of realization was a memory of an old Little Rascals show in which Dicky had a stiff neck. Dicky's parents spent the whole program taking him to specialists, but in the end Stymie cured him simply by yanking his head around.

Eugene stayed inside her five minutes without moving, just enjoying the thought of where he finally was. Nancy wriggled impatiently under his body.

Buddy felt like he was wearing damp towels for underwear. Marie had been studying his bowling trophies for half an hour. As he stalked her around the room she focused on everything from the paint job on the walls to the loose-leaf on his desk. He thought of Eugene in the next bedroom, wondering what

he would do in a case like this. Just as Buddy reached twenty in the twenty-eight count he was making before jumping Marie, Eugene and Nancy came into the room holding hands and looking mildly drugged. "Sonovabitch," Buddy muttered, "he did it again."

"So, Ace, what's new?" Al wore a red brocade smoking jacket with black silk lapels.

Eugene high-jumped the back of the couch, landing ass-first on the cushion. He breathed heavily.

"I got laid!"

"Good. Thirty-five, right?"

"What?"

"Thirty-five, ain't it?" He offered his son a cigarette from the case.

"Thirty-five?" Eugene experimented with the number as if it were a new concept in modern living. "Thirty-five? Fifty! A hundred! Who cares!" He jumped over the couch again and bounded out of the living room.

Breathless, he sat at his desk, turning quickly to the DIAL page in the black book. In large letters he wrote NANCY CROSS-EYES. Then he put a line through DIAL and wrote LAID. Turning to the EVERYTHING BUT page, his eyes roamed slowly down the list of names, and his expression was that of a starving man reading a menu.

7

The Death of Hang On Sloopy

IN DECEMBER, in a drunken fit of patriotic passion, ten of the toughest Fordham Baldies joined the navy. This involved a twenty-foot walk from one end of the kidney-shaped traffic island where the Baldies hung out to the other end where a trailer had been set up as a navy recruiting center. For more than a year the recruiting officer had stared from his office window at the black-jacketed scum and cursed the day he enlisted for the Big One. The idea of making the world safe for democracy so that these little, actually not so little, pricks could spend their days and nights standing around drinking out of brown paper bags, leering at women, occasionally grabbing an ass, and in general terrorizing decent civilians made him sick with rage.

The day they staggered into the trailer his first reaction was to go for his forty-five in the desk drawer. When he realized they wanted to sign up, the ten of them leaning and staggering around his desk, eyes at half-mast, breath smelling like the tail end of a distillery, he whipped out the papers, hustled their signatures, and booted them out with, "At least you guys don't need no navy haircuts, har har har." The navy needed these bastards like they needed lead lifeboats but at least they'd be off the traffic island — out of his sight for good.

Later, after they sobered up they came back to say it was all a joke. He had prayed they would do that. "Sorry, boys."

"Whadya mean, sorry, boys. I ain't twenty-one."

"You don't gotta be. Har har har."

"C'mon, give us a break."

"Nope, them's the rules."

"My muther'll die wit'out me."

"You shoulda thought a that before."

"Whad you say about my mother?"

He took out his forty-five. They clammed up. "Now get outta here. Don't worry, the navy'll make men outtaya, har har har." They stared balefully at his leather face, at his steel blue gun, muttered, and left.

The only guy rejected after the examinations was Terror. He tried to maul the psychiatrist when the man asked him if he ever had wet dreams about his mother. When three MPs dragged Terror from the shrink's office, the psychiatrist wrote in a trembling hand on Terror's card, "The only uniform this man should wear is a strait jacket." But Terror's official rejection was for physical reasons — he had asthma. This was ironic because he was as strong as any two men. He had hands as big as coal shovels and a head the size and shape of a diving helmet. He was a mean mother and might have enjoyed a war.

So Terror was back on the traffic island, along with Joey DiMassi, Cookie Scalisi, who was busy with the dry heaves when his friends signed up, and ten to twenty faces that kept changing.

This was the end for the Fordham Baldies and Joey Di-Massi knew it. The heart and muscle were gone, Jay-Jay, Butler, Peter DiLuca, Fat Sally, the Martin brothers, Big Chief, Gussie, even the gang nigger Roger — although no one except Terror would dare call him a nigger, because to be a nigger and to be in the Baldies you had to be twice as tough as a white guy — all gone. At least they didn't take Terror, though Terror cut his own value with unpredictable rampages. Also, the new guys weren't the same. The old guys who didn't enlist started dropping out because a lot of their friends weren't around anymore. Joey knew his own days as a Baldie were numbered, and when he left that would be it. The heart and muscle were gone; and he was the brain. No brain, no gang.

*

A low concrete wall bordered the traffic island. When the Baldies got tired of standing they sat on the ground, backs against the wall, and watched the constant stream of shoppers walking across the island from Alexander's and smaller stores.

Saturday, February 14, Valentine's night. Terror, Joey, Hang On Sloopy, and Cookie sat against the wall, smashed on Tango, each in his own private rage. Cookie picked his nose, rolled the snot on his fingertips into a ball, and flicked it at the leg of a passing shopper. Terror was amused but didn't say anything. Joey DiMassi, on the other hand, was pissed and slapped Cookie across the back of his head.

"What's wrong wit' you?" Joey had bright eyes. Cookie winced.

"C'mon, Joey, man, hah?"

"Ain't you got no manners?" Joey sneered with irritation. Terror snickered. "How'd you like me to fling snot at you?"

"Awright, awright."

"You guys are hopeless!" he shouted.

"O.K., awready! Shit, you ain't no . . . no . . ." Cookie was stuck for a word.

Terror lifted his leg and bounced a fart off the pavement. This cracked up Cookie and Sloopy. Terror giggled like a little kid. Joey got up, dusted the seat of his pants, and started to walk away.

"Where you goin'?" Terror asked.

"Away from you pigs." Joey stood with his back to them, surveying Fordham Road.

"You gonna go to the movies?"

"Yeah."

Terror struggled to his feet. "I'll go wit' you."

"Don' do me no favors." Joey walked toward the Loew's. Terror tagged behind like Joey's pet gorilla.

"What's playin'?"

"*Mondo Cane*."

"It's Italian?" Joey didn't answer. "What's it about?"

Cookie and Hang On Sloopy watched Joey and Terror disappear down the hill. It started to snow, and the wind picked up.

"Fuck. What you wanna do, Sloop?"

Cookie took another slug of Tango and belched up some burning bile. Sloopy grabbed the bottle from Cookie, taking a wet gulp.

"Wha' time is it?"

Cookie looked over his shoulder at the big clock atop the Dollar Savings Bank three blocks away. "Half-past nine."

Sloopy took another belt and handed the bottle to Cookie. Cookie wiped the mouth with his sleeve. The idea of drinking from Sloopy's lips made him nauseous. Hang On Sloopy had a mouth that looked like it was put in his face with a can opener. A small bloodless, lipless hole with multicolored teeth going in four directions. Cookie was no stud either, but he thanked God daily that he didn't look like Sloopy. Sloopy's head was a narrow skull wrapped in skin. He had no nose save for two flaring holes and his ears were the size of quarters. His eyes were pale blue — not bad in a normal face, but nice eyes in Hang On Sloopy's face looked awful. Tommy Tatti said that Sloopy looked like somebody went over his face with a jumbo eraser and quit halfway through the job. But what God left out in the way of facial features he substituted with a galaxy of pimples. Not just the overnight breakout type, but permanent dark brown, sunk-in ones that had been nesting for years, the type that could withstand a laser beam. And the final touch was that Hang On Sloopy, like all the Baldies, shaved his head down to the scalp.

The wind whipped the snow sideways. Cookie and Sloopy stood up, turned up the collars of their Fordham Baldies' jackets, and jiggled in place to keep warm. The Fordham Baldies' jackets were better suited to the spring but snow or no, they had class. Black silk with butter yellow piping on the sleeves. The back was a work of art. Across the shoulder blades was "Fordham" in Gothic lettering. Below the letters was the profile of a grinning skull wearing a top hat like some dude ready for a night out on the town. Beneath the skull were two crossed ebony canes with silver tips. Everything lay on a background of orange-and-red flames, and at the bottom was "Baldies" in the same painstakingly beautiful print.

"Whoo, shit! C'mon, let's go somewhere!"

They walked down Fordham toward the Third Avenue el. Sloopy went into a liquor store to buy another quart of Tango.

*

Every year on February 14 Bronx House Community Center had a Valentine's Dance. The gym was decked out in crepe streamers and big cardboard hearts were hung every ten feet along the walls. Girls wearing ankle bracelets could get in for half price providing they were accompanied by their boyfriends who had proof that their name was the name on the ankle bracelet and providing that they both had Bronx House membership cards. Rumor had it that either Dion or Johnny Maestro and the Crests was going to be there, and the Wanderers decided to make the scene — Richie and Buddy with their girl friends, Perry, Joey, and Eugene stag. Once inside, the five guys went straight to the john to tease and pat their already frozen pompadours and waterfalls, elbowing twenty other guys for a good position in front of the mirror. Buddy and Richie split as the band warmed up. The other three stayed to piss. Joey and Eugene finished first, and after Joey zipped his fly, he gave Perry a little shove as he was peeing, making Perry spray his light gray sharkskins from knee to thigh. Laughing, Eugene and Joey split, leaving Perry cursing and pulling wads of sandpaper-like brown towels from the towel machine. He rubbed furiously at the stain, feeling the creepy wetness of piss on his leg. By the time he made it to the dance floor, both Joey and Eugene were dancing. He was upset. Joey's girl was a royal skank, so that wasn't too bad, but Eugene's was a real cunt. When the music stopped, Joey started talking to his dancing partner, but she walked away. Perry felt better.

"Jeez, what a skank," Joey said defensively.

"I seen you wit' worse."

Perry and Joey anxiously watched Eugene. Eugene and his girl were talking and laughing like old friends. The music started again. Eugene and his girl started dancing.

"Fuckin' Eugene."

"That guy mus' brush his teeth with Spanish fly."

The next song was slow. In a controlled panic, the stag guys pushed through the crowd asking first the nice-looking girls, then anything without a dick to dance. Joey got a girl right off. Perry got shot down straight across the dance floor. The song was half over, and Perry started to sweat. He checked Joey out — Joey was dancing close but he wasn't grinding. Eugene was dancing like he should be wearing a Trojan. A girl stood next to Perry, smiling into space, her hands clasped in front of her. She had orange hair and the biggest tits Perry had ever seen. He tapped her on the arm.

" 'Scuse me." She didn't notice him. He felt like everybody

was watching. " 'Scuse me." She smiled dumbly. "You wanna dance?"

She put her arms around his neck and socked right in there. Yes. She was grinding. And her tits were like two fireballs pressed into his chest. He moved his leg between hers for two beats, then she moved her leg between his for two beats. Joey saw him. And Perry was in heaven. Too soon it was over. They separated.

"Ah, you go to Columbus?"

"Yeah, do you?"

"Nah. Tully."

"Do you know a guy named Steve?"

And so it went. Three dances. Then another slow one. They forgot the two-beat grinding rhythm in a delirium of new-found passion and stood in one spot frantically banging crotches. Perry's boner. He wanted to split for the john to jerk off, but he was afraid she would find someone else before he came back. He smiled at her as they waited, sweating, for the next dance. She looked up at him.

"Are you Jewish?"

Cave-in. "Ah . . . no." He noticed the Jewish star around her neck — heavy enough to kill — and kill it did.

"Uh, 'scuse me, I wanna see where my friends went." She smiled. Perry stood there drowning.

"She wasn't your type," said Joey, "she was nice."

Eugene and his girl were making out against the wall. Richie and Buddy were irrelevant — they had dates.

The band was a piece of shit. Little Domenick and the Sharktones. Three guineas and two niggers — couldn't harmonize for squat. The drummer used only one drumstick because he'd lost the other one. Eugene and his pickup won the twist contest with Buddy and Despie taking second — a Wanderer sweep. Richie and C smooched it up in a corner. Joey and Perry stood in the middle of the dance floor not even bothering to ask anybody to dance. Two shattered egos, having been shot down a total of twenty-six times. Perry cupped his hand in front of his face, checking his breath. Joey pretended to look at the back of his shirt and checked his armpits.

*

Hang On Sloopy and Cookie took the el to Pelham Parkway. They finished the Tango on the train. When they got off they were staggering drunk. They saw two girls walking to Bronx House and followed them, making sucking noises and discreet inquiries into their sex lives, family heritage, and toilet training. The girls walked briskly through the storm, the Baldies stumbling six feet behind like two retarded snow demons. During the last block, the girls broke into a genteel trot for the safety of bright lights and a crowd.

"You wanna go in?" Sloopy proposed.

"Nah." Cookie was self-conscious about his baldness. "Too many Jews."

"Bullshit. C'mon."

"Nah."

"Lissen, man."

"I don' wanna. You deaf?"

"Fuck ya!" Sloopy marched in, leaving Cookie outside in the snow.

The minute he got inside people cleared a path. He was older, he was drunk, and his skinhead and Baldie jacket were more obvious than an American flag. Oblivious to everyone around him, he started dancing alone like a monkey, hunching his shoulders, eyes closed, head bouncing in tune to the music. Joey nudged Perry. "Look who's here."

"Oh Christ, what an asshole."

Sloopy fell down, scrambled to his feet, and continued dancing.

"Who let *him* in?" Eugene asked, his arm around his new

girl friend. Joey and Perry stared at this new addition to Eugene's long list of conquests. "Oh yeah. Fred, this is the guys. This is Fred."

"My real name's Frederika but everybody calls me Fred," she giggled.

Joey and Perry nodded dumbly.

Eugene stared at the ceiling. She'd said that five times in the last two hours. Perry noticed she wore one of those Jewish thermometers they taped in doorways. He wondered if Eugene had told her he was a rabbi. Eugene looked more guinea than the Pope.

"Hey, Eugene," Perry started, "you gonna mass tomorrow?"

"What?"

"You gonna mass? You know, church? Mass?"

"What're you talkin' about?" Eugene hadn't been to church in four years.

"I think all good Catholics . . ." Perry didn't finish because a girl screamed right behind him. Wheeling around he saw Hang on Sloopy grabbing the orange-haired girl and trying to kiss her. She was screaming, trying to give him the straight arm like in the movies. They were surrounded by guys who were afraid of Sloopy, so instead of breaking it up, they just hovered like butterflies around the couple. Without thinking about the pros and cons, Perry busted through the crowd. Grabbing Sloopy by the waist, he yanked him clear off the ground. Sloopy landed on his feet, staring at Perry in amazement. Perry was a big boy. Sloopy was scrawny, mainly window dressing.

He clenched his teeth, shaking his finger at Perry. "I'm gonna *kill* you, motherfucker!" Perry knew he could take Sloopy, but he was afraid of the Baldies. Whatever happened, he couldn't go to Fordham Road anymore.

Sloopy backed through the door, shaking his finger and

cursing Perry. Perry felt nauseous with fear. The orange-haired girl ran crying with her friends into the bathroom. Joey came over to comfort Perry. "Now you did it." He shook his head. "Now you *really* did it."

Sloopy staggered through the snow, tears of rage freezing on his cheeks. He was so cold his back hurt. He tripped over a curbstone and split his lip. "SHIITTTT!" — one long cry of agony bouncing off rows of sleeping buildings. "FUUUUUUUUCK!" — roaring in harmony with the elevated train directly overhead.

"CUUUUUUUNNT!" The blood stained the front of his jacket.

Somewhere a window opened. "Shut the hell up, ya bastad!"

Sloopy rose to his knees. "Kiss my ass, ya cocksucka!" He laughed like a cretin.

Another window opened, and the yellow light made the five-story tenement look like a winking giant. "Shaddap, ya moron."

"Suck mah cock!" Sloopy got up, took his prick out, and pissed straight up in the air. When he was finished he spread his legs, jiggling it like a rubber cigar. A pot came crashing down through the shroud of plummeting snow.

"Who threw that?"

"Get outta here or I'll call a cop."

Sloopy yelled something back, but his voice was drowned out by another train.

An egg hit him on the head, splattering over his face and jacket. Sloopy bellowed at the buildings. He roared tears and in his fury started picking up rocks and smashing windows. He ran down Allerton Avenue smashing store windows. He ran down to the park and smashed car windows. Howling like a berserk Indian he ran through snowdrifts and over benches until he came to Webster Avenue. Once out of the park he sat exhausted on a bench near a huge church. Gasping, he listened to his heart pound like a car needing a tune-up. His tongue hung out like a dog's, and he started scraping egg off his head with his fingernails. His jacket was ruined. Totally ruined.

*

Bobby Cuddahy was a Ducky Boy. And like most Ducky Boys he was Irish, under five-foot-six, and crazy. Webster Avenue was Ducky Boy country. They roamed their turf like midget dinosaurs, brainless and fearless. They respected only nuns and priests. They would fight anyone and everyone and they'd never lose. They'd never lose because there were hundreds of them. Hundreds of stunted Irish madmen with crucifixes tattooed on their arms and chests, lunatics with that terrifying, slightly cross-eyed stare of the one-dimensional, semihuman, urban punk killing machine. And they were nasty — used tire chains, car aerials, and the "Webster Avenue walking stick," a baseball bat studded with razors.

Their ladies' auxiliary was even meaner. They would attack single guys and sometimes groups of guys. They used car aerials and in a single singing flash could pare a cheek so skin would be hanging down to the neck.

Periodically, the entire Ducky Boy nation would descend and destroy a neighborhood. Neither the Ducky Boys nor their victims knew why or when. It was more a natural calamity, an unthinking massive impulse, a quirk in gland secretions than anything thought out or even mentioned. One moment they would be sitting on stoops quietly drinking beer; an hour later, a housing project, a high school, or a playground would look like London after the blitz — complete with sirens and moaning wounded. And they'd be back on the stoops sipping beer, like they'd never left. They didn't wink, laugh, or bitch.

They ignored injuries. They'd sit there and bleed. Or they'd amble to confession covered with blood. They'd confess things like using the Lord's name in vain or farting in public. And Father O'Brian would also ignore the blood, listen to their droning, and give them a few Hail Marys to do. If he was in a particularly good or bad mood, he would march the confessor to the tiny concrete courtyard in back and administer ten lashes with a car aerial. No one complained. They could barely communicate verbally. Conversation was unknown. The only thing they did along with the rest of the human race was go to church. They'd go six, seven, sometimes ten times a week. They loved "Faddah O'Brian," an ex-Fordham University football star, who unlike most poverty area priests didn't give a shit what the youth did as long as they came to church. He didn't believe in baseball leagues or social work. He believed in confession and physical punishment. Father O'Brian was one of the original Ducky Boys of the early fifties who made good.

Father O'Brian watched Bobby Cuddahy get up and leave. The priest was sitting on a hard stool below the altar facing the eight Ducky Boys sitting in the front pew. Like every Saturday night only the Ducky Boys showed up for midnight mass. O'Brian faced them like a class and they stared blankly back at him. They'd sit like that for an hour. O'Brian would sigh, swallow phlegm, and crack his knuckles. The Ducky Boys would pick their noses, study their fingernails, and yawn. Sometimes the Ducky Boys would leave, sometimes O'Brian would leave. That Saturday Bobby left first, and fifteen minutes later the rest of them followed. O'Brian watched them get up wordlessly without a signal and silently file out of the church. O'Brian checked his watch. Twelve-thirty. He wondered where they were going. He wished he was still a Ducky Boy. He wondered if they were going home or going to kill somebody. He wished he was still a football star. He wished he was drunk.

Hang on Sloopy came out of the shadows as Bobby Cuddahy rounded the corner by the church.

"Hey, yo! C'mere!" Sloopy said. Bobby stared up at the mixture of blood, egg, pimples, and Technicolor teeth that made up Sloopy's blitzkrieged skull.

"Yo! C'mere!" Sloopy was about six inches taller than Bobby. He was still drunk and he didn't realize he was on Webster Avenue. "C'mere. I ain't gonna hurtcha." A curious halfsmile crossed Bobby's thick lips as he approached Sloopy. "Where you comin' from?" Sloopy snake-eyed him. Bobby didn't answer, just stared with that slight smile. "You go to high school, hah?" Sloopy's breath came out in clouds. His teeth chattered. The snow had stopped but the midnight chill was deadly. "You go to high school?" Bobby said nothing, stepping back out of the narrow circle of light cast by the old iron streetlight. Sloopy grabbed his arm. "Kid, you wanna blowjob? C'mon I ain't drunk, I'm serious. You wanna blowjob? We can go inta the park."

Sloopy squeezed Bobby's arm. Bobby's nostrils flared. Something shiny flashed in front of Sloopy's face, and he felt a cool mustache of blood creep into his mouth. He screamed, letting go of Bobby's arm. In a flash he realized where he was, who Bobby probably was.

Bobby's eyes shone. He raised his old-fashioned pearl-handled razor. "Blowjob?"

Sloopy ran down Webster Avenue. Behind him sprinted six Ducky Boys lazily swinging walking sticks. Sloopy ran faster; they continued at the same pace. They made a noise approaching laughter and shouted, "Blowjob?" Sloopy ran on cartoon legs. When he turned around again there were ten. They materialized from doorways, from the park, from the sidewalk. Sloopy came up to a high mesh fence and jumped on it, the force of the leap making the mesh wobble back and forth. He scrambled higher, each step up yielding a noise like clinking chain armor. When he got to the top, about fifteen feet up, and straddled the narrow metal bar, there were twenty Ducky Boys right under him, swishing the air with walking sticks, wandering around, snapping off car aerials, not seeming to pay him any attention. Every once in a while one of them would look up and say, "Blowjob?"

Sloopy was beyond panic. This was the end. The knotted ends of wire sticking up over the bar he straddled cut into his groin. Across the park he saw sporadic lights from apartments in high-rise buildings. He wished, by magic, he could vanish into the blackness and reappear by one of those lights — on a couch, a chair, a bed — safe. He looked down. To his left the Ducky Boys still milled around, ignoring him. To his right, a flat sheet of snow disappeared into darkness. He could barely make out the gallows-like silhouette of a basketball pole and backboard. A playground. He was on the fence of a playground. Staring hard across the playground he made out another fence. Beyond that, rumbles and speeding lights — the parkway. A chance that brought back the panic. If he could climb down into the playground, cut across the darkness, climb the other fence, run to the parkway. He looked to his left again. No one was even looking up at him. Do it. He lifted his leg. It was numb from staying in one position and from the cold. As he started to scramble down the inside of the fence, a Ducky Boy leaped onto the mesh, hands and feet clutching the wire, and thrust a walking stick at his face. Terrified, Sloopy let go and fell headfirst fifteen feet. His forehead struck the ice and concrete. His eyes rolled up under his eyelids.

*

Cars driving through the slush made a hushing sound as they came down the hill, and the reflections of their lights traveled across the walls and ceiling of Perry's bedroom. He lay in bed, hands clasped behind his head, watching the shifting beam-shadows illuminate his closet door, his record player, move across and up and disappear as the cars passed his building. He couldn't sleep — he thought about Sloopy. He thought about Terror. He thought about Debbie, the orange-haired girl whose bony cunt was thrust up against his cock only hours ago. He got a hard-on, started to jerk off, but his mind wandered. He thought of the Baldies, and his cock drooped over his fist like a dead flower. He chewed his nails thoughtfully. He thought about Terror. He could take on most of the Baldies, but not Terror, and Terror would come after him. If Joey DiMassi was around Perry would be safe. Joey was the only guy who could control Terror. And Joey was a good guy — he would understand what happened and call Terror off. Maybe Joey would decide that Perry would have to fight Sloopy. That would be O.K. Perry wouldn't beat him too bad, then he would offer to help him up, extend his hand — bygones be bygones and all that bullshit. Maybe the Baldies would like his style and offer him membership. He would turn it down of course, but would be grateful, swear undying friendship to Joey. Terror would growl but admire Perry's class. Maybe offer him a belt of Tango. Yeah. He thought of Debbie's tits and started jerking off again. But what if Sloopy went right to Terror without telling Joey? Terror knew Joey would stop him, so he'd keep it between him and Sloopy and come around to Big Playground and open Perry's skull on a pole like Perry's mother would split a peach. His cock fainted.

*

The Ducky Boy who poked Sloopy off his perch was the only one to see him fall. The others had their backs to the fence. When Sloopy's head hit the ground with a sickening THOCK they turned around and stared at his still form. Like a battalion of paratroopers, they slowly climbed the fence and dropped to the other side. They stood over his body, gently poking and prodding him with walking sticks, rolling him onto his back.

Bobby lightly drew a walking stick across Sloopy's cheek leaving a pencil line of blood. The Ducky Boys looked at each other for a long minute, then Bobby leaned down and raised Sloopy to a sitting position. Bobby removed Sloopy's stained jacket and shirt and gently laid him back on the ground, naked to the waist. Then they reclimbed the fence, the Fordham Baldies' jacket hanging from Bobby Cuddahy's belt like a scalp.

*

The news of Hang On Sloopy's death sent shock waves through the playgrounds, candy stores, and deserted lots of the North Bronx. Everyone became a philosopher. Some guys talked in whispers for the first time in their lives. The *Daily News* gave it three inches:

FOUND FROZEN IN BRONX

The seminude, razor-slashed, and battered body of a 19-year-old man identified as James Sloop of 2332 Valentine Avenue was found this morning in a playground at 203rd Street and Webster Avenue in the Bronx. He had apparently frozen to death during the night. Police are investigating the possibility of foul play.

"It was fate," said Eugene.
"What's it all mean?" asked Richie, shaking his head. "You

know, we're like specks of dust in a vacuum cleaner. It's like
. . . like everything you do, everything you feel is like . . ."

"Like for shit, man. You could go just like that." Joey
snapped his fingers.

"Just like Sloop," said Perry morosely.

"I mean like why go to fuckin' school? You spend eight
hours on math homework and walkin' to class some boogie
knifes you in the heart, and it's all over," said Richie.

"Yeah, homework's for shit," said Buddy.

"Sloopy was an O.K. guy," said Eugene.

"Hang On Sloopy," said Perry vacantly.

"I didn't even know his name was James until I read it in
the paper."

"Your name's Mario ain't it, Buddy?"

"What's Turkey's real name?"

"Ira."

"Ira?"

"Yeah."

"What an asshole."

"Ah, he's O.K."

Eugene lit a cigarette.

"Gimme a light," said Joey, steering Eugene's hand.

"Me too," said Buddy.

"Hey, that's three on a match."

"So?"

"So it's bad luck."

"Wit' all this bullshit goin' on I gotta worry about bad
luck?" Buddy asked.

"Din't you ever hear about the three soldiers?"

"You gonna tell us a story?"

Richie ignored Eugene. "It was night, right? An' these
guys were in the trenches. I dunno, I guess in Germany. Anyways, one guy lights his cigarette an' a sniper sees the light,
right? Then the guy gives a light to his buddy so the sniper

got time to aim. Then he gives a light to the third guy and —
pschoo!" Richie sighted down an imaginary gun barrel and
shot at Eugene.

"Was they Americans or Krauts?"

"How the fuck should I know?"

"Let's change the subject," said Perry.

"Let's get a Coke," said Richie.

"Let's do something," said Eugene.

The Wanderers dawdled along White Plains Road looking
for something to do. They stopped in Pizza World Pizzeria
and bought Cokes. Then they walked to the empty Safeway
parking lot across the street. The towering fluorescent lights
were on, and if there'd been no ice and snow they would have
played touch football. No one drank his Coke — it was too
cold to enjoy soda.

"Anybody wanna buy my Coke?" Richie offered.

"How much?"

"A quarter."

"Fuck you, they're fifteen."

"O.K. Fifteen."

"Nah."

Eugene put his thumb on the top of his bottle, shook up the
contents, and sprayed Richie. Laughing, they ran and slid on
the ice. Richie got pissed and didn't bother to shake his soda
up, he just threw the bottle at Eugene, hitting him square in
the head, knocking him out cold. They stopped running. Eugene lay on his face in the snow.

"You're a fuckin' asshole!" Perry yelled at Richie.

"I didn't mean it, I swear!" They kneeled around Eugene.
In a moment he came to. Moaning, he rolled over on his back
and stared at the faces and the towering lights. "I'm sorry,
Eugene, you O.K.?" Eugene stared at Richie like he wasn't
sure who he was. "Help 'im up." They lifted Eugene by the
armpits, and he stood like a drunk on wobbly legs.

"You O.K.?"

Eugene looked puzzled.

"Here." Richie gave Eugene the Coke bottle, which didn't break when he threw it. "Here, gimme five to run and you can throw it at me, O.K.?"

Eugene stared at the bottle placed in his hand and dropped it on the ground. He looked from face to face and rubbed the back of his head. "I wanna go home." A worried look passed around the Wanderers. Eugene started to walk out of the parking lot. The guys crowded around him.

"You O.K.?"

"You awright?"

"Yeah . . . yeah." His voice, little more than a whisper and very sleepy, sounded as if he'd just been roused from bed.

"Let's walk him home," said Richie, feeling guilty and anxious about Eugene's lack of anger and desire for revenge.

"Nah, nah, it's O.K. Just . . . just." Eugene waved his hand weakly as if to dismiss everything and walked away.

They watched him go down Burke Avenue. He didn't seem to wobble anymore.

"That was really stupid, Richie."

"Well, shit, he started."

"Yeah, well, you didn't have to throw the fuckin' bottle at 'im."

"I said I was sorry."

"What if he got a brain tumor now?"

"What?" Richie got a cold flash in his gut. "You can't get no brain tumor."

Perry continued in righteous anger. "Oh, yeah? Well if he got a brain tumor what are you gonna say to his parents? 'Well, he started'?"

Richie envisioned the funeral — Eugene's father maddened by grief charging blindly across the grave to kill him. Richie started to cry.

*

Eugene was O.K. He wasn't out for more than a few seconds. He knew he was O.K. Physically. But something had happened to him when he was coming to, when he didn't know if he was dreaming or awake, when he saw not the Wanderers but a painting of the Wanderers, when above their unreal faces he saw the giant lights of the parking lot — at that moment he'd realized that some day, like Sloopy, he, Eugene Caputo, was going to die. And it scared him shitless. It wasn't pain that made him wobbly-legged, but terror.

His reflex protective impulse was to watch TV. And he watched TV for hours and hours with a savage concentration until his neck muscles felt like pincushions. When only test patterns were on he turned off the TV and turned on the radio. When the radio station signed off, he turned on his record player, dressed up in his sharpest clothes, and practiced dancing as if as long as Kookie Byrnes or Cousin Brucie or Mad Daddy or Babalu or Murray the K or Dion or Frankie Valli could be heard, as long as there was some kind of hip ditty bop noise, as long as there was boss action, as long as there was something to remind him of the nowness and coolness of being seventeen and hip, he was safe. At six in the morning he collapsed, trembling with exhaustion. It was no use. He couldn't dance it out of his system. He couldn't stick two fingers down his throat and puke it up like too much Tango. Death was for keeps. He fell asleep and dreamed he was a rock-and-roll star.

8

Perry — Days of Rage

JOEY SAT in the living room watching cartoons. His school-books were sprawled over the big marble coffee table. He heard the elevator door open in the hallway, and his gut tightened instinctively. Outside the door, a splash of dropped keys and change. A muttered curse. Joey turned off the television. The door swung open, knocking over Joey's bicycle parked in the foyer. Emilio came crashing down on top of the crazily spinning wheels. Staggering to his feet, he picked up the bicycle and flung it the length of the apartment. He turned his eyes on his son, who stood frozen in the center of the living room.

"I tol' you to get rid of that goddamn thing!"

Joey stared at his father, the former Mr. New York City, the anchor tattoos, the thick old Italian-style mustache, the hawk nose, the burning eyes ignited by liquor and hatred for his weakling son. Joey took a deep breath and started the long walk past Emilio to his room.

"Whereya goin'?" Emilio demanded.

"I'm gonna pick up the bike," muttered Joey.

"What?" Emilio cupped an ear and squinted, standing dangerously close to Joey. "Talk like a man."

Joey didn't know whether to leave himself exposed or cover his front for an attack. If he put up his hands, he'd be asking for trouble. If he stood defenseless, his father could deck him in a second. But whatever he did, he couldn't walk past his father without answering — that would be suicide. "I'm gonna pick up the bike."

"What? I gotta fairy bad hearing problem." He brought his ear close to Joey's mouth.

"I'm gonna pick up the fuckin' bike!" Joey screamed. He had a split second to curse himself for losing his temper before a blur of flesh zoomed in on the tip of his nose, sending him sprawling, blood cascading from both nostrils. That was Emilio's favorite shot — the flat of his palm square in the nose.

"Jesus Christ." He looked down at his son. "You bleed just like a goddamn girl!" He walked down the foyer into his bedroom, giving Joey's bike a kick for good measure. "If I see this here when I get up," he said, pointing to the bike, "I'm gonna wrap it around your head."

Joey played dead until the bedroom door slammed. He went into the bathroom, took two Q-Tips from the medicine cabinet, ran them under cold water, and plugged one in each nostril until the bleeding stopped.

Joey rode the seven blocks to Eugene's house. "Hey, man."

"Hey, Joey. Hey, what's on your shirt?"

"Ah, I dripped some chocolate ices."

"What's up?"

"Ah, lissen, you think I could leave my bike in your basement a couple of days?"

"Sure, hey, your nose is bleedin'."

Joey wiped his nose with the back of his hand. He never carried a handkerchief.

After school the next day Joey invited the guys to his house for a taste of his old man's homemade wine. "This is good shit. He made it from apricots." Joey offered a glass to Eugene. Everyone else helped themselves.

"Feh!" Richie swallowed with difficulty. The others also had trouble drinking the bitter brew.

"It gets better the more you drink," said Joey, on his third. After a while everyone was plowed.

"Hey, man," Buddy grinned, "where's Mr. America?"

"He's sleepin', the fuckin' musclehead," Joey sneered.

"Aw, he ain't bad," said Perry.

"Aw, he ain't bad," mimicked Joey. "I'd like to cut his balls off and jam 'em down his throat."

"Hey, don't say that, man, he's your father," said Perry.

"Yeah? You just say that cause your old man's dead, Perry." Everyone stiffened. No one ever said anything to Perry about not having a father. Joey was really drunk. "I'd trade places with you any day a the week, Perry," Joey said. Perry's neck veins bulged. "Any day a the week, man," Joey repeated.

"Hey, Joey." Richie glared at him. "Whyncha shut up."

There was a taut silence for ten minutes. What could have been a shit-faced blast turned into a wake.

"My old man ain't any better," said Eugene. "He thinks he's like Marlon Brando. Spends whole fuckin' days in the bathroom combin' his hair. He fucks more pussy than you ever kissed."

"Gowan," said Buddy, "you're full a shit."

"Yeah? You shoulda heard the fight las' night, man. My ol' lady was gonna kick 'im outta the house. Dinky was scared shitless. It ain't right for parents to fight in fronna a eight-year-old girl. I had to take her for a comic book just to get 'er outta there. Paid for it wit' my own money. I don't want my sister windin' up wit' no ulcer, man."

The Wanderers sat in shocked silence.

"My mom's O.K.," said Perry. They all turned to him, watching his face. Because of what Joey said, the guys now looked at Perry as if he were naked. No one ever had the nerve to ask Perry about his father's death. Perry was the biggest Wanderer, standing over six feet, weighing over two hundred pounds. Perry looked around, confused by the abrupt silence and the weird looks the Wanderers were giving him. He didn't know that each of them was waiting for him to start talking about how his old man died. Each of them imagined a different death — guns, cancer, explosions, war, nothing as mundane as the heart attack that did in his father when Perry was twelve. "My mom's O.K.," repeated Perry. "The real douchebag is Raymond." He stared at their faces. They wanted more. He continued unsteadily. "Ever since he married that Jewish cunt and moved out to the Island he's been breakin' my mom's heart." Everybody knew Raymond Jr., Perry's older brother. Raymond was the projects' celebrity because he was almost a millionaire and not even thirty years old. "My mom drags me out to the fuckin' Island every month to see Raymond's kids. We always come back on that fuckin' train an' Mom's always cryin' 'cause that stupid blond twat thinks Mom's some kinda Mustache Pete and'll contaminate her kids." He took another gulp of wine. "Raymond's a fuckin' jellyfish. I don't care how much dough he got."

The sound of slippers shuffling on linoleum broke the spell. Emilio wearing a baggy pair of boxer shorts, scratching his balls, his eyes half-closed in sleep, stood in the doorway. His eyes traveled slowly from Wanderer to Wanderer, finally settling on Perry. "Hey, you come inta my house," he said, pointing a thick finger at Perry, "an' you watch your language. God lives in this house." They stared at his incredible biceps flexing effortlessly with every movement of his arms. "I don't want no cursin' here." He absently picked his nose as he sized up Perry, wondering if he could still kick a big man's ass as fast as he could twenty years ago. "Don't your father teach you no manners?" Emilio leaned against the door frame, tensing his body almost seductively. His words were angry, but his facial expression was slick and cool. "Ain't you got no tongue in your head? I ast you a question." Joey's eyes darted from his father to Perry and back to his father. Perry gripped the sides of the padded easy chair. The other Wanderers sat as if nailed into their chairs. "That's the trouble with you rotten kids today." He raised his hand over his head, a riot of muscle movement in his arm, and caressed the arch of the door frame. "The fathers are afraid to kick some sense inta their heads."

Perry half rose, still gripping the doily-covered arms. Emilio smiled, sizing up Perry again — he liked them big. "Your father mus' be some kinda piss ant 'cause . . ." He never finished the sentence. Perry flew across the room. Emilio stood poised, relishing the sensation of his iron fist sinking into soft flesh. But Perry didn't get close enough to be hit because Joey knew what his father was up to, and he tackled the big Wanderer as soon as Perry moved. Emilio stood there with his fist cocked watching his scrawny son trying to hold down the enraged giant. The other Wanderers also jumped on Perry. Perry bellowed in fury and frustration as his friends stopped him from getting to his feet.

"Perry!" Joey shouted. "He'll kill you, man, he'll kill you!"

"Lemme up! Lem-me up!" He struggled, his face almost purple, but the Wanderers held him. Emilio chuckled. Joey looked up as his father turned to leave the room. Snarling, Joey sprang to his feet, grabbed a wine bottle, and smashed it across the back of his father's head. The Wanderers ran like hell, dragging Perry with them. Eugene grabbed Joey's hand, almost jerking him off the ground.

"C'mon, man!" They flew down the stairs into the sunlight and raced for the park. Emilio Capra slept in a pool of blood and homemade apricot wine. They sat on the stone wall circling the park, gulping the cold air into their overworked lungs.

"H-hey, Joey." Richie labored to catch his breath. "Y-you shouldna done that."

Joey stared sullenly at the ground. "I hope I bashed his fuckin' brains out."

Perry grabbed Joey by the front of the shirt, pulled him to his feet, and slammed him against the wall. "Don't ever say that." He eyed Joey coldly. "He's your father and don't you forget it."

Perry walked home with a mean head. He was confused and angry. He would have liked to paste that rotten scumbag Emilio, yet in a funny way he liked him. He was sorry that he got pissed at Joey, but he didn't feel like apologizing. Fuckit. His mother was still at work. He threw himself on his bed and listened to Babalu on the radio. Half an hour later, he heard her come in. He didn't feel like talking so he turned off the radio and pretended to be asleep.

"Perry! C'mon, honey. I gotcha supper on the table."

"I ain't hungry." He rolled over on his side.

"C'mon, it's gonna get cold."

"I ain't hungry."

"You wan' me to bring it onna tray?"

Sighing, he got up to wash his face.

"I'm gonna be at Tillie's," she said, slamming the door.

He sat down to a dinner of hamburgers and three mounds of mashed potatoes. The phone rang. "Hey, Ma! Get the phone." He remembered she was next door. "Hullo?"

"Perry?"

"Hi, Ray."

"Hi, is Mom there?"

"She's over by Tillie's."

"Good. Ah, lissen, buddy, you gotta do me a favor."

"What?"

"Ah, Mom is supposed to be comin' out Sunday."

"So?"

"Well, we're gonna have some company and, ah . . ."

"You don't want her to come."

"Yeah. I mean whatehell, she'll be out in a couple of weeks for Christmas anyhow."

"So? I'll call 'er in, you can tell 'er."

"Hey! Perry? Ah, you tell 'er."

"Why don't you tell 'er."

"Ah, you know. She'll keep me on the phone for hours."

"Awright."

"Make up somethin' good."

"Sure."

"Take care, babe." Ray hung up.

"Rotten douchebag," Perry muttered.

"Was that the phone?" Perry's mother walked in.

"Yeah."

"Yeah what?"

"It was Ray."

Her face brightened. "How is my sweetie?"

Perry stiffened with anger. "Your sweetie's fine. Your sweetie said he can't wait to see you on Sunday."

Perry's mother sat down at the table as if in a trance — her eyes glazed with happiness. She was a short, fat woman with a face so sexless that if she wore the right clothes she would look like an old man. Perry took after his father — big and powerful, but with a soft baby face, round, full cheeks, and slightly pouting mouth. His eyes were like his mother's though, deep blue, pulled down at the corners. They gave the impression he was much older and more weary than his seventeen years would seem to permit.

"You know," his mother smiled, "I'm sixty years old, I ain't got more than a couple a years. But when I hear my sweetie gotta call me long distance *just* to tell me he can't wait to see me, I don't care if I die tomorrow. As long as I can see my sweetie on Sunday."

"You got more mashed potatoes?"

His mother drifted into the kitchen, took the ice cream scoop off the counter, and dipped it into the two-quart pot. She plopped the ball of mashed potatoes on Perry's plate and took her seat. "Hey! That's funny!" She smiled.

"What?"

"If I die tomorrow, how could I see Ray on Sunday? Hah hah!"

"You oughta be on television, Ma."

"Yeah, like on 'Ed Sullivan,' " she offered.

"I was thinkin' more like 'Queen for a Day.' "

That night Perry had a nightmare; he dreamed he was lying in bed. He heard the limp jangle of a cowbell from his mother's room and he jumped out of bed, his candy-striped pajamas soaked with sweat.

"Per-ee, Per-ee, Per-ee," in her weak, petulant voice.

He closed his eyes, trying to slow down his racing heart. "Hold on, Ma, I'm comin'." He lit a cigarette, exhaled heavily, and walked into her room. The stench of human shit assaulted his nostrils. She lay in bed — a vague collection of flesh and damp bedsheets.

"Per-ee, Per-ee, the man was here, yeah?"

He took the cover off the bed. She was laying in a pool of diarrhea. He pinched the skin between his eyes and clenched his teeth. "Jesus Christ. I'll be right back, Ma." He walked into the bathroom, grabbed a towel, and a small blue plastic pail. On the way back he took a clean bedsheet from the linen closet. He rolled her on her stomach. Then he pulled the dirty sheet from under her, carefully rolled it into a ball, and threw it out the window. He went back into the bathroom for a sponge to wipe down the rubber sheets. When he returned he saw she had partially missed. "Jesus fuck! You got it onna mattress! Goddamnit! That's it! You did it an' you're gonna lay in it!" He rubbed furiously with the sponge, but the stain was deep. He threw the sponge in the bucket. He opened all the windows in the room — the smell was causing his eyes to tear. Then he went to the other side of the bed where his mother lay motionless on her stomach. He removed her soiled nightgown and tossed it into the bucket. For a moment he stared down at her nude frame — bloodless and fleshless. He spread her legs delicately and turning his head away wiped her ass with the towel.

"Per-ee, the man was gonna hurt me, yeah?" She started to cry.

So did Perry. He went to his room. He took the thirty-eight from his dresser drawer, placed it on his desk, and sat down. Wiping the tears from his cheeks he smelled the shit on his hands. No matter how careful he was when he wiped her, no matter how big a towel he used, the same smell was always on his hands when he finished.

The cowbell again. Perry picked up the gun. His mother still lay in the same position. "Oh, Jesus." With two hands Perry aimed the gun at her head, closed his eyes, and fired. The shot missed its mark, blasting the pillow into a cloud of feathers.

She remained motionless as Perry dropped the gun at his bare feet. Then she calmly turned her head until she could see Perry. "Where's Raymond? I want Raymond."

"Aw-nuld! Aw-nuld!"
Perry's eyes opened wide.
"Hey, Aw-nuld!"

He got out of the bed and went to the window. Two kids sat on the green wooden bench downstairs in front of his building shouting for their friend. A little head appeared at a window two floors down. "C'mon, man. It's twelve-thirty."

The head disappeared, a window slammed. Perry sat on the window sill. It was a cold, sunny day. He spit, watching his saliva spiral and twist until it hit the pavement. He closed the window. The doorbell rang.

"Hey, man, it's twelve-thirty."

Perry scratched his ass through his pajamas and sleepily regarded Joey. "C'mon in."

"Whadya wanna do today, man?"

"I dunno. Hey, boil me some coffee, O.K.?" Perry headed for the bathroom. When he came out, Joey had poured him coffee and was sitting in the dinette eating a salami sandwich. "Help yourself!" Perry smirked.

Joey opened a bottle of soda.

"What happened wit' your old man?" Perry asked.

"Nothin'," Joey answered.

"What!"

"Yeah, nothin'."

"It don't make no sense." Perry sat down and sipped his coffee.

Joey shrugged. "Well, as near as I can figure it, that was the first time I ever hit back, you know what I mean?"

"Yeah?"

"Yeah, so like . . . I dunno, maybe he got respec' for me now, you know what I mean?"

"I'd still like to mix wit' 'im. No offense." Perry poured another cup of coffee.

"Don't," Joey said, "don't even think about it."

"Ah, he ain't so tough."

"Perry, I know that cocksucker. He'll tear you to shreds."

"Well, just tell 'im to stay outta my way."

Joey shook his head sadly. "Hey look, man, nothin's happenin' so I think I'll go over to my cousin's. I gotta get some shit over there." He headed for the door. "Dig you later."

Perry sat in moody silence for twenty minutes holding but not drinking his coffee.

"Perry?" His mother came through the door with a full shopping cart. He ducked through the kitchen and into his room. Dressing quickly, he left the house before she had taken her coat off.

He wandered over to Big Playground. No one was around except Turkey.

"Hey." Turkey waved.

"Hey. What's goin' on?" Perry didn't like Turkey, didn't especially want to be alone with him.

"Nothin'." Turkey felt self-conscious alone with any of the Wanderers. A big group was O.K., but one guy made him want to run away.

"You doin' anything?" Perry jammed his hands into his coat pockets, hunching his shoulders against the cold.

"Well, I gotta go downtown. I wanna check out this new bookstore."

"How you goin'?"

"Train."

"Let's go." As much as Perry disliked Turkey he didn't want to be left alone to think about Emilio.

"Sure." Turkey was amazed at Perry's confidence. He could never just walk up to a guy and say "Let's go" like that. They walked to the train station. Turkey felt like he had to entertain Perry, but everything he said fell flat. He talked about the skull he'd seen for sale on 46th Street, but Perry only scowled and stared across the street. He mentioned the Nazi armbands he'd just bought off this guy on Radcliffe Avenue, and it was like Perry wasn't even there.

On the train, Perry thought about the possibilities of fighting Emilio. This made him nervous, so he searched his brain for something else to think about. He flashed on Debbie Luloff, the orange-haired girl from the Bronx House dance. Maybe he should take her out. He imagined diving between her huge breasts and staying there for a week — maybe taking food and water with him.

". . . and he also has the original soundtrack from 'War of the Worlds.' "

"What?"

"He has all of them."

"Turkey, what the fuck are you talkin' about?"

"This guy Lowell Tucker down in the village got all the . . ."

"Turkey, I ain't interested. You broke my train of thought. Shut up."

Turkey wondered why he thought that *he* had to keep Perry amused. At Times Square, Perry walked off the train without even saying goodbye. Turkey felt hurt but relieved.

Perry wandered past the row of dirty movies off Broadway. Although he wasn't eighteen he could get into the "be 21-or-be gone" bookstores because he was a big guy. In one narrow shop with pegboard-covered walls, he examined a magazine called *Hand-Job*. One of the girls looked just like Debbie Luloff. He found a phone booth outside.

"Hullo?" An older woman's voice.

"Oh. Is Debbie there?"

"Who's calling?"

"A friend from school."

"What's your name?"

"Perry."

"What do you want with Debbie?"

"Oh, I gotta get the homework."

"Well, Debbie doesn't have it. She's been in bed for a week."

"Well can I . . ."

The lady hung up on him. "Rotten cunt," he muttered. He walked around the streets in a mixture of rage, embarrassment, and horniness. A storefront caught his eye:

TROPICAL JACK'S BOOK STORE
MOVIES — MOVIES — MOVIES
Private Booths
With SOUND!!!

Two life-sized big-titted nudes were painted in silhouette against the white windows. Perry walked through the brightly lit dirty-book section past the cashier into a dark hallway lined on both sides with curtained booths. The only light came from red bulbs over each booth: on if occupied, off if available. Perry picked a booth and stepped inside, drawing the curtain. He checked out the interior — a square closet with a wooden box on one wall, a coin slot, and two eyeholes. He dropped in a quarter. The screen lit up — the show began. He pressed his eyes against the peepholes. Two teen-age kids grinded mechanically from all angles for about three minutes. A tiny speaker from somewhere in the booth played a recording of a woman's voice, "Ohhh-oh-ohhh," alternating with a man's voice, "Yeah baby oh yeah baby oh baby."

Perry debated whether to whack off or not. Some guys must — why else would they give them their own booths. The screen went blank. He left the booth and slipped into the next one down the line. Dropped in a quarter. He squawked — two guys going at it. He watched anyhow. They stroked each other's chests. Then a close-up of mingling tongues. Then slightly hairy asses rolling over and over in bed. Against all mental protest Perry was excited. They don't show cock. He thought he saw a flash of cock but wasn't sure.

He ran to the next booth. Dropped in a quarter. Two dykes. That's more like it. They show bush. A close-up of a lipsticked mouth over a tit. Perry frantically rubbed his prick through his pants.

He ran to the next booth. He was out of quarters. He put in two dimes and a nickel. Nothing happened. He cursed, spraying spit. He stormed to the book section to get his money back from the guy behind the counter, but as soon as he left the darkness of the booths and entered the brightly lit storefront he felt ashamed and lost his hard-on. The guy behind the counter was a good-looking kid with long hair. Perry left Tropical Jack's and went home.

"Hallo, Perry, you have a good time? We gonna eat soon." Perry pushed past his mother. The thought of food gave him a stomach ache. She bustled after him, Lou Costello in a housedress. "Perry, whassamatter? You sick?"

"Lemme alone, hah?"

"I bet you're sick, c'mere." She put a wet, raw-meat-smelling hand on his forehead. The coldness and the food smell made him nauseous.

"Get outta here, willya?"

She started jabbering at him. Sidestepping her beefy clutches, locked himself in the bathroom. She yelled at him through the door. "Per-ry, Per-ry, opena door!"

"Go 'way!"

"Perry, come outta there an' lemme take your temperature!"

Pacing the bathroom Perry thought of the guy behind the counter looking in on him now and laughing.

"GET THE FUCK OUTTA HERE!" He punched the door, turning his knuckles red. He heard a gasp. Deathly silence. A little choke. A siren went off deep within her throat. The wail filled Perry's ears and eyes and mouth. He didn't know which to cover first and slammed his hands to his ears, screaming back, "SHADDUP SHADDUP SHADDUP SHADDUP."

The siren walked toward the kitchen, competing with the crashing of pots and pans.

Sweating, Perry flopped down on the toilet seat, exhaled heavily, and wiped his face on his sleeve. Then he stood up and combed his hair. He lit a cigarette and sat back down on the toilet. The trapped smoke in the tiny room made him wheeze. He was still wearing his coat. He stood up and flicked the butt in the bowl. "MOTHERFUCKIN' SHIT!" He slammed the seat back down and went into his room, threw off his coat, took off his damp shirt, and wiped his underarms with it. He splashed cologne in his armpits, put on a clean T-shirt, and walked into the kitchen.

"I'm sorry, Ma, I wasn't feelin' too good."

She turned to him — her long-suffering eyes as red as torn flesh. "Oh, Perry, Perry." She started crying again, holding him around the gut in a bear hug. He awkwardly returned the embrace, revolted by the burning sensation of her tears on his chest. He tried to disentangle himself. "O.K., Mom, O.K., Mom, I'm sorry. Hey, I'm sorry, awright?"

"I don't believe I should live to hear my younges' son, my *baby* . . . my *baby* call me a bad word like that. Perry, I'm a old woman now an' soon I'm gonna be wicha father up there." She let go to shake a finger at him. "An' he's gonna as' me how the boys treated me these las' few years . . ." Her voice died to a choked whisper. "An' I'm gonna hafta tell 'im, Perry." She shook her head. "I'm gonna hafta tell 'im . . ." She grabbed Perry again, sobbing in mighty bellows. Perry couldn't breathe. Suddenly she stopped, brought her tear-stained face up to his, and touched him lightly on the cheek.

Perry imagined plunging his tongue in her mouth, grabbing those big fat tits, twisting and squeezing them, ripping off that stinking housedress, and ramming his cock in her so hard that he'd break her fucking ribs.

"Perry, your face is hot. You got a fever, get in bed."

"G'wan, I ain't sick."

He disentangled himself from her arms, aware of the wet spot on his chest. He went into the bedroom again to change his T-shirt. She followed right behind: "Perry, please, lemme take your temperature?"

"No!" She started to cry again. "O.K., O.K., take my temperature."

She kissed him. "Lay down." She went to the bathroom. He dropped his pants and lay belly-down on his bed. She returned with a jar of Vaseline and a thermometer. As she walked in he covered his ass with a corner of the bedspread. She laughed. "Mister Bigshot." She sat down next to him, shook down the thermometer, scooped up a blob of Vaseline on the tip, and tried to remove the cover from his behind. He grabbed the thermometer from her hand and held the cover tighter around him.

"Jus' gimme the goddamn thing. I'll put it in myself."

She rose smiling. "Mister Bigshot. I knew you when . . ." She started to leave the room but turned around just as he took the cover from his ass: "I knew you when . . ."

9

The Funeral

LEANDER TULLY HIGH SCHOOL had 8000 male students and no girls. It was probably the toughest school in the city. Social Studies 326 was a special class for punks. The students were hand-picked troublemakers and although it was nominally a history class, the teacher was supposed to teach discipline. In past years the class had been taught by guidance counselors, but after one of them was beaten up by his students, it was given to gym teachers.

For the current year Mr. Sharp was chosen. Mr. Sharp was a tall, lean, athletic guy with a hawk face and stooped shoulders. He was young, in his thirties, and didn't mind the assignment. In his late teens he'd been Warlord of the Red Wings, the most feared gang in New York City after the war. He wouldn't tell that to his students, not because he was ashamed but because the Red Wings were notorious "nigger chasers" and half his students were colored. Some of them might have older brothers who remembered the Red Wings, and it wouldn't be too cool for them to know their teacher used to get his kicks busting woolly heads. Besides, the past was the past, and now his name was Mr. Sharp.

For some weird administrative reason the thirty-five students in 326 were colored or Italian except for one Jew. A similar class, Social Studies 381, was composed of Irish and Puerto Rican with a sprinkling of Polish and Germans. Mr.

Sharp didn't understand the logic behind this, but he didn't mind the setup. He didn't like Puerto Ricans.

He sat behind his desk as the class filtered in, banging books on their desks, sprawling into their seats like they'd just finished ten laps around the gym. Colored sat on the left side of the room, whites on the right side. He didn't assign seats because he knew they'd sit with their own kind anyway.

The room was composed of six rows of nailed down old-fashioned combination chair-desks, his chair and desk, and a blackboard. The walls were bare. He didn't believe in arts and crafts or displays. Besides, what would these guys like to see up there, six easy steps to putting someone in the hospital? Maybe portraits of famous gangsters. Once he'd cut out pictures of an electric chair, a gas chamber, a firing squad in action, and a gallows. He'd even printed a title, "The Way to Go," but he junked the idea on a last-minute impulse.

The classroom was filling up. He opened his Delaney book and read off the names of the students he didn't see present.

"Rocco?"

"He ain't here."

"Capra?"

"He ain't here."

"Jenkins?"

"He ain't here."

"White?"

"He ain't here."

"La Guardia, take your feet off the desk." Perry smiled, looked around at his audience, and slowly moved his feet. "It smells bad enough in here," said Sharp.

"Ahhhh-ha-ha."

"Whooooooooooo!"

Perry sat up and shot Sharp the finger when he turned his back.

"Oh! Oh! Oh!" Boo-Boo hammed. Boo-Boo was in the Viceroys, a colored gang. "Mistah Sharp, you shoulda seen what La Guardiah did."

"Woooooooo!"

"Shaddup, stoopit!" Perry glowered across the room.

"Woooo! Fight! Fight! Fight!"

"You gonna make me?" Boo-Boo stuck out his chin at Perry.

"O.K. O.K., shaddup, both a you."

"See you later!" Perry whispered loudly.

"Any time." Boo-Boo stood up and gave Perry crossed forearms, guinea for fuck you. Everyone laughed.

Sharp decided to teach: "O.K. Does anybody know what this week is?"

Joey Capra waltzed into the room, slamming the door.

"Capra," Sharp said, marking the Delaney book, "come on time or don't come at all." Joey shrugged and started to leave. "Capra! Siddown!!"

In mock fear Joey scrambled for his seat and slid in next to Perry. Joey smiled around the room at the laughter.

"Hey, Mistah Sharp, them white boys is getting obstreperous." A teacher once called Ray Barrett obstreperous, and he liked the word and used it twice a day.

Five or six white guys stood up, mouthing threats and pointing fingers across the room. The colored guys stared bug-eyed, stuffing their knuckles in their mouths, trembling with mock palsy.

The door slammed again, and Curly White bopped in. He walked like he had a record playing in his head — dipping his hips left then right in slow motion, eyes almost closed, snapping his fingers. The colored guys cheered in approval. Joey Capra, wiggling his ass, shaking his shoulders, eyes closed, lips moving, did a gross imitation down the aisle. The white guys cheered.

"Capra, you got detention." The colored guys cheered. "Awright, everybody is gonna get detention if you don't shut up." Sharp was getting pissed. "White, I'll tell you the same I told Capra — come in on time or don't come in at all."

Curly sat down covering his face with his hand. He eyed Sharp through spread fingers. "Sssshoo, man, ah jus' wanna go to sleep." Everyone shouted their approval.

"O.K., White, you got detention."

"Awwwww, ma-a-a-a-n! Sheee-it." He waved his hand in disgust but knew he'd made a big mistake.

"Wooooooo!"

"You're gettin' a pink card, White."

"Awwwww, ma-a-an, I was only kiddin'!"

"Well I'm not." A pink meant suspension. Everyone was silent in respect for the sentence just passed.

"Now." Sharp looked over the faces of his army of misfits. "Who knows what this week is?"

" 's Bruthahood week," mumbled Curly White, sulking behind his hand.

Sharp was impressed. "Good, White."

"You still goin' gimme a pink, Mistah Shahp?"

Sharp ignored the question and wrote "Brotherhood Week" on the blackboard. Then he wrote, "All men are created equal." "Anybody know who said that?"

Perry mumbled, "Your mother," but Sharp didn't hear it, although those around Perry cracked up. Perry slunk lower in his seat, trying not to smile at his own wit. Sharp wrote: "A. Lincoln" under the quote. "Abraham Lincoln."

There was a bored silence in the room. Sharp tried a more radical approach. He numbered one to five on the blackboard. Above the numbers he wrote: "Race, Creed, Color." "O.K." He swept the slightly interested faces with his eyes. "I wanna see how many different races, creeds, and colors we got just in this classroom. Ah, all Joosh people stand up." Embarrassed, Dushie Melnick, the smallest kid in the class, stood up. Mr. Sharp wrote, "Jewish," putting a chicken scratch next to the word.

"O.K., how many Italians here?"

Half the class stood up, cheering and shouting, clasping hands over heads like "champeens." The colored guys booed, holding their noses. Ricky Leopoldi started singing an aria. "Awright! Awright! Awright!" Joey yelled as if at a football game. "O.K., sit down." Sharp shouted. Slowly, the Italian delegation sat down still congratulating each other. Sharp had forgotten to count, but he wasn't going to ask them to stand again, so he wrote "Italian — 18."

He cursed himself. This was a stupid idea. "O.K., how many" — he debated what word to use — "colored?"

The colored guys jumped up, cheering and shouting twice as loud as the Italians. They danced down the aisle, giving each other skin. The Italians also stood up, booed, and made farting noises. Sharp slammed a dictionary on the desk. The noise sounded like an explosion. Everybody froze in place. "Awright," he said softly. He noticed that Curly White wasn't standing with the rest of his people. "Everybody sit down." They sat, murmurs of laughter and good times. "White, din't we pick a group to suit you?"

Curly's face was still covered, his legs dangling in the aisle.

"Ahm a Eskimo."

"Ah — ha-ha."

Just to show that he wasn't a straight-neck, Sharp wrote "Colored — 15" and under that "Eskimo — 1." Curly White fought back a smile.

Sharp was struck with a giddy thought. When he was a Red Wing he was known for leading charges against armed gangs with the recklessness of a kamikaze. He was often overcome with a crazy feeling, a disregard for danger that made him one of the scariest guys in a very scary gang. Over the years he'd mellowed, but every once in a while he got a flash of the old insanity, that courting of disaster which earned him the nickname "Jap" as a teen-ager. And Jap was in control now. With a flourish of the eraser he eliminated Dushie Melnick and the Jewish people, leaving the universe to Italians and colored.

"O.K., Italian and colored. Italian and colored. Izzat the way people talk? I mean" — he looked at the white side of the room — "is that the way your old man talks. The Cullid?" They snickered, intrigued, trying to figure out what he was getting at. "And how 'bout you guys?" He addressed the left side of the room. "Whada you say outside a class? Eyetalians?" They roared. "Let's be straight." He almost said, let's call a spade a spade, but he didn't. He faced the board, touched the chalk to the surface, and said, "Gimme some names."

Embarrassed silence. Then Perry said, "Nigger."

Sucking in of breath. The sound of writing on the blackboard. Perry looked down at his desk.

"Greaseball," said one of the Dukes. Angry glances.

"Jungle Bunny," said Peter Udo.

"Swamp Guinea," shot back Ray Barrett.

"Han'kerchief Head," said Ricky Leopoldi.

"Mountin' Wop," said Curly. The colored guys slapped palms.

"Boogie!" Perry shouted, rising from his seat. A chorus of "yeahs" from the whites.

"Guinea!"

"Coon."

"Dago."

"Spearchukka."

"Motherfuckah, ahm gonna chuck a spear at you!"

Jap wrote them as fast as he could. He laughed low and

crazy, but no one heard. They were all shouting again, standing like two opposing armies separated by a ravine.

"Fuckin' black bastids."

"Greaseball guinea honkywops."

"Rug head."

"Yo' mama."

"You ain't got one."

"Fucked yo's."

"Say that again."

"Fucked yo's."

Riot. Perry led the charge. The first victim was Dushie Melnick, who got beaned with a loose-leaf. Peter Udo got kicked in the balls. Books went flying. Curly White stomped Joey, who was down anyhow. Perry almost socked Ray Barrett through a window. Boo-Boo jumped on Perry's back and pounded his head. Sharp watched the fight, debating whether to help the white guys or to beat everybody up. He decided to stop the fight. In a sweeping rush he knocked down six guys, grabbed Perry by the back of the neck and Boo-Boo by the front of his shirt, raising them both off the ground. His sudden violence stopped the war. He dropped them, after rejecting the idea of banging their heads together. Everybody walked or crawled back to their seats. Sharp straightened his tie and smoothed back his hair. They stared at him with awe.

"Shoo!" Sharp caught his breath, and tucked his shirt into his pants. "You guys are a bunch of azzoles, all a you." He dismissed everybody with a wave. "You can't fight wort' dick." They laughed, uneasy at his words.

"Yeah, that's right, I said azzole. You stoopit jerks . . . whadya think, I live inna desk? Yeah, I was inna gang too. We coulda took on this whole school. I useta eat guys like you for breakfast. Shit." He sucked air noisily through his nose. "Yeah." He erased the jumble of scrawls on the blackboard. He felt good. Everybody was digging it.

"Hey, Mistah Sharp, you still gonna gimme a pink?" Curly asked, a trace of sarcasm in his voice.

Mr. Sharp bopped over to Curly's desk imitating his strut just like Joey had. "Wha, sheeeee-it, would ah give mah main man uh pink cahd?"

The white guys were laughing so hard some of them started crying. The blacks didn't see what was so funny. Then Sharp turned to the other side of the room, gesturing with his hand in front of him — fingertips touching. "Ey Ey Ey, whada you thinka so fonny, you stoonatz spaghetti-heads?" He staggered around the room, a brutish, stupid look on his face, talking with his hands and grunting. They rolled in the aisles — all of them except Dushie Melnick, who sat in terror, waiting to be next.

Mr. Sharp zeroed in on Dushie. He pursed his lips, raised his eyebrows, and shuffled over to Dushie, sitting next to him. Putting an arm around his shoulder, he shoved his face within an inch of the kid's nose. "Tal me, Dushie, do you dink dis iss funny? Nu, so vat could be fonnier?" Dushie giggled nervously.

At that moment, someone knocked on the classroom door. A black kid bopped into the room, swaggering more like Sharp's imitation of Curly than Curly.

"Hey, Earl!"

"Hey, baby."

Earl waved to his friends as he made his way to Mr. Sharp. Mr. Sharp met him halfway, bopping like Earl, dragging his left foot. The kid didn't know that Mr. Sharp's imitation of strutting had been considered very hip among the Red Wings. It was called the Cocksackie Shuffle back then. When Sharp had been a teen-ager the shuffle was almost an involuntary action, like breathing. "Whutchoo want, baby?" Sharp asked. The whole class screamed. Earl was perplexed. Mr. Sharp took the white slip from Earl's hand.

"It's a cawl slip fo' Perry La Guardia, yo got a Perry La Guardia?" Earl asked.

"Meee, do we gotta Perry La Guardia! Hey Carminootch, whadja do disa time?"

Perry left with Earl. "What's wrong wit' that man?" asked Earl.

"Ah nothin', he's O.K."

They heard sporadic bursts of laughter from the room. "What's goin' on?" Perry asked.

"Ah dunno, they's some lady here to see you."

They walked into the principal's office, and Perry saw his aunt standing by the time clock. She was wearing her coat, her face was a red slash of tears. "Rosie!"

She hugged Perry, sniffing back more tears. "Whassamatter, Aunt Rosie?"

She blew her nose and ushered Perry into the hall. Like Perry's mother, she was short and dumpy, had the same old man face. Perry was scared. "P-Perry, your momma had a accident."

Perry got a cold flash. His legs trembled as if he were standing on a nerve. He grabbed her elbows. "What happened? Where is she?" Aunt Rosie let out a thick roar of grief. Perry started crying in anger. He shook her. "What happened?"

"She's dead."

Perry saw the walls take off down the hall, and the next thing he knew he was sitting on the floor, his legs straight out in front of him. Rosie was making "mmm" sounds into her handkerchief. He shook his head and looked up at Rosie. "Shaddup!" he bellowed. He felt very rational, very calm. He knew he had to leave school now, so he walked back to Mr. Sharp's class to get his lunch, which was in a brown paper bag in his desk. Halfway down the hall he turned around, yelled "shaddup" again. He pushed the door open, strode toward his desk, and extracted the bag.

"Ey paisan, you gonna eat luncha so early?" The class still laughed. Perry straightened up and spoke in a calm voice. "Shaddup, my mother's dead."

He stood there trying to put the brown bag in his pants pocket, but the bag wouldn't fit. There was a confused silence in the classroom. Perry stuffed one third of the bag in his pocket and marched purposefully into the hall. He swung his arms back and forth, taking long steps. Joey ran down the hall and caught up with him. Perry kept marching, eyes forward.

"Perry, you're kiddin', ain'tcha?"

"Hello, Joey."

"Perry!" Joey grabbed his elbow, yanking him out of cadence. His lunch fell out of his pocket. He picked it up and tried to lodge it into the chest pocket of his shirt, ripping it. Finally, he gave the bag to Joey.

"Don't eat it, Joey, just hold it for me." He marched to the principal's office where his aunt, Mr. Kaufman, his counselor, and the school nurse waited for him. "Hello, Mr. Kaufman, did you hear what happened?"

Mr. Kaufman had a raw, cratered face, with bloodless lips and almost transparent eyes. "How do you feel, Perry?"

"Fine thank you. How are you feeling?"

"Would you like to lie down?"

"No thank you, but I would like some water." He marched to the water fountain, took a sip, patted his lips dry, walked back. "I lost my lunch. Could I borrow fifty cents. I'll pay you back tomorrow."

Between seven-thirty and nine o'clock that morning, there was a power failure in four buildings of the housing project. Perry's mother was alone in an elevator stuck between floors. She rang the alarm bell. No one came, and she was trapped with a screaming, shrill siren for ninety minutes. When the elevator started moving, she went upstairs to her apartment and had a heart attack. She weighed over two hundred pounds and barely stood five feet tall. No one was home. At eleven o'clock a neighbor found her lying in the foyer. The neighbor ran back to her own apartment for a cool damp rag, but Perry's mother was already dead.

Perry moved to New Jersey to live with his aunt. She ran the funeral, so the Wanderers weren't invited. But they came to the house in Trenton to pay their respects. Buddy couldn't get his father's car, and they had to take a bus from Port Authority. They met in Big Playground. Their mood was strange. It was a school day, and with the exception of mothers and babies the playground was deserted. It was like a horrible holiday. Waiting for Eugene, Joey, Richie, and Buddy sat on a bench, straightening their ties, smoothing back hair, inspecting creases.

"Hey." Eugene showed up in a green iridescent suit. The rest of them wore black.

"Where you think you goin', to a prom?"

Eugene looked at himself. "What the fuck?"

"You can't go to a funeral in that."

"Hey!" he said, pissed off. "This suit's a hundred bills." Eugene was a natty dresser.

"Great. You'll be the life of the party."

They proceeded in silence to the el train. Eugene kept examining his suit, flicking off imaginary dirt, lint, and dust. Everybody seemed angry, cranky. The bus ride was boring and long. Joey sat with a narrow, gift-wrapped box in his lap.

"What's that?" asked Richie.

"Candy."

"Candy?"

"Yeah, candy."

"Jesus Christ, you'n Diamond Jim oughta be a team." He nodded in Eugene's direction. "We could have a real circus wit' clown costumes 'n refreshnents 'n everything."

"Aw, suck my dick," said Eugene.

"Take it out," Richie challenged.

Eugene looked to see if anyone else on the bus was watching as he unzipped his fly. Still watching the front of the bus he stood up and whipped it out. He quickly sat down, putting it back. They choked on subdued hysterical laughter.

"Christ, Eugene, a hundred-dollar suit. Wow, you got class." The mood was broken. They laughed easy.

"I still say you don't bring no candy to a funeral," insisted Richie.

"What the hell *do* you bring?" asked Buddy.

"I dunno, not candy, that's for sure." Joey frowned and examined the box. "Oh well," he sighed, tearing the wrapper, "anybody want candy?"

It was a small box and it was gone in fifteen minutes. In higher spirits, they got off the bus and into a cab, but when the cab pulled up in front of Perry's new home, stomachs knotted, ties were straightened, and invisible dirt removed again. They had a brief debate about the tip, then walked up a narrow concrete path separating two large lawns, leading up to the apartment. Perry met them in front of the house. They were scared. He shook hands with them in silence. They had never shaken hands with each other before, and in his nervousness Joey shook hands with Eugene. Perry wore a white shirt without a jacket. He looked older and angry, his face a fist.

"How you doin', man?" Buddy half whispered.

"Great," Perry smirked. "Let's stay out here." He extended his left hand as if to intercept anybody trying to make it to the house.

"Sure."

"Lissen, ah . . . thanks for comin'." He rubbed his forehead with the bridge of his palm. "You hungry or anything?"

They guiltily remembered the candy. "Nah."

"No thanks."

"I could go inside an' make some sandwiches."

" 'S'awright."

"Well, let's siddown."

He sat heavily on the stoop, and they followed his cue. Perry rested his elbows on his knees, his hands supporting his head. Lost in thought, he stared across the street. "Aaach." He hunched his back, straightened his arms in front of him, and yawned. "So what's been doin' in the projects?" he asked.

They shrugged. Joey stared at the yellow-gray lines of sweat half-mooning Perry's armpits.

The apartment house door opened and a heavily made up grizzly bear came blubbering out followed by her silent mate. Perry turned around, sighed, and stood up. " 'S'awright, Aunt Mary."

"Awwwww," she whined as a prelude to more tears and smothered Perry in fake fur. "Yah such a brave boy." She crushed him to her bosom, her lipstick-stained, tear-crumpled Kleenex leaving a red blot on the back of his white shirt. "You mama loved you so much."

"Yeah . . . you too, Aunt Mary."

Her husband looked away and lit a torpedo-sized cigar. "You can't wait, Lou, hah? You gotta smoke right away."

"Ah, shaddup." He spat neatly into a bush.

"Perry . . ." she held him at arms length. "Perry . . . you come to our house for a meal and a bed any time you want. I'd make you a . . . awwwwww." Her husband looked skyward, smirking.

"Sure." Perry patted her arm diplomatically and detaching himself held out his hand to his uncle. "Lou?"

Uncle Lou smiled and shook Perry's hand. "Come around any time, kid." He winked, and when Perry withdrew his hand there was a twenty-dollar bill folded into a chunky square.

They walked down the path to their car, shreds of an argument wafting back to Perry and his friends on the stoop.

"That's my people," Perry sneered, sitting down. He unfolded the bill and held it in front of him. He turned to the Wanderers. "Kinda makes it all worth it, doncha think?" They smiled in embarrassment.

"Hey, Perry?" Joey frowned. "You gonna live here?"

"Yeah." Perry looked at the ground.

" 'S'a long way, man."

"I know."

"How 'bout school?"

"I dunno. There's some school aroun' here." He crumpled the bill absent-mindedly. "Hey!" He startled them. "You guys *don't* forget about me!"

"Whadya mean?"

"Yeah, whadya kiddin'?"

"You're our main man, man."

"Awright," he said.

They sat in silence, each figuring out how he would come out to Trenton every week, Perry planning trips to New York. But in their hearts they knew this was the end for Perry as a Wanderer. Suddenly, as if to certify that fact and a few other facts, Perry furiously jammed his face into his palms and started to cry. Tears dripped through the crotch of his fingers and rolled down his forearms.

Tongues thick in their heads, they sat helpless. Joey choked hard, but the tears came. Richie was next. Then Buddy. Only Eugene couldn't cry but turned his face away.

"Hey, man," Richie sniffed after a while, "we're like a bunch of faggots."

"Ah, shaddup," said Buddy.

Perry stopped crying and stared into the distance, resting his chin on his knuckles. "I can't believe it," he said to no one in particular.

Joey noticed Perry's knuckles on his left hand were red and enlarged. He touched his friend gently on the arm. "Hey, what happened to your hand?"

Perry examined his fingers as if he had never before realized there was anything on the end of that wrist. He jerked his head back a few inches and snickered, but said nothing. They sat silently for a long while. Suddenly, Perry raised his fist in front of him, his first two fingers rigidly pressed together. "We were like that . . . I mean just like *that!*" He shook his fist for emphasis, then stood up and paced in front of them.

"Christ, Perry, we're sorry, man . . . what can we say?" Eugene asked weakly.

"What *can* you say? . . . she was a goddamn saint . . . loved everybody . . . she used to cry for people allatime . . . people wit' trouble who she hardly even knew . . . two weeks after my old man died this lady downstairs lost her husband . . . Mom din't even know her last name . . . she went down to that lady's house every night for five weeks . . . useta clean for her . . . cook for her . . . and Mom was hurtin' too. Don't you think she wasn't. For two months after my old man died she slept in the living room because she couldn't even lay in the same bed where she useta sleep with Pop. Every once in a while I would walk in on her and she'd be talking to him as if he was there as plain as me. She had a lotta heartache these last few years, don't you think she didn't."

"From Raymond too, hah?" offered Richie.

"Ah, don't even mention that cocksucker's name. Christ, I'm tellin' you, what he did to Mom — him and that bitch — I don't wanna talk about it." He spit in the grass at the side of the stoop. "She was a good lady, Richie. A good lady. Every month she couldn't wait to go to the Island to see the kids and every fuckin' time she would leave that house in tears, Raymond and that bitch would make her feel so bad. Like she was some kinda immigrant lowlife, you know? An' I kept

pleadin' wit' her — Mom — don't go this month, don't go
. . . just this month. No . . . she forgot what happened last
time. Every month she would forget." Stretching his arms
over his head, he squeezed out a yawn.

"Ah . . . an' the funeral! Me an' Aunt Rosie had to run the
whole show . . . that bastard never even showed up at the
wake . . . he even came to the cemetery late. You know what
that hard-on did? He comes by late, right? He rolls up in his
big-ass Caddy in the middle of the service . . . his wife . . .
she don't even got the decency to get her ass out of the damn
car . . . he comes over to me, puts his arm around my shoulder, says . . . 'Perry, I'm sick, I'm sick. I loved that woman
so. Oh God, what am I gonna do, what am I gonna do?' It
took all my willpower to hold back from smashing his face in.
I just twisted away so his hand fell off my shoulder and walked
over to the other side of the grave so I'm facin' him. You
know? Anyways, they bring out the casket an' I'm watchin'
his face, see, an' he's cryin' a little too. I mean most of the
people are cryin', mainly old widows. Mom's friends. Anyways, they bring the casket to the side of the grave an' before
anyone could stop him, Raymond runs over to the side of the
casket, falls on top of it, an' starts screamin', 'Momma,
Momma, forgive me, forgive me.' I just stood there shakin',
just shakin'."

Perry started trembling, raising his hands, which were shaking too. His face was twisted in a snarl of black rage. "I was
gonna murder the bastard! I felt like jumping over the grave
an' breaking both his arms. *Now* he's sorry! *Now* he's sorry!
An' all the old ladies are screamin' and shriekin', they're fallin'
all over him an' cryin', 'He'sa socha gooda son, socha gooda
son, he *lova* his mama.' I tell you I was so . . . so tight I almost chipped a fuckin' tooth. I was just standin' there. I was
cryin' too, but God forgive me I wasn't cryin' for Mom. I
don't even know why, but when they helped Raymond up I

was so sick. Anyways, after the casket was lowered an' we threw some dirt in an' everybody started goin' home, I went over to Raymond and put my arm around his shoulder. He said, 'Perry, I loved that woman, I just loved her.' I said, 'Sure, Ray, sure, she loved you too' — an' then I asked him to take a walk wit' me, an' he said, 'I'd love to, Perry. But I gotta go to the office,' an' he looks at his fuckin' watch. I was controllin' myself, I was cool. I said, 'Just for a minute, Ray, just for a minute. I wanna tell you some of the things Mom said before she died.' Well, we walked over to this little area wit' trees around so no one could see us, an' I face him an' I say, 'Ray, I got somethin' for you from Mom,' an' I belted him on the jaw so fuckin' hard I almost broke these two knuckles." He held up his hammy fist. "An' you wanna know what that bastard did?" he challenged his friends.

They didn't want to know. They were wiped out by Perry's sudden fury. They sat there staring at their shoes. They wanted to go home. Perry was a stranger.

"I'll tell you what that . . . that *pussy* did. He sat on his ass 'cause he knew if he got up I'd put 'im right back down again. An' then he pulls out his fuckin' checkbook an' writes Rosie a check payin' for the funeral. Yeah, sittin' right there onna goddamn grass he writes out a five-hunnert-dollar check. You know what I did?"

No one answered.

"I'll tell you what I did. I took the fuckin' check, ripped it in pieces, an' threw it right back in his face." He stabbed Richie in the chest with a fat finger. "He ain't payin' his way outta this!"

Richie absently massaged his chest where Perry stabbed him. Perry walked to the edge of the sidewalk twenty feet away and stared up at the rapidly darkening sky. "She's up there now and she's sayin', 'Perry, what you wanna fight for? He's your brotha, I forgive, you forgive.' " He stared up at the sky for a moment, a scowl curling on his face. Turning, he stormed back to the stoop. The Wanderers jumped up and scattered in fear. Perry grabbed the doorknob and yanked open the door. He turned to them. "I ain't never! NEVER! forgivin' him." And then he was gone.

10

The Hustlers

EVERY FRIDAY NIGHT the Wanderers bowled as house hustlers at Galasso's Paradise Lanes. This meant they would take on any comers from the city or the Island or New Jersey, and Chubby, his six brothers, and other regulars would match any bets on the game against bankrollers who accompanied the visiting hustlers. The Wanderers rarely lost. Chubby and company would clean up to the tune of a thousand dollars or more on Friday nights. In return for this easy money, the Wanderers would get ten dollars a man, plus they could bowl for free any time they wanted. All they had to do was keep winning.

The week before Buddy and Richie got wiped out by two guys from Long Island. Even though they rolled the best games they had in the last six months they lost by sixty pins. They were scared, because Chubby dropped almost two thousand dollars, and Chubby Galasso was a big fat ball-buster who didn't want to know from best games in the last six years. The Wanderers lost by ridiculous spreads and when they slunk out of the bowling alley, Chubby was spitting fire.

The Wanderers had a thing about the bowling. Two guys would bowl as a team on Friday night. If they won, two different guys would bowl the next week; but if they lost, the same two guys would have to bowl again. And if they lost a second time they bowled the week after, and they'd bowl week after week until they won. Bowling was serious business, and nobody was coming off those lanes a loser no matter how long it took to win.

So this Friday, scared as they were, Buddy and Richie were honor-bound to represent the Wanderers again.

"Richie here?" Buddy stood at Richie's apartment door.

"Ri-chie!" Randy shouted back along the foyer to the bedroom. "It's Buddy."

"S'let 'im in, asshole!" Richie shouted.

"Hey, sewer mout'!" his father's voice echoed from the bathroom.

Buddy lugged his bowling bag into Richie's room where Richie was sitting on his bed running a rag over his bowling ball — a milky green beauty spangled with gold-metal flakes. "I got the car downstairs." Richie slipped the ball into the bag, took his bowling shoes out of the closet, and they left the apartment. Richie pushed the elevator button and ran his hand over his gut. "I think I'm gonna vomit." He winced.

Buddy shrugged. "Don't sweat it, we win tonight."

Richie stood on his toes and peered through the elevator window along the motionless cables. He slammed his hand on the elevator door. "C'mon, you bastads!" He pounded the door. "The fuckin' thing ain't movin'. It's the goddamn niggers on the first floor. You know what they like to do? They like to hold the fuckin' elevator so they can piss in it an' then they send it up to you wit' a little swimmin' pool on the floor so you can track piss into your house so a little baby that's crawlin' on the floor will get piss germs on his hands an' in his mouth and get sick." Richie viciously kicked the bottom of the elevator door. "Move it, bastads!"

Machinery was grinding at the bottom of the shaft, and the elevator slowly glided up to the third floor. Buddy was scared that the boogies heard Richie and were coming up to kick ass. When the door rolled open, Eugene and Joey were in the car. "You guys playin' games?" Richie growled as he and Buddy stepped inside.

Eugene and Joey looked at each other. "What's wit' you?" Joey asked.

Richie didn't answer. Buddy shrugged.

As Buddy pulled up in front of the bowling alley, all conversation stopped. He thought of Chubby's fat puss last week. Buddy felt weak. Richie hadn't said a word since the elevator. Joey and Eugene got tight and sweaty. The reflection of the neon sign washed their faces on alternating seconds.

"You guys better win tonight." Eugene laughed weakly.

"Fuck off," Richie said flatly as he got out, almost slamming the car door on Joey's foot.

Chubby was waiting for them, leaning on the shoe-lined counter, his six brothers standing around the cash register. Mary Wells's "The One Who Really Loves You" played on the juke box at the far end of the alley. Chubby smiled, slapping Richie on the back. Richie cringed. The six brothers moved forward. They were all big boys. Fifteen hundred pounds of mean meat. "You guys feel hot tonight?" Chubby wheezed. He had asthma.

The alley was deserted, which meant Chubby had kicked people out, which meant a lot of money was going down on the match. Chubby was still smiling, and he started massaging Richie's shoulder. A cigarette hung at an impossible angle from the corner of his mouth.

"Sure. We're always hot," said Buddy, his voice cracking on the last word.

"Yeah. Sure." Chubby's face cracked into a wider grin, the cigarette smoke obscuring his features, making his eyes narrow into slits as he nodded in amused agreement. Richie focused his eyes on the big man's nose squatting in the middle of his face like a chubby bear paw. "You know who you guys are rollin' against tonight?" The four of them shook their heads in dumb unison. "The same guys as last week."

Buddy gasped. Richie's shoulder started to hurt where Chubby's fingers dug in.

"You know how much we're bettin' tonight?" Chubby kept his grin, but his wheeze became more pronounced as his chest heaved under his short-sleeve, open-necked shirt with pineapples and hula girls on it.

Joey and Eugene started backing toward the door but Albert, one of the brothers, caught their eye, stopping them in their tracks.

"A grand?" Richie managed. Albert laughed. Chubby removed his hand from Richie's shoulder and spread his fingers in front of Richie's nose. "Five?" Richie gasped. Buddy felt faint. From his back pocket, Chubby took out a fat roll of hundred-dollar bills wrapped in a rubber band.

"You know who's gonna win tonight?" No one answered.

Chubby dug in his pocket again and took out two twenty-dollar bills. He gave one to Buddy, one to Richie, and nodded in the direction of the bar/lounge in the back of the alley. "Getchaselves some Cokes." They dropped their bags, and the four of them walked to the dimly lit amber-glassed lounge that was paneled off from the lanes.

Eugene nervously spun himself around on a barstool. Joey hunched over the counter and lit a cigarette. "I think Chubby wants you guys to throw the game," said Eugene.

"No he don't," Peppy Dio cackled. Peppy, an old uncle of the Galasso brothers, ran the bar. He wiped the counter clean in front of the Wanderers. "You guys is gonna win big tonight." Peppy laughed. His teeth looked like a set of broken dishes.

"Peppy, what's happening? We can't beat those guys. They're good enough to be pros."

Peppy winked and tapped a finger against a hairless temple. "Now you thinkin'. They *is* pros."

"What!" in unison.

"Yeah. Yeah. Chubby got to thinkin' how good they was last week, and he checked up an' found out they was pros."

Silence.

"Yeah. Yeah. They goes aroun' to different lanes an' hustles house bowlers like you guys."

"Sonovabitch!" Buddy declared.

"Yeah. Yeah. Anyways, so Chubby got 'em to come back tonight for a rematch."

"We oughta kick their asses." Eugene rose, tight-lipped.

Peppy Dio giggled. "You guys got nothin' to worry about."

"Whada they comin' back for? They cleaned up las' week."

Peppy rubbed his thumb and forefinger together. "They greedy boys. Want some more a this."

"Don't they know Chubby knows?"

"They don't know shit. Chubby's a smart boy." He winked and tapped his temple again.

"We still can't beat 'em," said Richie. Peppy only smiled and set a bottle of Canadian and four glasses on the bar.

A half-hour later Buddy and Richie were rolling practice frames when the two ringers walked in with three other guys who the Wanderers figured for bankrollers. They recognized one guy from last week, the two other bettors probably heard what a sucker Chubby was. They all looked uneasy, as if they didn't think it was a good idea to hit the same place twice in a row, but as Peppy said, they greedy boys. Buddy and Richie stopped bowling, sat down with Eugene and Joey, and watched Chubby come from behind the counter, a shit-eating grin on his face. The brothers were nowhere to be seen. Chubby waved for Richie and Buddy.

"You guys was lucky last week," Chubby said jovially to

the ringers. "Let's give my boys here another chance." Richie and Buddy exchanged hostile stares with the hustlers.

One of the backers shrugged. "Why not?" Before he could say anything else one of his bowlers put a hand on his shoulder and motioned his group back five paces where they got into a whispered debate. Chubby just kept smiling, sensing that at least one guy smelled a rat. For a split second, when it looked like they were going to balk, Chubby dropped the grin and nodded in the direction of the bar. Richie saw the silhouettes of Chubby's brothers behind the dark glass partition.

"So what's gonna be?" Chubby wheezed and forced another grin. "You guys bowlin' tonight or what?"

Last-minute eye contact between the hustlers and their backers. Joey saw Peppy Dio on the street sneak up and lock the front doors from the outside. Chubby saw him too. Peppy Dio vanished.

"What's it gonna be?" Chubby repeated. Richie saw movement behind the amber glass partition.

"I dunno," said one of the bowlers, a tall skinny guy with a face made for pushing in.

Chubby raised his arm as if to scratch the back of his head. Albert Galasso emerged from the lounge.

"What the hell," the skinny guy said. Chubby casually waved Albert back inside before anyone noticed him.

"Good . . . good." Chubby rubbed his hands.

"Ah, same as last week?" one of the bankrollers asked.

"Well, I'll tell you, I had a good week, lotsa tournaments." Chubby dug in his pocket and tossed the five-thousand-dollar roll on the counter. The bankrollers tore off the rubber band and counted the hundred-dollar bills faster than the Wanderers could see the green flash from one hand to another.

"This is five grand!"

"I said I had a good week."

"We don't got that much."

Chubby shrugged. "Whadya got?"

Another conference. Hard stares at Chubby, Richie, and Buddy. Chubby winked at the Wanderers.

"We get to pick the alley."

Chubby graciously conceded.

One of the bowlers stared suspiciously at Eugene and Joey. "Who a' they?"

"They're kids."

"Whada they doin' here?"

"They're friends a the kids."

"I don't like 'em. Tell 'em to take a walk," said the bowler.

Chubby shrugged and started to tell Joey and Eugene to get lost, but he remembered he had Peppy lock the doors. "Look, they're punk kids." Chubby lifted them both off the ground by their shirts and threw them five feet. They landed on their asses. Trembling and confused, they got up. Richie and Buddy held their breath. Chubby laughed. "If I wanna try somethin', you think I'm gonna need them?" Chubby took another twenty out of his pocket. "Getchaselves Cokes." Joey took the bill and walked on rubber legs to the bar, Eugene close behind. "Enough a this bullshit awready, you gonna play or not?"

Richie prayed they would say O.K. He silently swore to God he would bowl the best, the most perfect game of his life, shake hands with everyone, and run like hell. But he had to start *now*. The sooner they began the sooner it would be over. His bladder and his asshole and the nagging terror nibbling on the inside of his forehead with tiny teeth were making him walk in small circles, preventing his eyes from focusing on anything but Buddy's shoes.

Buddy stared self-consciously at his shoes. What the fuck was Richie looking at? He tried to catch Richie's eye but Richie wouldn't look up. Buddy peered into the bar, but Eugene and Joey were out of sight. Suddenly he sensed that he shouldn't be looking into the bar, that there was something forbidden and dangerously out of bounds behind the smoky gold glass. His eyes snapped straight ahead, and he felt ten points of ice on his legs as his fingertips chilled him through his pants. He balled his hands and the chill swirled in endless spirals within his tightly curled fists.

Eye contact. Digging into pockets. "Forty-eight hundred is all we got." A bankroller tossed a stack of bills on the counter. Chubby laid his money on top of it.

"Good enough. I'll leave the money right here." Chubby slapped his hand over the pile. "Whynchoo guys take some practice frames?" he offered the ringers. "Richie, whynchoo an' Buddy get some Cokes?"

"I ain't thirsty."

Chubby glowered at them, and they took off for the bar.

"Look a' this!" Buddy held out a trembling hand. "I can't even hold a fuckin' ball."

Inside the bar Eugene and Joey sat helpless at a corner table. The six Galasso brothers stood flat against the amber glass. Soon the thunder and hollow crashes of the ringers taking practice frames echoed through the building.

"You kids just sit tight till it's time for the game," said Henry Galasso, who wore a pineapple shirt like his brother Chubby.

They had no intention of moving. It was as if somebody had shouted "Freeze!" in a game of Red Light, Green Light. Joey stared unblinking at his freshly lit cigarette burned down to a fragile and perfect cylinder of ash before crumbling across his knuckles. Eugene's Banlon shirt stuck to his back like a mustard plaster. He closed his eyes and fell into a twenty-second sleep, waking with a shudder and a circular wetness around his stomach.

Five minutes later Albert nodded to his brothers, and the

six of them filed out of the bar. The Wanderers sat wide-eyed and motionless.

As soon as Jerry Rosen, the main bankroller, saw the Galasso brothers emerge from the lounge, he bolted for the money, scooped it up, and ran for the door. He pushed, pulled, and banged on the glass. Chubby calmly walked over to him. "Where you goin'?" Jerry turned around wild-eyed and opened his mouth to say something, but Chubby slammed him in the heart, and he dropped to his knees, the money descending like green snow across his back and shoulders. "We got a match here." Chubby dragged him along the floor by the collar, dumping him at his brothers' feet. The other two bankrollers stood trapped and terrified. Chubby motioned them to sit in the hard sky-blue plastic chairs at the head of the lane where the ringers were taking their practice frames. "You guys can keep score. I'm just a dumb guinea." They collapsed in the chairs. A score sheet lay neatly clipped to a white Formica table in front of them.

The ringers started backing down the alley toward the pins. "Where you guys goin'?" Chubby laughed. They looked around. There was no place to run.

"You can't bowl over there, that's cheatin'," said Albert. His brothers laughed.

"C'mere." Chubby motioned. "I wanna get started awready." Unsteadily they walked up the lane to the bankrollers. Jerry moaned and struggled to his feet. Albert and Henry lifted him onto a sky-blue plastic chair next to his colleagues.

"I wanna fair match tonight," Chubby said. "You guys are very, very good bowlers. You're good enough to be pros." The ringers looked at each other and ran for the door, but Albert, Henry, and Chickie, the two-hundred-pound baby of the family, grabbed them.

"Look, take the fuckin' money," Jerry sobbed. "Let us get outta here."

"I wouldn't think of it," said Chubby. "We agreed on a game, so we got a game to roll."

"We just think that you guys are so good," said Henry, "that it wouldn't be fair unless you bowled wit' a handicap."

"Fifty pins!" said Jerry.

"That wasn't what I was thinkin' about," said Chubby.

"Seventy-five!" Jerry offered.

"No good," said Chubby, as he nodded to his brothers. Henry took a ball from the rack, and Albert and Chickie threw one of the ringers on the ground. Louie and Jimmy Galasso forced him onto his stomach and sat on his back. Albert yanked his hand out straight and spread his fingers. The other ringer ran for the door again, but Chickie decked him. Henry knelt by the outstretched hand. The ringer screamed and tried to buck Louis and Jimmy off his back, but the two brothers sat tight.

A sixth brother, Ronnie, watched the three bankrollers for any sudden moves. "Sit tight," he growled, as two of them started to stand up.

Henry made sure the fingers lay straight on the waxed floor. He raised the bowling ball over his head like a big rock and brought it down hard, crushing three fingers. The ringer let out a horrible womanish scream and passed out. "Chubby, you wanna do the thumb too?"

Chubby walked over to examine the smashed fingers with the toe of his shoe. They were reddish-purple with deep gashes at the knuckles where bone protruded. Chubby didn't answer. Louie and Jimmy stood up, hoisted the unconscious hustler by his armpits, and dumped him in Jerry's lap. Jerry started to retch and threw him off his legs onto the floor, where he lay in a heap.

"Do the other prick," said Chubby.

The first ringer's scream had the Wanderers standing up. Richie knocked over his chair and quickly bent down to pick it up — maybe if the room was very neat when Chubby walked in they could all go home. He smacked his forehead on the corner of the table and saw stars for a moment, but the second scream from the alley straightened him up as if he had been stuck in the ass with a hot poker. They all ran for the bar entrance where they slammed nose first into Chubby Galasso's chest.

"Those guys are hustlers. They fucked with me, and they fucked with my money. They fucked with you guys too." He motioned for Buddy and Richie to come out. Richie stumbled after him, almost stepping on his heels. Buddy wandered in an erratic line.

"Now that you guys are handicapped we can have us a match," said Henry cheerfully. Chickie slapped the two ringers awake.

"Let us go home," one of the bankrollers pleaded. "Take the goddamn money."

"If I took the money wit'out a match I would be hustling," said Chubby.

"You guys warmed up?" he asked Buddy and Richie. "Lemme see." He peered over Jerry's shoulder. "Hey, Jerry, you gotta write down everybody's name." He pointed to the blank lines of the score sheet. Jerry cursed and wrote four names in a hasty scrawl.

"Buddy." Chubby motioned Buddy to bowl. Buddy staggered to the line in his street shoes, grabbed a lightweight red ball from the ball return, and threw it blindly down the alley. He knocked down five pins. The Galasso brothers jeered and laughed.

"C'mon, Borsalino! Booo."

Buddy took a deep breath, tried not to look at the two ringers writhing in agony on a long plastic bench, and rolled a spare.

"Yeah! Awright! Way to go," they cheered.

Chubby looked at the score sheet. "Which one a you guys

is Larry?" he asked the two ringers. Chubby yanked one of
them to his feet. "C'mon, Larry. It's your turn!" He shoved
Larry to the ball return. Larry just stood there swooning.
"C'mon, do I gotta show you how to bowl?" Chubby grabbed
Larry's mangled hand and rammed the fingers into the holes
of a bowling ball. Larry howled, falling to his knees. "I'm
just tryin' to help." Chubby shrugged. Larry struggled to his
feet and grabbed a bowling ball with his other hand.

"Cheata! Cheata!" The Galassos laughed.

Larry moved like a drunk. He managed to hang the bowling ball by his unbroken thumb and with a stiff motion, he
rolled the ball ineffectively into the gutter.

Eugene and Joey sat at the table in the bar listening to the
cheers and the catcalls. "I'm gettin' the fuck outta here," said
Joey.

"Where you gonna go, shithead?"

Joey nervously pulled at his hair. "We're gonna get killed."

"Shut up."

"We are."

A loud roar went up from the alley.

"I ain't *never* bowlin' again," said Eugene. He started pacing the bar, but stayed away from the entrance to the alley.

"Where you goin'?" Joey stood up in panic.

"I'm goin' dancin' . . . whereya think I'm goin'?"

"Sit down, hah?" Joey started crying.

"That's it, start cryin'. That'll take care of everything."

"Shut up." Joey held back more tears.

"Capra, you're such a faggot, I swear to God."

Joey stood up and grabbed Eugene by the front of his shirt.
"Start somethin', cocksucker!" he snarled and grabbed the
bottle of Canadian.

"Forget it." Eugene was shaken by Joey's rage.

Joey sat down. "Big fuckin' hero . . . cool man."

"Forget it," Eugene said.

"You think just because you get laid you're somethin' else."

Eugene said nothing.

"Well you ain't shit, Caputo, you ain't . . ." Eugene reached for the bottle, but Joey's hand darted out like a snake clutching his wrist. He tripped Eugene backward over his extended leg and sat on his chest, knees pinned like nails into Eugene's shoulders. Joey drew back his fist, ready to let loose when Richie and Buddy walked in. Their faces were white. Neither of them looked at Eugene or Joey.

"Let's go," said Buddy.

Joey stood up. "How'd it go?"

They didn't answer. Eugene stood up, straightening his shirt and smoothing back his hair. Joey shot him a contemptuous glance. Eugene was silent, knowing that whatever happened from now on, Joey could kick his ass and knowing that Joey knew that too.

As the four of them left the building, Chubby was Scotch-taping the score sheet onto the glass door.

BUDDY — 102
LARRY —   7
RICHIE — 97
TEDDY —   10

"See you next week, boys." The glass caught their reflection as they left Paradise Lanes.

11

Buddy Borsalino's Wedding Day

DRIVING ALONE to Despie's house one night after dropping the guys off from bowling, Buddy saw some blond cunt waiting for a bus under the el. "You wanna ride?"

Her whitish-yellow hair was piled on her head like custard. Meaty legs and a sneering mouth. "Get lost."

"You wanna fuck?" Buddy burned rubber, laughing, shooting a red light and missing a panel truck by inches. He debated going around the block again. No, yes, no, yes, no, yes, yes. The second time around she was standing with some monster guinea with a leather jacket and no teeth. She pointed at Buddy. The big greaseball lumbered over to the car, and Buddy took off again, running lights and taking corners like a drunken stunt driver laughing in his terror.

Buddy sat on a cracked vinyl revolving stool under a filthy light in Pioneer's candy store nursing a too-hot cup of coffee. He watched Maxie pile dishes in a gray plastic bus box, the overhead light converting his rimless glasses into blinding reflectors. Maxie was a crazy fuck. Buddy had come into Pioneer at least four times a week, since he was old enough to cross the street himself, and Maxie never once in all those years showed any sign that he'd ever seen Buddy before in his life.

Buddy thought of Despie and savored the twisting in his gut. Somebody put Chuck Jackson's "Any Day Now" on the juke box and Buddy felt his stomach shrink to the size of a marble.

> "Any day now, . . . mah beau-ti-ful bird
>   You will have flo-o-o-wn"

Things were going bad, and he was returning to his old ways, smoking two packs a day, taking eight-hour naps, not eating, finding secret meanings in every new song he heard. Buddy looked up at the Pepsi clock. Ten to ten. Fifteen minutes to go, then he could walk in five minutes late like he did every Friday night, just to show her how cool a man could be.

When Buddy came to the door he started to kiss Despie, but she turned her head, and he wound up lipping her ear. "Whadya wanna do t'night?" He frowned.

She shrugged. "I don' care."

"You wanna go to the Duke?"

"If you wanna go."

"You wanna stay home?"

"If you wanna stay home we'll stay home."

"You wanna go to Nathan's?"

"I said I don't care, you deaf?"

They drove to Nathan's in silence. Under death-white overheads Buddy counted a number of flies that took off and landed on their small Formica table. Despie took a piss. They each drank a grape soda, walked once around the pinball machines, and headed home.

Turning the car into the Sprain Parkway, Buddy floored the accelerator, one eye on the road, one eye on Despie. She yawned and took a cigarette from his shirt pocket.

"Who do you think you are, Steve McQueen?"

Embarrassed, Buddy slowed down. "What's wit' you?" he asked.

"What's wit' you?" she countered.

"Nothin'. What's wit' you?"

She ignored him, turned up the radio very loud, and stared out the window, moving her head and legs in time to a song they both hated.

"I rolled two-o-five tonight."

Nothing.

"Joey rolled two-twenty."

Exhaled smoke ricocheted off the window to Buddy's side.

"What's wit' you, you got the rag on or somethin'?"

She turned abruptly toward him, her face glowing with rage. "You wish!"

"What the hell is that supposed to mean?"

She turned up the radio so loud that Buddy couldn't recognize the songs anymore.

At two in the morning Buddy sat drunk and alone in the dark, hunched over the kitchen table — his head buried in the crook of his elbow, a cigarette dangling between relaxed fingers. He burned a hole in his mother's oilcloth. The insect volume of a weak transistor radio wafted through the kitchen. He thought of Humphrey Bogart in "Casablanca" sitting at that table alone in the middle of the night getting drunk and flipping out over Ingrid Bergman. There were no more ice cubes. He poured a fourth Scotch in a milk glass, added half as much cold water from the sink, and resumed his posture at the table. He couldn't think of the song that made Humphrey Bogart crack up. He tried to figure out what his and Despie's song was. He once dedicated Smokey Robinson's "You've Really Got a Hold on Me" to Despie over the radio. That was it. Their song. He thought of the painful sweetness in Smokey Robinson's voice. He took a big gulp of Scotch and almost vomited. The phone rang.

"Yeah?"

"What you mean, yeah."

"Despie!"

"I'm pissed as shit at you."

"For what?" The Scotch curled his teeth and made his ears burn.

"You don't give a shit about me!"

"Whada you talkin' about?"

"Forget it."

"Forget what?"

"None of your goddamn business!"

She slammed down the phone. Buddy lurched forward. He couldn't believe he could get so drunk by himself. He took another gulp. The phone rang again. Buddy fell down and banged his head. "Ah fuck . . . yeah?" He lay on the floor, pain like an ice pick right over his eyes.

"You wouldn't marry me even if I killed myself."

"What?"

"I thought so."

"What's goin' on with you?"

"You don't know what true love is." Buddy's eyes were walking around somewhere in the back of his head. "You don't know what true love is . . . do you?"

"What?" His eyes came back but now the kitchen was walking around.

"Do you want me to tell you what true love means to me?"

"What?"

"True love means standing by the person you love through thick and thin."

"What time is it?"

"And do you know what true love means especially to a woman? Do you know what a real sign of true love is in a woman? True love in a woman means wanting to have the baby of the man she loves."

"Yeah I know. Is it really three-thirty?" The numbers on the sunburst clock were holding hands.

"And do you know what true love in a man is? True love in

a man is *wanting* that woman who loves him to have his baby. Don't you feel that's what true love is? Huh?"

"What? Yeah." Buddy realized that a sure-fire way of vomiting was thinking about raspberry ice cream coated with chocolate.

"Do you love me, Buddy? I mean do you feel true love for me? Because I really feel true love for you, and I just would like to know if you feel true love for me?"

"Yeah." He contemplated sticking a finger down his throat and ending it all.

"I'm glad to hear that, Buddy. I'm very glad to hear that . . ."

Buddy hallucinated a six-foot-high raspberry sundae and tasted bile on the back of his tongue. ". . . because I'm pregnant."

"Uh-huh . . ."

"I'm very glad to hear that, because I'd probably kill myself right after I hung up if you weren't going to stand by me, and if we weren't going to get married. But now I can go to sleep."

"Sleep."

"I love you, Buddy."

"Sleep."

Buddy awoke in the morning to find himself curled on top of the washing machine. The phone was somewhere in the washing machine making siren whoops. He groped for the receiver and grabbed a fistful of puke. Recoiling he leaped to the floor and did a small dance of pain as his head and lower back competed for attention. The clock said seven-thirty. The Wilson's Scotch bottle was empty, and the milk glass lay busted on the linoleum. The transistor radio played on in its minute scratchy voice. The toilet flushed. Fuck and double fuck. He recognized his mother's cough. He bent down to

pick up the empty bottle. Somebody punched him in the forehead and down he went, sitting on the floor, his back against
the washing machine.

"G'morning, honey . . . what're you doing up so early?"
Buddy's mother shuffled into the kitchen, the tail end of a cigarette between her lips, a fresh one in her hand.

"I don't feel so good." Buddy slipped the empty bottle behind his back as his mother lit the new cigarette with the smol-
dering filter of the old one.

"You want some coffee?" She wrinkled her nose. "Jesus,
what a stink!"

Buddy hoisted himself to his feet, kicked the Scotch bottle
behind the refrigerator, and tried to close the washing machine. It wouldn't close completely because the receiver was
still laying in the vomit and the cord kept the top ajar.

She put on a pot of coffee and turned around to look at
Buddy. His shirt and pants had folds in them like an accor-
dion. Everything was splotched with puke. "How was your
date with what's-her-name, honey?"

The question filled Buddy with a vague but nagging dread.
Something happened last night, or he had a real drag of a
dream — something about something about Despie. "It was
good."

"I'm glad. I gotta get dressed. I'm going to Helen's mother's funeral." She put out the second cigarette and shuffled
out of the room, leaving the coffee to burn.

Buddy daintily picked out the receiver from the washing
machine, wiped it off, and put it back on the hook. He turned
off the coffee and started the washing machine — to wash out
the puke.

Buddy's mother came back into the kitchen in a bra and
girdle. "You wanna zip me up, honey?" she asked, her back
to him.

"Zip you up what?"

She stared at him blankly for a second, then raised her eyebrows, opened her mouth in a small o, and lifted her fingers to her lips. "Jesus!" she giggled and slapped Buddy weakly on the shoulder. "I forgot to put my dress on." She exited again. Buddy flash-focused on something Despie said about true babies last night or something.

A splash of dropped keys in the hallway signaled the return of Buddy's father from his job as night manager of Times Square transient hotels. The washing machine made noises like a Colonial Sand & Stone concrete mixer as it hit the rinse cycle. His mother started belting out opera in a voice like a singing saw. The door slammed.

"Who the hell is doin' a wash?" Vito Borsalino came in, throwing his travel bag at Buddy's head. His eyes were puffy red disks. "You doin' a wash? You doin' a wash?" He advanced on Buddy, slapping him around the ears. "Your father comes home he gotta listen to a fuckin' washin' machine? Hah? Hah?" Buddy retreated into the dinette under the steady barrage of slaps. "You gonna do me in? You gonna do me in?" Suddenly he stopped as he picked up the siren of his wife's singing over the roar of his own voice and the din of the washing machine.

"AHM THE BARBA AH SA-VI-I-I-I-LLE, AHM THE BARBA AH SA-VI- I- I- I -I-LLE, AHM THE BARBA AH SA-VI-I-I-LLE."

The tiny motor that ran the two facial ticks in Vito's face clicked into high gear. The corner of his left eye started dancing, the right corner of his mouth started jerking up and down.

"AHM THE BARBA AH SA-VI-I-I-I-LLE, AHM THE BARBA AH SA-VI-I-I-I-LLE."

Turning from his son he tiptoed into the bedroom.

"AHM THE BARBA AH SA-VI-I-I-I-LLE, AHM THE, EEEAAGH!"

Buddy heard furniture crash, slaps and snarls echo through

the foyer, a grunt from Vito followed by a sharp intake of breath from his mother, the wet slap of a fist in contact with soft flesh, a crack that was either wood or bone, and then heavy breathing.

"You wanna do me in? You wanna do me in, bitch? Hah? Hah? Hah, bitch?"

"NNNFF . . . NNNFFF . . . NNNNNFF . . ."

"Sing! Sing! You rotten *cunt!*"

"NNNNGGG . . . NNNNNGG."

Buddy ran to the bedroom and saw his mother in a head-lock, trapped between the beefy forearm and rib cage of his father. Vito's bald head was carmine. A thin rope of saliva looped from his mother's lips to her leg. Vito had an ashtray in his free hand, and he raised it to throw at Buddy. "Get outta here, you sonovabitchbastad!" The washing machine started making noises like a jet taking off as it hit Final Spin. "Shut that fuckin' thing off!" He flung the ashtray in Buddy's general direction, but Buddy was back in the kitchen franti-cally pulling and pushing knobs and dials and plugs until the washing machine shuddered, kicked, and died.

"NNNFFF! NNNNGG! NNNNNFF!"

"Sing, bitch! I wancha to sing!"

Did she say she was pregnant?!!

Buddy gasped and fell back against the washing machine as the whole conversation ran through his head like an electronic news bulletin above Times Square. He staggered into the liv-ing room ignoring the sounds of his wrestling parents. He sat back in the armchair amid the din and pondered the future. Only spics and niggers got abortions, so that was out, besides, Despie would go to hell along with the dead baby and prob-ably him too, so the only thing to do was get married, and be-sides, he really loved Despie, and they would get married any-way sooner or later, and this way they wouldn't have to sneak around when they wanted to fuck, but pregnant women can't fuck anyway. At least he would be out of this shit-dump and away from these two asswipes, and it wasn't like he couldn't hang around with the guys anymore, and now at least he wouldn't have to jerk off, and at least he wasn't sterile like Big George, and he could get the fuck out of fucking Leander Tully and get a job. He really loved Despie like nobody's business, and the wedding would be boss, and Tommy Tooky could get the Zircons, and maybe they could get them cheap and rent out the dance floor at the Duke. Nobody would have to know she was knocked up — besides love was love. SHADDUP! SHADDUP! Buddy leapt to his feet, ran into the bedroom, and screamed at his parents. They were rolling around, pummeling each other. They stopped in midroll, staring in animal dumbness at their son.

Buddy clenched his teeth and his fists. His breathing became asthmatic. He grabbed one of the remaining lamps in the room and threw it against the wall over their heads. They flattened against the floor.

"Whadya crazy?" his father shouted. But Buddy was gone.

*

Buddy sat in a hardback chair in the middle of the living room. Despie and her weeping mother sat huddled together in a corner of the couch against the wall. Al Carabella paced up and down in front of Buddy. Buddy held his knees and rocked slightly. Every time he looked at Despie her face was four slits of reproach. Her mother's mouth was contorted into such a convulsion of silent grief that Buddy found it hard to believe that all he'd done was bang her daughter.

"You got a job?" Al Carabella barked. He was short, red, bald, and thick like Buddy's father. He rocked on the balls of his feet as if any second he would explode into violence and go for Buddy's throat.

"Nah, I ain't graduated yet."

A sneer. "Awright. I'll getcha into the printers. You twenny-one? You gotta be twenny-one."

"I ain't eighteen yet."

"Jesus Christ . . . you goddamn kids . . . Jesus Christ." Despie's mother started weeping, and Despie hugged her. "You got a place to live?"

"Nah . . . I . . ."

"Jesus Christ . . . no job . . . no house . . . nothin' here." Al tapped Buddy's forehead. "It's all down here." He grabbed Buddy's crotch and squeezed. Buddy yelped and almost fell over backward. "Jesus Christ . . . you goddamn kids . . . awright . . . you live in the basement . . . we got wood paneling." Buddy nodded dumbly. "Despie, take your mother and go upstairs now. I wanna talk to him."

Despie almost carried her mother past Buddy, who avoided her murderous glances.

"Awright, Borsalino, I wanna have a man-to-man talk." He pulled up a chair in the middle of the living room almost touching Buddy's knees. "Look, I ain't a hard guy. I was your age once an' I used to put 'em away like there was no tomorrow. But one thing . . . I never did it with nobody's daughter." He stared at Buddy and stabbed him in the chest with a cigar-like finger. Buddy stared at the ground. "Not only did you do it wit' *my* daughter, but you knocked her up, you dumb wop." Buddy blinked hard, trying not to cry. "Awright, like I said, I ain't a hard guy an' it takes two to tango an' all that bullshit. For all I know, she's been bangin' away since junior high school, an' you're the first jerk to get caught. It don't make no difference to me. Now, the thing is you knocked her up so you gotta pay the price an' do the right thing."

Buddy sucked up the wetness in his nose, and his face buckled as he started losing the fight against tears.

"Hey, what's this?" Al straightened up in his chair. "Awww

. . . *now* you're scared." He got up and poured Buddy a shot of Scotch, started to put the bottle away, then changed his mind and poured himself a shot. Sniffling, Buddy held the glass and stared at the floor.

"Get up," said Al. Buddy raised himself slowly. "To my son-in-law." Al tried to clink glasses, and Buddy cringed — half expecting to get punched. Al put his arm around Buddy's shoulder and ushered him toward the basement. "You wanna see your new apartment?"

"I awready seen it."

"So that's where you did it," Al muttered more to himself than to Buddy. "Hey, Gloria!" Al shouted upstairs, "c'mon down wit' Despie!" He turned to Buddy again. "You like clams? I'll take you all to City Island for some clams."

Buddy nodded grimly.

"I ain't no hard guy," Al said, shrugging his shoulders and smiling.

*

Buddy walked to Big Playground, his hip pocket full of wedding invitations. For the millionth time he hashed over in his head the story he was going to tell the guys. When he got to the playground Richie and Eugene were playing colored guys in two-on-two baseball. Buddy sat on the bench holding the invitations with clammy hands and waiting for the stupid fucking game to be over. At one point Richie, seeing Buddy, waved hello, and Buddy almost jumped on the court to give him his invitation.

"Whew! I'm fuckin' wiped out!" Eugene sprawled on the bench next to Buddy.

Richie nodded. "Those guys are good."

"I'm getting married," said Buddy.

"That big nigger can jump . . . bawh," said Richie, leaning over, elbows on thighs, as he fanned himself with the wedding invitation Buddy handed him.

"Me an' Despie decided to do it up right. Here." Buddy gave Eugene an invitation.

"You into goin' to Bronx House tonight?" Eugene asked. Like Richie, Eugene used the invitation as a fan.

"Nah, you wanna go next week? Tooky's playin'," said Richie.

"Tooky can't play for dick," said Eugene.

"Fuck you, Jack!" Tommy Tooky was Richie's cousin. "He'll play your ass off any day, man." Eugene had just started taking sax lessons.

"Big fuckin' deal. If I was playin' as long as him I'd be giggin' the Duke every week."

"You'd be giggin' my sazeech every week," Richie said.

"I blow sax not the kazoo," said Eugene.

"Ahhhhhhaaa . . . woooo!!" They were surrounded by a dozen Big Playground regulars who sensed a major cut-down fight coming up.

"Your mama blows the tuba!"

"Wooo! OOO! OOO! OOO! OOO!"

"Yours blows the bandleader!"

The regulars were draped over the bench and mesh fence shrieking and freaking like a strung-out Greek chorus.

"Aha — haaa!"

"Your mama went to the circus an' gave the clap to a dyin' bull elephant." Eugene, red and tense, sat on the edge of the bench. Richie was on his feet.

"The elephant was *dyin'* from eatin' out your gramma!"

"I'm getting married next Friday," Buddy said more to himself than to anyone else.

"Your mama rides shotgun on the Cocoa Puff train."

"They made a commercial about your mama — so spreadable it's incredible!"

"Ahhhh-woooo! Uh! Uh! Uh!"

"Oh yeah? They made one about yours . . ."

"Lissen *god*damit!" Buddy stood up on the bench and

kicked at the mesh. "I'm *fuck*in' gettin' *fuck*in' married next
Friday. You guys deaf?"

Nobody knew exactly what to say. Somebody fell off the
fence and landed on his ass. Two guys walked away sensing
the fun was over. Richie sat back down. Both he and Eugene
searched Buddy's face for bullshit. "You shittin' us?" Eugene
asked.

"The fuck I am."

"Why?" Richie said hunching his shoulders.

"I want to." Buddy sat down. Silence. The crowd started
walking away.

Richie's frown broke into a grin.

"Borsalino, you bullshit so much your back teeth are
brown."

"We're goin' down to City Hall Friday an' we're havin' a
party Friday night." He gave Richie and Eugene another set
of invitations.

MR. AND MRS. AL CARABELLA
AND MR. AND MRS. VITO BORSALINO
REQUEST YOUR PRESENCE AT
A CELEBRATION FOR THE
WEDDING BETWEEN THEIR CHILDREN
DESPINOZA MARIE CARABELLA
AND MARIO PETER BORSALINO
ON JUNE I, 1962, AT THE COMMUNITY
CENTER RECREATION ROOM
AT 8:45 SHARP
RSVP

"Me an' Despie wrote it out ourselves, an' then we took it to a
printer."

"Why?" asked Eugene.

"It ain't that expensive."

"Why the fuck get married?" asked Eugene.

"I'm in love, Eugene. You guys don't know what it means to be in love like this . . . this is true love." Buddy was touched with his own sincerity and wiped away a tear. "This is really the once in a lifetime thing for me."

"Did you hear bells?" asked Richie.

"Did you knock her up?" asked Eugene.

"No."

"No what?"

"No I din't hear no *fuck*in' bells, an' no I din't knock her up."

"Buddy, you can tell us. You're our main man. She ain't pregnant?" Richie put an arm around Buddy's shoulder.

Buddy looked at their faces for any sign of mockery. They weren't even smiling.

"Hey, what's happenin'?" Joey came around the corner. "What's wit' him?" He nodded at Buddy. "You look like someone jus' died."

"Buddy's gettin married," said Eugene.

"No shit," Joey laughed.

"No shit," said Eugene.

"Jesus Fucking H. Christ, don't kid around like that."

"Nobody's kiddin' around, Joey." Richie gave him the invitation.

"What's this? A trick?" He looked at Buddy and squinted. "You ain't fuckin' aroun'.." Elbows on knees, Buddy hunched over, resting his face in the net of his fingers. Richie stared across the court and massaged Buddy's shoulders. Eugene lightly touched his arm, then withdrew. Joey knelt on the ground in front of him and looked up past his hands trying to catch his eye. He touched Buddy's knee. "You knock her up?" he asked softly and seriously.

"Yeah," Buddy said almost too low to be heard.

"Shit." Joey squeezed Buddy's knee, rose, sat on the other side of him, and put his arm around his shoulder.

"I know how to get an abortion," said Eugene, who felt squeezed out by Richie's and Joey's tenderness. "Just dial PEACHES backwards onna phone."

"That's for a cathouse stupid."

"Well, hookers get knocked up too."

"Ah shaddup, Eugene."

Eugene raised his hands briefly in small circles of desperation, opened his mouth to say something, clammed up, jammed his hands in his pockets, and left the playground.

Eugene walked home in a mixture of rage and terror. He'd fucked eleven girls in the last three months, and he'd fuck eleven more in the next two months at least, and he'd be goddamned if he would ever be stupid enough to knock anybody up. Buddy was a sap and a real pork to blow it all on the first roll. The jerk probably came before he could put on a bag — oh, Jesus, maybe I'm sterile. Eugene flashed on fucking Patricia Palladino with a busted bag, and she had her period two weeks *early*. Sterile. Then again that's fucking A-OK because who wants to have to get married and have kids. Maybe he should give up bags altogether. He unfolded the invitation and frowned. June 1. Next Friday. He had a thing going with Nina Becker next Friday. Number twelve. Maybe he could bring her to the wedding. Or maybe he could split early to pick her up. He'd have to give Borsalino a call.

*

Al Carabella was waiting for his daughter when she came home from school at three-thirty. He had a belt in his hand and every day since she'd told her parents she was pregnant, he marched her wordlessly into her bedroom, emerged ten minutes later, and locked the door until dinner time. Despie lay on her bed, her sore ass arched on a pillow. After the first two beatings, it didn't even feel worth crying about. Four more days to the wedding. Four more beatings. He wouldn't dare hit her after she was married. She lifted up her blouse, pulled down her skirt, and ran her fingers lightly along her lower belly. Doctor Pugliese said it was no bigger than a peanut. She felt for the possible outlines of a peanut-sized baby. She found it to the left and a few inches below her navel and fingered the outline. She found its mouth and eyes and hands and feet. She even felt it squirm under the pressure of her hand. She rested her fingernail on its tiny chest. Then she curled her hand into a fist and smashed it down on her belly again and again and again.

*

Tommy Tooky and the Zircons fell through for the party so Buddy went around to everybody's house collecting 45s for the reception. He made a list of records so he could return them when the whole thing was over.

Richie

Patches (S)
Pretty Little Angel Eyes (F)
Tell Laura I Love Her (S)
Runaway (F)
Tears on My Pillow (S)
Spanish Harlem (C)
Heartaches (F)

Joey

Sherry (C)
Big Girls Don't cry (C)
Walk Like a Man (C)
Ain't It a Shame (F)
The Wanderer (F)
Runaround Sue (F)
Lovers Who Wander (F)

Eugene

Could This Be Magic (S)
The Closer You Are (S)
The Wind (S)
Diamonds and Pearls (S)
Valerie (S)
Donna (S)
Every Beat of My Heart (S)

Little Diane (F)   I Only Have Eyes for
Quarter to Three (F)   You (S)
Barbara-Ann (F)   What Time Is It? (S)

C

Johnny Angel (C)
Blue Moon (F)
Any Day Now (S)
Soldier Boy (S)
Will You Still Love Me
   Tomorrow (C)
The End of the World (S)
Da Doo Run Run (F)
Duke of Earl (S)

He had a pretty good mix — sixteen slow, twelve fast, and six cha-chas. He was bringing 287 records himself, and Despie was bringing almost 400, but it was good to have some important doubles around.

*

Perry stood in front of Trenton High School in his Tully jacket, a cigarette dangling from his mouth and a tiny blue loose-leaf tucked under his arm. Two sidekicks stood on each side of him, like identical bookends. They kept one eye on the crowds and one eye on Perry. If he shifted his weight, they shifted their weight. If he used his thumb and forefinger to take the cigarette out of his mouth, then squint and blow out smoke through compressed lips, like the hitter he was, then they followed suit. Perry took a last drag, dropped the butt, and walked across the street to a playground. His flunkies ditched their butts and walked three feet behind, one on either side to form a wing. Perry scanned the basketball court, saw who he was looking for, handed his looseleaf to a flunky without turning around, lit another cigarette, and slipped a two-dollar roll of nickels into his right fist.

"His nose split open like a tomato." Perry spat a small ball of saliva. "An' I look down at him an' I says . . . keep the change." The flunkies laugh appreciatively even though they had seen the whole thing. "Fuckin' A." Perry squinted, took a long hard drag, and spat again.

Perry sat alone in the fake oriental living room of his Aunt Rosie's house watching reruns of "Rawhide" on the color TV, eating Fritos, and debating whether to do his homework. Fuck it. Fuck school. Fuck the world. He was getting left back because of his disciplinary record. The principal's office had him for eleven fights in three months, but Perry didn't see them as eleven fights. He saw them as three KOs, six TKOs, one unanimous, and a split decision. Besides, he was quitting school at the end of the month, going back to New York to see the guys one more time, and then shipping out for Africa or China or someplace. He heard that they had live fuck shows in Singapore where women fucked snakes, grizzly bears, and whirling dervishes. Tokyo had whorehouses where they did Japanese tongue fucks that drove a man crazy. Tasmania paid a grand for every Tasmanian devil captured. Slaves could still be bought in Angola. A guy could buy a fucking goddamn harem in Saudi Arabia. He read that good manners for an Eskimo was to offer you his wife, like you would offer a guy a drink. Tattoo artists in Casablanca knew a way of tattooing a barber pole on a guy's cock so that it rotated when he got a hard-on.

Trenton New Fucking Jersey. "Eat me out backwards," Perry snorted.

The telephone rang. "Yo."

"Yo yourself."

"Who the hell . . . ?"

"Hey! Mistah Chooch!"

"Joey!"

"Dig it!"

"Joey!"

"Hey, mah main man, how's it hangin'?"

"In there, how's it goin'?"

"In an' out."

"Jesus Christ, Joey . . . goddamn . . . I can't believe . . ."

"Lissen, Buddy's gettin' married."

"You shittin' me?"

"No way. He knocked up Despie."

"He was *fuckin'* her?"

"No, he knocked her up by sixty-nine."

"He was fuckin' her?" Perry was still cherry.

"He's gettin' married next Friday. You comin' in?"

"I can't believe he was *fuckin'* her. Yeah! I'm comin' in."

"You can stay here."

"Dig it."

"Dig it yourself. How's it goin'?"

"I got left back."

"Shit. How'd you manage that?"

"I kicked some ass. You wouldn't believe the faggots aroun' here. I'm the toughest guy in the whole fuckin' state."

"You asshole."

"It don't mean squat. I'm quittin' school."

"You gettin' a job?"

"Nah, I'm gettin' seaman's papers."

"Where you gonna go?"

"I dunno . . . China."

"You can't go to China."

"Why the fuck not?"

"It's Communist."

"So I'll go to Africa."

"Why the hell you goin' to Africa? You got boogies in Tully."

"I don't go to Tully no more."

"I ain't gonna be goin' there no more either."

"You quittin'?"

"Graduatin'."

"Fuck you."

"Big deal. It don't make no difference."

"You gonna college?"

"Whada you kiddin'?"

"Whada you gonna do?"

"I dunno. I'm gettin' the fuck outta here. That's for sure."

"Whadya mean?"

"It's no good no more. You're gone. Buddy's good as gone. I had a fight wit' Eugene so it's me an' Richie. Nobody to play with no more."

"How's Emilio?"

"I can't live in the same house wit' that fuckin' maniac."

"Jus' tell 'im I said he should dig himself."

"He should fuckin' dig himself six feet under."

"Don' worry, babe, he's gonna get hit."

"I gotta get outta here, Perry."

"You wanna come wit' me?"

"Where you goin'?"

"I got a uncle up in Boston in the Seafarers. He can get us papers an' we're off."

"Jus' like that?"

"Jus' like that . . . jus' like that, Joey."

*

Thursday night after dinner Buddy went downstairs to take a ride. As he was getting in his father's car, he saw Perry sitting in the passenger seat. "La Guardiah!"

"Heeeyyy!" Joey, Richie, and Eugene jumped up from behind the car, and they all grabbed Buddy. Laughing, they rammed him against the door, lifted him on their shoulders, and carried him back to his building. They dumped Buddy into the elevator and jammed in with him, still shouting and laughing. "What the fuck is goin' on?" Buddy yelled, as they tried to get him on the bottom of a pile-up.

"Bachelor party!" they shouted. They hustled Buddy into his apartment, into a fresh Banlon shirt, and back to his car.

"Where we goin'?"

"The Duke!"

"Mom's!"

"Ain't got one!"

"The Duke!"

Joey took the wheel, heading the car toward the Duke on Central Avenue in Yonkers.

"Perry! Where the fuck you been?"

"Fuckin' Trenton, New Jersey."

Buddy took a good look at Perry. He'd lost a lot of weight. "You fat tub a shit, I missed you."

"I wasn't gonna miss this for nothin'." Perry leaned over the front seat and flicked Buddy's ear. Buddy ducked, then half leaped over the seat and wrestled with Perry. Richie and Eugene piled on. Joey laughed and swerved the car sharply to knock everybody against the door. Everybody started laughing and yelling at Joey. Eugene pulled out a pint of bourbon, and Richie pulled out a quart of Tango. By the time Joey screeched into a parking spot, Eugene's green iridescents were soaked with Tango, Perry had lost a shoe somewhere in the car, and Richie had a lump like a softball on his forehead.

After the second pitcher of seventy-sevens, Richie stood up and raised his hands to quiet everybody at the table. "We got a present here for you, Bors'lino." He staggered away from the table to the checkroom and came back with a big, shiny green package. He flipped it to Buddy. "Open it!"

"C'mon, c'mon, open it!"

"Yeah. Wait! Give 'im the card!"

"Yeah, the card!"

"Give 'im the card!"

Nobody could find the card. People at other tables were watching and took up the cry. "Where's the card! We want the card!" Soon all the people were laughing and shouting for the card. Finally Richie found the card and held it in front of the packed club. On the card was a drawing of a farmer locking a barn door and two horses running in the distance.

"Open a package!"

"Open it!" The crowd shouted encouragement.

Buddy ripped open the green paper, and four hundred foil-wrapped Trojans cascaded across the floor.

*

Perry and Joey stumbled through the dimly lit hallway to Joey's door.

"I can't fuckin' believe it." Joey giggled.

"Did you see the look on 'is face?" Perry imitated Buddy's expression, opening his mouth to a big O.

Joey doubled over in breathless laughter, extending a palm that Perry slapped loudly.

Suddenly the door opened. Emilio stood in his shorts rubbing the sleep from his eyes. He yanked Joey inside. The door slammed shut before Perry could react. Perry stood startled, staring at the closed door, a horrible fear snaking through his guts. A slap. Another. A sharp intake of breath. Muttered curses. Silence. The door slowly opened. Perry backed away. Joey emerged. His face was pinched with pain. Tears ran down his cheeks in fat tracks. Five red lines streaked across the side of his ear. He held his stomach.

"What the fuck!" Joey motioned to Perry to shut up, hesitated a few seconds, and ushered him inside the darkened apartment.

*

Richie got home at two-thirty in the morning and called C. After two rings he remembered she was sleeping at Despie's. He hoisted himself up on the kitchen counter and lit a cigarette. He sat in the darkness, idly swinging his legs, staring down at the deserted street. An el train passed outside the window. The rocketing cars washed his face with light. The train was empty.

*

Eugene undid his tie as he sauntered into the living room.

"Ace!" Eugene's father faced a dead television. He wore his red brocade smoking jacket, a small pyramid of cigarette butts in front of him on the coffee table.

"Whada you doin' up?"

Al shrugged. "Couldn't sleep. How was your friend's party?"

"Good." Eugene took a cigarette from the coffee table.

"You get 'im laid?"

"Nah."

"What kind of a send-off is that? You know when one a my friends was gettin' hitched we use to rent out a whole cathouse. There was this place, a brownstone down on Thirty-eighth Street." He lit another cigarette and exhaled through his nose. "Lefty Rao's bachelor party, we go down there," he chuckled, "and I put away . . . I put away *six* chicks . . . *six*."

Eugene pressed his fingers into his temples. "Look, I don' wanna hear that now, O.K.?"

Al was taken aback. "Whassamatter?"

"Nothin' . . . nothin'. I jus' don' wanna hear any a that bullshit right now, O.K.?" Al raised his eyebrows and lit a fresh cigarette from the butt in his mouth.

Eugene paced the living room. "Sorry."

Al shrugged, waving his cigarette hand.

"I'm just goin' nuts. I don' know what the fuck is goin' on anymore." He jammed his hands into his pockets.

Al's eyes darted around the room. He shifted uncomfortably on his buttocks.

"I had a fight with Joey about a month ago and ever since then . . . I dunno . . . it feels like . . . like I'm walkin' aroun' with my shirt buttoned wrong or somethin'." Al raised his eyebrows again and coughed. "An' las' week . . . I had this chick upstairs . . ." Eugene sat down again. "An' I couldn't get it up."

Al's face tightened. Eugene shrugged. "I mean the next night I gave her a double to make up for it but like . . . the thing was . . . that night I couldn't get it up. I didn't give a shit. I mean I wasn't scared about it or nothing'. I just didn't care if I ever got it up again for the rest of my goddamn life . . . it's weird!"

"You oughta see a doctor," Al said.

"A shrink?"

"You don't need none a that bullshit. Whyncha go over to Glassman tomorrow. Let 'im take a look."

"At what?"

"I dunno, maybe you got a pulled muscle or somethin'."

Eugene made a fist, and, forearm up, jerked off an invisible prick.

Al laughed. "You still jerkin' off?"

"Whada you kiddin'? I ain't jerked off since I was twelve."

"You got no time, hah?"

"I got better things to do with it."

Al laughed again and got up. "I'm gonna bed, Ace. You wanna see Glassman tomorrow, tell 'im to put it on my tab."

Eugene sat alone on the couch rubbing his face between his fists, feeling like he just got cheated out of something, but he couldn't put his finger on what it was.

*

Despie and C lay in Despie's bed staring at the ceiling.

"Whada you thinkin' about?" C asked.

"I forgot to invite Debby Tepper."

"Call her tomorrow."

"She'll be pissed off."

"So what? She's a skank."

"We're gonna get the license tomorrow."

"You scared?"

Despie shrugged. "I'm gonna be a married woman."

"How does it feel?"

Despie rolled over, her back to C. "Like shit."

*

Perry and Joey lay in Joey's bed.

"Rotten motherfucker." Joey fingered his face lightly where Emilio had slapped him.

"He'll get hit."

"Who's gonna do it?"

"Don't you worry."

"I gotta get outta here," said Joey.

Perry stared at the ceiling, his hands clasped behind his neck. "You think of comin' wit' me?"

A long silence. "Yeah."

"I'm leavin' Sunday."

"You goin' back to get your stuff?"

"No."

"You just goin' after the wedding?"

"Yeah."

"Up to Boston?"

"Yeah."

A long, slow exhale. "You takin' anybody?"

"Just you."

Another long, slow exhale. "I'm fuckin' scared, Perry."

"I'm hip."

A long silence. "How we gonna get there?"

"I got two bus tickets." He reached over Joey's chest and took his wallet from the dresser. "Two tickets, an' I copped two hundred bucks from Rosie."

"I got no money."

"Don't sweat it."

"Hey, Perry?"

"Yeah?"

"I don' wanna sound like no faggot . . . but I dig you . . . you're my best friend."

Another long silence.

"We gonna make it, man." Perry rolled on his side.

"I ain't gonna go to no Africa," said Joey.

"Let's get outta the Bronx first."

"I just ain't gonna go to no fuckin' Africa, that's all." Joey listened to Emilio's snoring through the wall.

*

Eugene dreamed that he was dressed and in bed at a party, his dick hanging out of his fly. He rolled over in bed, but no matter which way he turned, he couldn't hide the fact that his dick hung out of his fly. Handsome men and beautiful women stood around his bed with drinks in their hands, yakking away, and he couldn't hide his dick from them, no matter how much he tossed, turned, or contorted himself.

*

Buddy came home to an empty house. His father was at work, and his mother wasn't yet home from mahjong. He had all his shirts and shit packed to move to Despie's house tomorrow afternoon. The two suitcases were still open on top of his bed. He felt like he was going away to camp for two weeks. He went over the list of records for tomorrow night's party, and that cheered him up a little. He wasn't sure if his father knew about the wedding. When he told his mother she said not to tell Vito, because he would blow his top. She would tell him. But Buddy wasn't sure when she was going to tell him. What the fuck difference did it make. Vito would be working, and Buddy didn't want him at his goddamn party anyhow. She could stay home too. He heard the door open, his mother humming opera. Buddy dumped everything off his bed and pretended he was asleep. She walked right by his room.

*

Early Friday morning the Wanderers cut school and went to Fordham Road to buy new sport jackets for the wedding party. They got off the bus at Fordham and Webster Avenue in front of Sears Roebuck and started the long uphill trek.

"Where we goin'?" asked Eugene.

"Alexander's."

"Bullshit. I ain't buyin' that crap."

"Where you gonna go, Wallachs?"

"Slak Shak."

"That's the same shit as Alexander's."

"I ain't goin' to no Alexander's."

"You wanna split up?"

"I gotta go to Alexander's."

"Yeah, I only got twenty bucks."

"They got good stuff."

"Forget it, I'll meet you guys later." Eugene started to walk away.

"Hey, Eugene!"

"What!" He wheeled around.

"What's goin' on wit' you?"

He shrugged angrily. "I don't wanna go to no shithouse for a sport jacket. You wanna in-depth report?"

"You better start diggin' yourself, Caputo," Joey said. They stared at each other, both tight-lipped and unblinking. Eugene walked back down Fordham Road. Perry made a motion in his direction, but Joey grabbed his arm. "Fuck 'im."

The Wanderers continued up the hill toward Alexander's.

In Alexander's basement Richie found a silver sharkskin jacket with green felt lapels. Buddy grabbed a pale yellow mohair with no lapels.

"Dig it." Buddy slipped it on over his muscle shirt and stood in front of a four-paneled mirror.

"That's fuckin' beautiful," said Perry.

"I got this yellow tie." Buddy outlined a tie along his throat as he stared at his reflection. "An' a tab collar shirt . . . man."

"Dynamite."

"How you like this?" Richie paraded in front of them in his discovery.

"I didn't know Purina made sport jackets," said Joey.

"Hey, fuck you. Let's see what you're gettin'," said Richie. Joey and Perry exchanged brief glances. "I think I'm gonna wear one I got awready," said Joey.

"You ain't gonna buy a jacket?" asked Buddy.

"Nah, I got a good one at home."

"I'm fuckin' insulted," Buddy said half-seriously.

"Ah, c'mon, Buddy. I got one that cost thirty-five bucks. I only wore it twice."

"I ain't gonna buy one either," said Perry. "I ain't got no dough."

"Bullshit! I'll lend you the money," said Buddy.

"I brought one wit' me," Perry excused himself.

"Fuckin' guys. Richie, you don't buy that jacket I'll cut your balls off."

"It looks like shit," Richie sulked.

"It's outtasite."

"Bullshit."

"What the fuck is goin' on here!" Buddy grasped the coat-rack with a bloodless fist. "You guys say you're gonna get jackets for the wedding an' now nobody's buyin' shit."

People turned around and stared at Buddy. Nobody said anything.

"What's goin' on? Damnit!" Richie rolled the jacket into a ball. Joey and Perry studied the floor. "Well, fuck this!" Buddy tore off the yellow jacket, flung it across the floor, and stormed out of the basement.

"Hey, Buddy!" Richie took off after him.

Perry held Joey back. "We can't afford it, Joey."

"It's his fuckin' *wedding,* man."

"We don't got that much dough."

"It's *Buddy,* man."

Perry shook his head. "Can't do it." They walked slowly past pants and records and clocks and out into Fordham Road.

*

An hour after Buddy got back from Alexander's, Al picked him up and drove him and Despie to the Marriage Bureau. They were married in twenty minutes. On the way back Buddy decided he would like to see if any of the guys were around, so he asked Al to please drop him off at the projects. Despie said nothing. Al stopped the car in front of Buddy's building, then went home with his married daughter.

Buddy walked to Big Playground but none of the guys were

there. He went over to the campsite and wandered around, aimlessly kicking rocks and swiping at shoulder-high weeds.

"Hey."

Buddy whirled around to see Eugene sitting on the ground, his back against the sheet-metal garage that formed one of the perimeters of the hangout. An el train roared by overhead, casting running shadows across the garage and half the lot. Buddy sauntered over and sat down next to Eugene. He leaned back against the gray wall, propping his forearms on his knees. Eugene took out some smokes and passed the pack to Buddy. Buddy leaned into Eugene's cupped hands for a light and collapsed back against the garage. "You buy a jacket?" Buddy asked, his eyes closed, twin slips of smoke trickling from his nostrils.

"Yeah."

A long silence.

"I'm a married man, Eugene." Eugene rested his forehead in the bridge of his thumb and index finger, eyes closed, head cocked to an angle. "I'm a fuckin' married man."

"It could be worse."

Buddy idly pulled out clumps of grass around his shoe. "Eugene, you're a lucky guy." Eugene raised an eyebrow. "You got everything — looks, brains, dough, you musta screwed a hundred chicks, an' it's like nothing. My first piece an' boom! I'm a daddy." Both Buddy and Eugene laughed in spite of themselves. "I'm a fuckin' daddy." Buddy shook his head sadly.

"You're lucky, Buddy, not many guys got somebody to love like you."

"I shoulda bought her an ankle bracelet and stuck to jerkin' off."

"It's nice. A wife, a kid, your own place."

"I'm fuckin' seventeen."

"So what? We'll catch up soon enough." Another train

roared overhead. Eugene flicked his cigarette butt into the high weeds.

"If that kid is born retarded, I'm gonna stab it with a butcher knife an' dump it down the incinerator."

Eugene looked at Buddy but didn't say anything. He lit another cigarette and extended the pack to Buddy.

"Buddy." He blew a smoke ring. "Sex is bullshit. Cunt is bullshit. Love is bullshit. Everything is bullshit."

"Fuckin' man-a-the-world." Buddy smirked.

"Nah, I know it sounds like . . ."

"Bullshit," Buddy offered. They both laughed.

"There gotta be somethin' else goin' down," said Eugene. "I mean like . . . like, I don' wanna sound like a fuckin' philosopher but . . . pussy is pussy . . . you know what I mean?"

"No."

Eugene winced. "O.K., look. Jus' cause you can fuck it don't make you a better person. O.K.?"

"You mean like . . . the fucking you get ain't worth the screwing you take?"

"That's bullshit too. It's just that there's gotta be more to being a man than being a good fuck."

"I still think the fucking you get ain't worth the screwing you take," Buddy said, stabbing out the half-smoked cigarette into the earth.

*

Perry and Joey spent the rest of the afternoon in Army-Navy stores on Fordham Road. They bought dark blue, heavy-knit turtleneck sweaters, sailor hats, sea coats, ditty bags, knot-tying instruction manuals, and twenty feet of boat rope to practice with on the bus. They carried everything in the ditty bags. On the traffic island where the Fordham

Baldies used to hang out before Hang On Sloopy died, they stood in front of a navy recruiting center.

"This time tomorrow we'll be in Boston," Perry said.

"Your uncle know we're comin'?"

"Nah, but I know where he lives."

"You fuckin' jerk! What if he's on a ship someplace!"

Perry shook his head. "I don' think so. Las' time I saw him he was in a hospital."

"Well, maybe he got better!"

"Nah, he ain't goin' nowhere." Perry smirked. "He got no legs."

*

"Well, I guess I don't have to tell you about the wedding night," said Despie's mother, half-a-dozen curtain tacks extending between compressed lips as she began redecorating the basement.

*

Buddy walked home, stretched out on his bed, and fell asleep. On his way to work, Vito Borsalino stopped by his son's room, saw that he was asleep, and put two hundred dollars in Buddy's sport jacket, which was draped over a chair. Half an hour later, the telephone rang. Buddy bolted out of bed. "Hello?"

"Buddy? Where the hell have you been?"

Hearing Despie's voice, Buddy felt weak with terror. He hung up the phone and bent down to pick up a rubber band on the rug. The wedding party was two hours away.

*

The community center was across from Bronx Park. It was a squat, red brick building adjacent to the building where Scottie Hite had jumped to his death. The community center recreation room was a pale green cinder-block square. The floor was poured concrete. Water pipes ran along the ceiling. The porters were tipped to haul in two long collapsible tables for the food and about twenty folding chairs that they lined up against the walls. The room was reasonably clean with the exception of some sheets of colored construction paper left by the day center's arts and crafts class, scattered around the floor. The room smelled like glue.

"Good, they brought in the tables," said Al Carabella as he kicked open the door, his arms filled with shopping bags. Buddy followed right behind carrying a shopping bag and a phonograph. "It's a nice room." Al sniffed.

Buddy thought it sucked. It smelled like a day camp. Al unpacked the bags on one of the long tables. He took out a long paper tablecloth, paper plates, plastic silverware, party napkins, monster bags of M&Ms, Fritos, popcorn, cold cuts, potato salad, cole slaw, macaroni salad, plastic cups. While Buddy unrolled the tablecloth, Al brought in records, a case of Pepsi-Cola, a large Styrofoam cooler filled with ice, a dozen rolls of crepe streamers, a big bag of balloons, and Scotch tape.

"It's gonna be *some* goddamn party," Al said.

*

Perry and Joey examined themselves in the big mirror in Joey's room.

"These fuckin' pants are too baggy," said Perry, grabbing a fistful of material around the cuffs.

"If those pants were any fuckin' tighter I could see the veins on your balls."

"Yeah. Sure." Perry frowned, grabbing the material around the crotch.

Joey adjusted the tiebar pinching his neck, smoothed back his pompadour, and clapped his hands. "Lez go, bawh."

Perry made a face in the mirror, grabbed the material around the ass of his pants and started to leave the room.

"Take your bag," said Joey, hauling his ditty bag over his shoulder.

"What for? We can pick it up when we leave."

"We ain't comin' back."

"What?"

"I ain't sleepin' here again. We walk out that door an' that's it. I don' care if we gotta sleep in the goddamn bus station." Perry shrugged and hoisted his bag over his shoulder.

"Hey." Joey wheeled around to see Emilio standing in the foyer wearing a skin-tight, orange Fire Department T-shirt that made him look twice as big as he was. "What the hell you got in there?" Emilio asked nodding toward the ditty bags.

"Presents." "Laundry." They said simultaneously.

Emilio grabbed Joey's bag. Joey's eyes felt dry, but his neck was a damp ring of sweat. Staring hard at his son, Emilio ripped open the bag and looked in.

"They're presents," Perry started talking fast. "Buddy's goin' on a honeymoon."

"Sailin'," added Joey, "he's goin' sailin'."

"Sailin', hah?" Emilio stared at Joey, nodding his head slightly up and down. "Sailin'." He didn't say anything or move for a full minute. He just stared at Joey. Then he gave him back the bag, turned away, and went into his bedroom. Joey was puzzled.

"C'mon." Perry ushered him out the door to the elevator. "That was too fuckin' close for comfort." Perry adjusted the bag on his shoulder. Joey didn't answer.

*

When Richie picked up C she was sitting in her room, crying.

"Whassamatter?" he asked.

She looked up at him, twin furrows of makeup running

down her cheeks. "You bastad," she cried. "You don't know what true love is, do you?"

*

Despie left the house in the late twilight with her mother. She had her hair piled a foot high, ringlets Scotch-taped to her temples. They were about seven blocks from the community center. A summer wind was threatening to ruin Despie's hair. "You wanna take a cab?" she asked her mother.

"I think we should walk. We're not going to have that much money anymore, and you should start getting used to it."

*

Eugene went over to Gun Hill Projects to pick up his date, Nina Becker. Her parents were away for the weekend so, if she fucked at all, he was in. He'd met her two weeks ago at a friend's party. He was pretty drunk but straight enough to get her number and set tonight up. The only problem was that he couldn't remember what she looked like. The girl who answered the apartment door had such a simple and pure beauty that Eugene immediately fell in love. She had long ash-blond hair to her ass, big gray eyes, a long thin nose, lips as thin and delicate as Communion wafers, and a look of such devastating, seductive innocence that Eugene found himself almost laughing in drunken delight.

"Hi." She smiled.

Eugene laughed. He was totally wiped out.

*

Perry and Joey were the first to arrive at the party. Al Carabella and Buddy were sitting in folding chairs drinking Pepsis when they walked in and dumped their ditty bags in the corner.

"Hey! Where were you guys when we needed yah?" Al asked. Buddy raised his eyes to heaven and got up.

"How you doin', man?"

"Good."

The three of them stood arm in arm.

"Look at this fuckin' place," Buddy muttered. The entire ceiling was a veinwork of red, blue, green, and yellow crepe streamers and balloons. "This ain't a wedding. It's a carnival," he said. Joey snickered. "You want somethin' to eat?"

"Nah, you got any booze?"

"Fuck . . . no . . . you wanna go with me, Perry?"

"Sure."

"Joey, stay here with Bozo the Clown."

"Bullshit, I'm goin' with you guys."

Buddy turned to his father-in-law. "Ah, Al, we'll be right back."

"Don' run away, hah hah hah."

"Haha hah hah." Buddy turned toward the door. "Asshole."

Two seconds after Buddy split with Joey and Perry, Despie and her mother came in. Al stood up and frowned. Despie had a Brownie camera strapped on her wrist.

Richie and C walked in. C and Despie hugged each other. C was still crying. Despie started crying. Richie shook hands with Al like a man, like his father taught him to do.

"Richie Gennaro."

"Al Carabella."

"Congratulations."

"Thanks." Al winked.

Richie excused himself, walked over to the food, took one M&M, walked over to the phonograph, and began to study the records with an intensity that could melt wax.

*

Eugene was in such a daze with Nina Becker sitting next to him in the car that he almost hit an el pillar on Gun Hill Road. Nina slipped an arm through his and curled her fingers around his forearm. He grinned like a moron and totally forgot his lines. After he parked the car they walked hand in hand to the community center. In high heels she was almost as tall as he was. She had a great ass, firm tits, and dynamite legs, but all Eugene could focus on was that face and the dry warmth of her hand in his.

"Eugene!" Richie was so glad to see one of the guys that he dropped half-a-dozen records on the floor. Eugene padded in Richie's direction and sat down with Nina. He didn't even say hello to Despie or C. Richie felt hurt and was about to walk outside when Perry, Joey, and Buddy came back in with small brown bags. The four of them walked outside for a taste.

"Eugene!" Perry held up his bag and nodded in the direction of the door. Eugene smiled, waved, and returned to his conversation with Nina.

"Who's the cunt?" asked Buddy.

"Who the fuck cares," said Richie.

They leaned against the red brick building watching the sun disappear behind the treetops.

"You goin' on a honeymoon?"

"Maybe later. I dunno. I gotta finish school."

"Shit." Richie took a hit of Tango. "My old man went to Niagara Falls."

"So did mine," said Perry.

"I think mine went to Devil's Island," said Joey.

"I'll drink to that," said Perry.

"You sleepin' over there tonight?"

"I guess so . . . yeah . . . I guess I am . . . shit, I dunno . . . I guess so." Buddy took a long gulp.

"Lissen, I want you guys to come over tomorrow night for a house warmin', O.K.?"

"Sure," Richie said.

Perry and Joey said nothing.

"O.K. you guys?"

"Sure," Joey said.

"Perry?"

"Sure."

When they went back inside, the place was filled with fifteen or twenty of Despie's girl friends from school and the guys they were dating. Eugene was still talking to Nina. Despie and C were dancing. Al was standing by the record player with a handful of potato chips, tapping his foot in tune with the music. Despie's grandmother drooled on her dress and made noises. Despie's mother stood behind her, arms folded across her chest like an evil Indian. The room was hot as a bitch. Buddy avoided Despie. Richie avoided C. Eugene was lost for the night. Perry and Joey stuck together like glue. Somebody spilled soda on the record player. Somebody called somebody an asshole. Somebody started popping balloons— jumping up and getting them with a tie pin. Despie started taking pictures with her Brownie. Somebody yelled shaddup and put Johnny Maestro and the Crests' "Sixteen Candles" on. Al wanted to dance slow with Despie. He waltzed her around the room. Despie wanted to brain him with the camera. Buddy and all the guys agreed that his father-in-law was the biggest jerk in the world. C scowled at Richie, and Richie shot her the finger. Eugene walked out of the room arm in arm with Nina. After the dance somebody put on a twist record, and Despie's grandmother wandered into the middle of the dancers and got knocked down. Despie took a picture of her mother standing like a guard at the Tomb of the Unknown Soldier. She took a picture of Buddy. Buddy looked at her. She lowered the camera and smiled. Buddy smiled, grabbed her, and hugged her as hard as he could. This was the first time they'd touched each other since Despie found out she was pregnant. Buddy told her he loved her. Despie kissed his neck and told him she loved him too. Perry looked at his watch and nodded to Joey. Joey turned white. Perry moved to get his ditty bag. Joey laid a hand on his arm.

"Wait."

"We gotta go, Joey."

Joey grabbed Richie and Buddy and pulled them over to Perry. "Stay right here." He found Eugene outside necking on a park bench.

"Eugene, c'mere a minute."

"Later."

"Eugene get the fuck in here now, or I swear to God, I'll kick your ass."

Silence, an exhale of breath. Whispers. Eugene followed Joey into the building. Buddy, Richie, Eugene and Perry stood around wondering what the fuck was going on with Joey. Joey feverishly rifled through the mountain of 45s on the table. He found the record he was looking for and took off the one that was playing. People started yelling. Joey ignored them and put on his record. As the first dirty piano notes of "The Wanderer" filled the room people started dancing again. Joey faced his four friends and started singing. One by one they started singing along too.

> "I roam from town to town
> I go through life wi-thout a care"

Joey cried as he sang. Perry felt a great mantle of sadness creep over his head and shoulders. Richie felt terrified of what he did not know. Eugene got shook by Joey's tears, but he had more than half a mind on Nina Becker. Buddy put his arms around Richie's and Joey's shoulders and squeezed tight as he could, as if the tighter he held on the more things would always be the same. Soon all of them stood with arms around each other's shoulders, fingers pressing into flesh, trying to make a circle which nothing could penetrate — school, women, babies, weddings, mothers, fathers.

The song was over. Some other shit came on, and the circle broke. It was twelve-thirty and Perry motioned to Joey. Eugene thought about Nina. Richie caught C's eye and winked; Buddy started thinking about being a father; Eugene wandered outside looking for Nina. Perry and Joey finally split. Richie and C took off; Despie and Buddy left, touching each other in a mixture of terror and love. Soon the only people left in the room were a bunch of dancing assholes.

12

Coda: The Rape

"ANYWAYS, when I was fourteen I noticed that when I got a hard-on my dick went down instead of up. We were havin' this circle jerk at Gennaro's house, an' I saw that all these guys had hard-ons that went up, an' I was the only one who had one that went down. So I figure holy shit, I'm built wrong, you know? So I flipped. I mean I figured unless I got some chick to stand on her head an' spread her legs so I could, you know, like lower myself into her, there was no way I could get laid. What the fuck did I know? I was like fourteen."

"You ever talk to anybody about it?" Nina pulled the covers over her bare shoulders and nestled her head on Eugene's shoulder.

"Well, that was the bitch. My father . . . I mean ever since I was twelve I would come into the house from some movie or somethin' with a girl an' he would say . . . 'Hey Ace! Get any?' you know. An' first I din't even know like . . . any *what?* An' then he would be tellin' me all these stories about how like he was eleven an' got sucked off by his teacher, an' how he bagged two girls at his confirmation, an' shit. So like by the time I was thirteen I was sayin', 'Yeah! I got laid,' an' 'Yeah! She sucked me off, whadya think!' You know, an' I wasn't even gettin' tit or anything. So like by the time I was fifteen my ol' man thought I spent half my day fuckin'. To tell you the truth I was cherry as the day I was born but I couldn't go up to him an' say . . . 'Hey, Dad, I think my dick goes the wrong way, an' I'm flippin' cause I think that means I can't fuck a girl.' 'Cause he would jus' say, 'Whadya mean! I thought you was fuckin' girls since the year one. Whadya bullshittin' me all this time?' I was too ashamed to tell him, an' I couldn't tell the guys either 'cause when I started tellin' him I was gettin' laid, I started tellin' them too. I tried to tell my ol' lady but she's a real ball-buster about that shit, because she thinks my ol' man bangs anything that moves. I mean in a way I don't blame her. My father even used to bring women home at lunchtime. When I was a little kid I had so many fuckin' aunts comin' in with my father that I couldn't keep track a them. I use to tell everybody I had the biggest god-damn family in the Bronx. One time I got into a fight with this kid in fourth grade. Silvio Rusciano. That kid had like fourteen brothers and sisters. We had a fight about who had a bigger family. He gave me a fuckin' shot in the nose, I thought I din't have no face left. I came home, an' I'm bleedin', an' my mother starts yellin' at me about I should be a man, an' she starts pushin' me out the door an' tellin' me not to come back to the house until I beat 'im up, an' fuck that, you know? The kid could eat apples off my head. I ain't fightin' him with a goddamn Sherman tank on my side. Anyways, she keeps me outta the house all day. I was just sittin' on the stoop waitin' for my father to come home." Eugene laughed.

"She's a maniac," said Nina.

"Ah, she's O.K.," said Eugene, turning off the light.

"No, she's not, Eugene. And your father's a prick and an asshole."

"Ah, he's O.K. Anyways, so since I was fourteen I been walkin' aroun' thinkin' I'm impotent. When I was ol' enough to score, you know like fifteen, sixteen, what I would do was I would get 'em in bed, an' I would do *anything* an' I mean *any-*

thing — you know foreplay stuff, but I wouldn't stick it in because I was scared that, I dunno, it wouldn't work. It was a real drag because they would get real turned on, an' soon they would wanna fuck an' then I would have to *insult* them or . . . you know, just *do* something to turn them off so they would get mad and go away. It was a bitch. I could never . . . never go out with a girl I liked, because if she ever wanted to fuck I would have to make her mad at me. If we're in bed, an' she splits, it ain't *my* fault we didn't fuck, an' my reputation ain't hurt, an' nobody knows my little secret. I had it all figured out." He lit another cigarette and readjusted the pillow. Nina leaned on her elbow, her long hair brushing against his neck.

"Then . . . about three months ago I met this chick at a bar, an' I go bring her back to Buddy's house, an' we're gettin' it on, an' all of a sudden she takes my dick before I could say or do anything, an' she just slips it right in. That's all she did. An' I was cured an' saved an' all that bullshit . . . *dah dah!*" He turned his face up to Nina's. "Except I ain't saved. You ever hear that thing — miles to go before I sleep? That's me, miles to go before I sleep. Sex don't mean shit. I mean I dig sleepin' with you, Nina, an' I love you like I never loved anybody, but there's more to bein' a man, you know? I useta think once I got it on, boy, no more problems, no more hassles. But sometimes, sometimes now I feel worse than I ever did. I ain't a kid anymore. I gotta start movin', make decisions."

"What're you goin' to decide?"

"I dunno. Maybe I'll go to college. Maybe I'll get married. "You wanna get married?"

"No."

"Why the hell not?"

"I like you too much." She briefly kissed him on the mouth, then leaned over and reached for a cigarette on the night table. The pack was empty. She jumped out of bed and turned on the light.

"Where you goin'?" he asked.

"I wanna go down an' get cigarettes." She slipped her dress over her head.

"It's twelve-thirty, where you gonna go?"

"Candy store on the corner is open . . ."

"You want me to walk you?"

"It's O.K. I'll be back in a second."

"Hey! You gonna put on any underwear?"

"No, I'll be back in a second."

"Whyncha put on underwear?" Eugene felt himself getting angry.

"It's hot out."

Eugene leaned back as the front door slammed. That was really fuckin' stupid. You wanna get married? Why the hell not? Christ. Eugene winced. He noticed Nina's shoes on the area rug. They were gray suede soft against the palm of his hand. He thought of her touch and her face. No way out of it, he was doin' a hurtin' dance when it came to Nina Becker. Just touching her goddamn shoes had him sucking wind. Eugene jerked up. If her goddamn shoes are here, then she's walking around barefoot. He saw her brassiere hanging across his desk chair, her panties in a crumpled ball on the seat. He jumped out of bed, furious. She'd been gone fifteen minutes. He put on his pants. Barefoot and bare-chested, he went downstairs and stood on the porch. The street was as silent as the hour was late. He stepped lightly to the sidewalk and peered down the block. He could see the candy store. The lights were out. He cursed and started walking down the street. The air was cool. Tree branches dipped like palm fronds in a lay back wind. A white cat crouched on top of a garbage can and watched him walk by. Eugene felt weird walking around without shoes and a shirt. He heard laughter from one of the houses. The candy store was closed, an iron gate locked over the door. Eugene peered into the darkness — the clock on the wall showed one o'clock. He looked both ways down the street. Nina wasn't anywhere in sight. Stupid fucking cunt. He looked back the way he'd come. Maybe he'd missed her walking back. He started trotting back to the house, stopped, and turned back to the candy store. He would have seen her walk back, motherfucking cocksucker. He didn't know where to look for her. Maybe she went home. Bullshit. He walked into the dingy lobby of an old apartment building next to the candy store. Total silence. An old mirror and an elevator. He stood there for a few minutes deciding where else to look. Maybe he should run down to the candy store on Radcliffe Avenue. He'd reached for the door when he noticed a passageway leading behind the elevator. Eugene decided to check it out. He found a narrow alcove with mailboxes and a big black guy with dungaree shorts down to his knees laying on top of a white woman. All Eugene could see of her was her spread legs. The blood drained from the top half of his body.

" 'Scuse me," he mumbled. The black guy turned impassively toward Eugene. The woman was motionless beneath him. The terrible silence. Eugene thought he saw something shiny. Knife. Nigger. Rape. For a terrible second Eugene froze, not knowing whether to leap forward or back. He heard a soft, wavering moan. Knife. Nigger. He wheeled back to the lobby. The backs of his eyes itched with panic. He noticed a ground-floor apartment. He reached out to ring the buzzer, held back, and tore out of the building. The street was deserted. Two blocks down he saw a couple walking his way. He started to run toward them, stopped. Fuck it, they wouldn't do anything. Can't explain. Across the street he saw a phone booth. He ran, pulling out change, dropping nickels, dimes, quarters in the street. "Operator? Police. Hurry. C'mon, hurry."

"I'm sorry. Whad you say?"

Eugene saw the guy walk out of the building. He looked at

Eugene in the phone booth and walked briskly toward Burke Avenue. Eugene dropped the phone and ran back into the building. The minute he opened the door he heard Nina crying hysterically. She staggered out from behind the elevator, nude, dragging her dress on one leg. Eugene grabbed her. She was shaking and screaming. Her trembling fingers pulled at his hair. Eugene's legs shook.

"It's O.K.,'s'O.K.," he mumbled.

She sobbed and gasped. "Oh God, h-h-h-he was g-g-gonna k-kill me! He w-woulda *k-killed* me!"

"'s'O.K., 's'O.K." He hugged her, mechanically smoothing her hair. "Did he hurt you?"

"He . . . he h-had a ra-razor!" she cried. The terror and tears bubbled in her throat. "He . . . he wuh-wuh-woulda k-killed muh-me." She made a high-pitched whine and almost collapsed. Eugene held her tight and helped her to the steps near the elevator. He sat on his haunches in front of her and held on.

"Nina! Nina! Did he hurt you?"

"H-he h-had a *razor!*" She dropped her head on his arm then pulled up straight. "He said he w-woulda k-killed muh-me, h-he h-had a r-razor!"

"'s'O.K., 's'O.K." Eugene saw the red lines running along the left side of Nina's throat.

"S-suh-suh-suh-somebody came. Su-somebody came, an', an' then th-they left! Th-they d-didn't s-say n-nothin'."

Eugene clenched his teeth and trembled. Coward, faggot, coward, pussy, cunt, coward, coward, coward.

"B-buh-but he got sc-scared and l-left. He-he woulda killed me, Eugene!" She fell against his shoulder. He stroked her hair. Knife. Eugene flashed on looking down and seeing him on top of her. He flashed on the terrible silence. Then that tiny moan. The whimper. That scene and that moan jerked at him like invisible fishhooks snagged into his guts. Nina settled into a weeping half-sleep. Eugene helped her stand up and pulled her dress on. He walked her out into the street. She stumbled forward, one arm limp across his shoulders. Coward. Cunt.

When Eugene's parents came home at three in the morning, Eugene was sitting on the stoop in front of the house.

"Whadya you doin' up?" his father asked.

He shrugged. "Can't sleep."

His parents stood arm in arm over him.

"You got a date tonight?"

Eugene winced. "I'll be in."

His parents went into the house. Eugene tried to make himself cry. A song popped into his head. The Four Seasons' "Walk Like a Man." He realized that if he ever started crying, he would never stop. He got up, sighed, and headed into the house. His mother was in the kitchen making coffee. He heard his father in the bathroom upstairs.

"Ma?" She looked at him without saying anything. "I gotta talk to you. Somethin' happened tonight."

She raised her eyebrows, continued making coffee. "I'm listening."

"My girl friend got raped."

"What?" She stopped moving.

"We were in the house, an' she went down to get cigarettes. She din't come back so I went out to look for her. I walked in on this nigger rapin' her down by the candy store. He dragged her into a building."

"You were *there!*"

"Yeah, an' . . ."

"What did you do?"

"I looked, an' I . . ."

"What did you *do?*"

Eugene raised his hands and stuttered, "I-I saw . . ."

"Eugene . . . what did you *do!*" Her lips were white slits, her eyes narrow bands.

"I saw an' . . . he had a *razor* to her throat."

"Eugene . . . what did you *do!*" She clenched her teeth. The neck veins stood out like roots along her throat.

"I called the cops."

"You ran."

"I called the cops."

"You ran," she pronounced sentence. "A *nigger* . . . was *raping* your *girl friend* and you *ran!*"

"No!" Tears welled and dripped down his face. He couldn't catch his breath. His mother sneered.

"Where is she?"

"I-I c-called h-huh f-father." His grief was pulling him down, and he sank into a kitchen chair, gasping for air.

His mother finished making the coffee. He looked at her as if she would grant him a boon. She nodded with contempt. "Go upstairs and take a bath," she said.

"Huh?" He hung on her every word.

"Just do it." She dismissed him with a disgusted wave.

Eugene dumbly obeyed and staggered up the stairs, passed his father in the hallway without a word, and went into the bathroom.

He sat numb in a steaming tub. Tears would come and go. His hands lay dead on his thighs. He stared at a bead of water condensed on a pipe underneath the sink. The bathroom door opened. His mother came in wearing a bathrobe. She leaned on the sink, folded her arms across her chest, and stared at Eugene unforgivingly. "Some day, my son, you are going to learn that the two greatest joys of being a man are beating the hell out of someone and getting the hell beaten out of *you,* good night." She walked out and closed the door.

Eugene stared at the water drop again. When it finally fell

off the pipe, he drew his hand into a fist, and smashed himself full in the face.

*

Eugene lay in bed all night staring at the wall. At six-thirty in the morning he heard his mother get up. He was terrified that she might walk into his bedroom. When he heard her leave the house half an hour later he got up, got dressed, and drove his father's car to Nina's.

"I hate him," she said through clenched teeth. They sat in the small dinette, the table littered with the remains of a light breakfast. "That motherfucker!" She laughed humorlessly, shaking her head.

Eugene looked down at the floor. "I shoulda jumped him."

Nina lightly fingered the cuts on her throat. "Whadya mean?"

"That was me that walked in when he was on you . . . I ran."

"What?" She didn't seem to understand.

"I'm a fuckin' coward, and I ran." Nina touched his hand. "I was standin' there just lookin', Nina . . . an' I tore ass outta there like a fuckin' coward."

"Babe." She tried to stare into his eyes, but he wouldn't look up. "If you jumped him like you think you should've, I wouldn't be here right now. I would've been dead in two seconds, and maybe you too."

Eugene shrugged. "Maybe him instead."

"Eugene, you don't understand."

"No! *You* don't understand!" He stood up and banged his fist against the wall. "You think any of the guys woulda ran?"

"If they had brains in their heads they would've! Eugene, when he saw you he got scared. If you hung around he would've had to hurt somebody. Maybe me. Maybe you. Maybe both of us. When you split that gave him his out.

That gave him his chance to get away. Eugene!" She pointed to the razor marks on her neck. "Just look at this. Just look."

Eugene glanced at her neck, winced, and looked away. "You don't understand," he repeated.

"The *hell* I don't! You don't care about me! All you care about is your goddamn pride. You wouldna cared if he sliced my head off."

"You don't under . . ."

"*Don't* say that anymore. I goddamn well understand better than you'll ever know!"

Eugene left the apartment and walked down the stairs.

"You wouldn't know what a real man is if he came up and bit you on the ass!" Nina shouted from the top of the stairs. She ran back to the apartment, slammed the door, and cried until the scratches on her throat started to burn.

Eugene raced down seven flights of stairs. He had just made a decision that he was sure Nina would never understand.

Dear Richie

Greetings from Beantown. Me and Perry are here to get semens papers and to ship out. Perry wants to go to Africa but I want to go to Japan so we compromised and are going to Arizona (ha ha). We left after the wedding. I guess Buddy is getting some now (ha ha). We will write from every port and send pictures. Say hello to Buddy and Eugene but not to the Scumbag (Emilio).

Your friend
Joey "Main Man Wanderer" Capra

P.S. We are living in a motel next door to a hore. I swear to God. We are going to get some tonight.

P.P.S. Don't take any wooden pussy.

Richie flipped the postcard over to the drawing of a big yellow pot full of brown beans superimposed on a photograph of

Boston; a legend curved like a rainbow in the sky: YOU DON'T
KNOW "BEANS" TILL YOU COME TO BOSTON!

Richie cursed. Big Playground was deserted. It was ten
o'clock Saturday morning. He read the card again. "Shit!" he
cried, punching the wooden bench. Three down. Why the
fuck didn't they tell anybody? I woulda gone. Jesus Christ
sonovabitchbastard. The day was going to be a hot ball-
buster. The Parky swept out the handball courts. Richie
watched his slow, mechanical movements. At the far end of
the basketball courts, he saw Buddy and Despie enter the
playground through the hole in the fence.

"Hey!"

"Hey, how you doin'?"

"Awright. How's married life?"

They smiled. "Awright." Buddy took a pack of cigarettes
from his Banlon shirt. Despie's hair was in curlers and she
had on a pound of black makeup. She wore pale blue short-
shorts and a red rayon halter. She didn't look pregnant.

"I'm gonna C's." She waved, then folded her arms across
her chest and walked away — her loose flats slapping the
pavement. Sighing, Buddy sat down.

"How's it going?" Gennaro slapped him on the knee.

"It's good. What's doin' wit' you?"

"Nothin'. Look." He handed Buddy the postcard.

Buddy read it and smiled. "Holy shit."

"Ain't that a bitch?" Richie frowned.

"It's somethin'."

What the fuck was this it's somethin' bullshit? Richie
thought. He was getting pissed off.

For the next ten minutes Buddy watched the Parky sweep
out the handball courts. Richie silently fumed.

Despie came back. "I wanna go, Buddy."

"See you, Richie." Buddy stood up, yawned, and squinted
at the sky. Richie watched them leave through the hole in the
fence.

Some little kids came in with a basketball and started playing, throwing the ball straight up into the air and watching it bounce away. Not one of them could hit the backboard let alone the hoop. Richie's brother Randy zoomed into the playground, hunched over a sleek black ten-speed racer. He screeched to a halt in front of his older brother. "Mom wants you to go shopping," he said, digging into his dungarees for a few crumpled bills.

"Go yourself!" said Richie.

"She said you."

"Fuck it. I ain't goin'."

"I don't care." He tried to hand the bills to Richie but Richie wouldn't take them. Randy had grown four inches in the last few months, and his body was filling out pretty solid. Richie was scared that his brother would soon be bigger than he was. Randy let the dollars fall at Richie's feet. "A white bread, two quarts a milk, and some floor polish," he said, getting back on his bike.

"Fuck you! I ain't goin'!"

Randy shrugged. "Don't go." And he was off — hurtling through the playground like a human rocket.

"Goddamn shit!" Richie cursed as he bent down to pick up the money.

Some more kids came into the playground and soon the place was filled with kids playing basketball, handball, riding bikes and running around. Richie was about ready to drag ass over to the supermarket when Eugene came in with the shortest haircut Richie had ever seen. "What the fuck you do, man?" Eugene laughed and sat down. He leaned back with his arms draped across the wooden planks of the bench. His haircut was so short the sides of his head looked bald. "You look like a egg."

"Fuck off."

"Jesus Christ, Nina'll take one look at you an' run the other way," said Richie.

Eugene looked away.

"Where you been this week? I called you six times," Richie said.

Eugene appeared exhausted. There were dark swaths under his eyes and his face was puffy.

"Look at this." Richie handed him the postcard. Eugene didn't take it but glanced down.

"I know."

"Ain't that a bitch?"

Eugene shrugged. "I can dig it."

"Whadya mean you can dig it? I think it's a bitch."

"Richie, it ain't a bitch. It's cool. I mean we gotta start doin' things. We gotta start movin'. We ain't kids no more."

"Like Buddy, huh?"

Eugene shrugged. "To each his own."

"They'll be back," Richie said bitterly.

"You gonna sit there and wait for them?"

"I got things to do," Richie said defensively.

"So do I." Eugene took out a folded piece of paper from his wallet and handed it over. Richie grunted, thinking about the first thing he had to do, which was go to the Safeway for his mother. As he read, his eyes widened.

"What the fuck!" he stared at Eugene in disbelief.

"I go in day after graduation."

"Why the goddamn marines for Chrissake?" Eugene was silent. "Why the motherfucking marines? You're fuckin' crazy! You wanna get killed, buy yourself a goddamn razor!"

"Richie, some day you're gonna learn that the two greatest joys of being a man are beating the hell out of someone and getting the hell beaten out of you."

"You can beat my meat! That's the stupidest thing I ever heard!"

Eugene got up to leave. Richie watched him walk out of the playground.

"An' you look like a *jerk* wit' that haircut!"

Eugene kept walking, his figure getting smaller and smaller. For a second it seemed to Richie that Big Playground was filled to the fencetops with millions of screaming ten-year-old maniacs. He sat back down on the bench and clapped his hands to his ears.